FROM
the
OUTSIDE

FROM
the
OUTSIDE

CLARE JOHNSTON

Urbane
PUBLICATIONS

urbanepublications.com

First published in Great Britain in 2019
by Urbane Publications Ltd
Suite 3, Brown Europe House, 33/34 Gleaming Wood Drive,
Chatham, Kent ME5 8RZ
Copyright © Clare Johnston, 2019

A CIP catalogue record for this book is available
from the British Library.

ISBN 978-1-912666-31-7
MOBI 978-1-912666-32-4

Design and Typeset by Michelle Morgan

Cover by Author Design Studio

Printed and bound by 4edge Limited, UK

URBANE

urbanepublications.com

For all those we've loved and lost.
May we meet again.

CHAPTER one

SITTING ON THE EMBANKMENT I took in the endless expanse of blue sky, the warmth from a sun I couldn't see melting away the worries that had been lodged in my head all morning.

The cars rushed by along the motorway in front of me, but their noise was muted. I could see them but the sound just didn't register.

It was then I noticed the mangled wreck of the silver Audi sitting so hopelessly to my left, smashed and broken like the driver slumped over the inflated airbag at the wheel.

Already, there were people all around the car. A bottle-blonde woman who looked to be in her late forties made a frantic call to the emergency services on her mobile, while others paced next to the driver's side, pausing now and then to peer in the window.

Finally, one of them plucked up the courage to prise open the door, only to stand stock still once he'd completed his daunting task, confronted by the terrible reality of what sat before him. He glanced nervously back at the blonde woman who was still on the phone as if to say: 'What now?'

'Check if he's breathing,' she said, pointing towards the lifeless victim – in doing so accepting the leadership role she had unwittingly been awarded.

Another pause as the man tried to work out the best way of checking for breath without actually touching the body. He put his hand over the driver's mouth, then leaned forward to put his ear next to it. A second flash of panic swept over his face. Poor guy. I'd say he was in his thirties, dressed in a non-descript dark suit, with the air of a hassled sales executive on his way to the next meeting when, sod's law, he just happened to be one of the first to pass the scene of a terrible accident. Good for him too that he actually stopped.

I'm hopeless in any medical situation, which is why I had absolutely no intention of getting involved. It had already become obvious to me that their efforts to assist the forty-something, Rolex-wearing man were futile.

After all, it was me sitting at the wheel of that mangled Audi, and me watching this scene of devastation from the safety of my ringside seat.

And I knew there was no way I was coming out of that one. I was most certainly dead.

It occurred to me this was a strange situation to find myself in. Here I was, witnessing my own death – or the aftermath of it – as though standing by a shore watching the waves lapping against the sand. There was no emotion, just a sense of perfect calm ... and something else, something harder to define. I will call it an understanding and appreciation of what was happening, as if I'd somehow been expecting it.

I felt more compelled to look at the people flapping anxiously around me than to study my own tragic form.

I've never seen a greater look of relief than the one I witnessed on the salesman as he first heard the siren and then looked around to see the flashing lights of a police car approaching.

As soon as it pulled over, an officer jumped out and ran to check the driver. I felt like walking over and telling him I could save him the trouble, but I knew they'd never hear me.

I understood that I had left that world. I was somewhere else now; on my own, but not alone. Somewhere I belonged.

It was time to move. I got to my feet, turned around and started walking up the side of the embankment towards the field of rapeseed that stretched before me – that light stronger than ever, its warmth enveloping me so that I could feel nothing else.

Where am I going? I didn't care. I just knew I should just keep walking.

I had not gone far before, in the distance and through the light, I could just make out the figure of a woman coming towards me. As she drew closer I could see she had jet-black hair. Then I recognised the deep-purple, flowing trouser suit she wore. I had seen it before – clung to it when I was a child, begging her not to leave me with the neighbour while she went out for the evening with my father.

I waved at her then ran, arms outstretched, she soon running too, smiling all the way until we met and clung to one another. 'Harry,' she said, so softly and lovingly. Just as I had remembered.

'Mum,' I whispered, pulling back to look into the face that had kissed me goodnight for fifteen years; fifteen years before I decided I was too old for motherly affection. The face I had yearned to see on my wedding day, ten years ago, and the face that told me all was as I had hoped. With nothing to fear, we walked hand in hand together.

~

Morningside Church in Edinburgh sits proudly at the heart of a community packed full of upstanding and well-heeled members who would never dream of moving from this affluent part of the city with its array of scone-selling coffee shops and little boutiques.

The church itself tells its own story of the genteel congregation it hosts with its immaculately-maintained gardens, ornate interior and perfectly-polished pews.

Today, the place of worship I had been dragged to every Sunday of my childhood was much fuller than I had expected. People I hadn't seen in years – some of whom I realised must have travelled from overseas – sat or stood among the friends, family and colleagues who had come to say goodbye to me.

The minister, Bob Cuddy, had come out of retirement to lead the service. As an old pal of my dad's, I knew he wouldn't have passed up the opportunity to do this favour for his lifelong friend.

My wife Sarah and I had once howled with laughter at him – most inappropriately – before he married us. He was passing on some of his unique wisdoms. The one that tipped us both overboard as he spoke so humourlessly, was a warning on the perils of the internet. Dad must have told him that I had set up an online auction house.

'The internet,' he said gravely in his strongly lilting Western Isles accent, 'may tempt us with the promise of great wealth and prosperity, but beneath its surface there lie many evils.' Then fixing us with a steely glare, he added the killer line: 'I know – because I've seen them.' As he raised his right eyebrow to reinforce this dramatic statement, we could no longer suppress the tide of laughter that erupted with volcanic force, spilling into every corner of the otherwise eerily silent church.

'I'm so sorry,' Sarah blurted out as she tried desperately to stifle what were now unstoppable fits of hysteria.

He continued to look somberly at both of us before quietly adding: 'Nerves can make fools of all of us.' With that he stood up and walked out of the church hall, leaving Sarah and I sheepishly wondering if we had just blown our chance of marrying in the same place as my parents. To his credit though Bob came good and, two weeks later, happily presided over what was to be the best day of my life. I can say that now, can't I?

Today, Sarah cuts a very different figure as she sits in the same pew we once huddled together on to meet Bob and receive our personal, pre-marital sermon. Her joy and tears of laughter that day have been replaced with grief and hopelessness, but no amount of pain can disguise her undeniable beauty. Though she has only a slight frame, she still reminds me of the finest thoroughbred mare with her prominent cheekbones, deep brown eyes and stunning mane of thick chestnut hair. I breathe in her scent without even being near. It is always the same fragrance; a mixture of the Coco Chanel perfume she loves and the pure, effortless class of someone totally at home in their own skin. She carries herself with dignity, even when burying her husband.

I know she too is remembering our happy times here. I wish I could tell her that it's okay, that I'm really not that far away, just out of reach for a while. Instead, I can only passively witness her pain.

I feel mum's hand in mine where it has remained since she led me here. She is my helper on this side. Without her, I wouldn't have been able to come. I wouldn't have found my way.

She is no stranger to sadness, Sarah. Having buried her beloved father at the tender age of 12, she thought the worst was behind her. But, some 20 years later, heartache dealt another devastating blow when we discovered we could not have children together. I will never forget the anguish etched on her face as she listened to the doctor tell her that I was infertile; that I could not give her the child she so longed for. Her silent grief was in stark contrast to the doctor's blustering demeanor – seemingly incapable of hiding the fact we were just one more couple on a long list of desperate people he would have to put straight on their fertility status before getting back to the golf course.

I wanted to walk behind that desk and punch him, but instead I sat there and watched him shatter the hopes of the woman I loved – a woman who had never had a single thing in life denied her. Yet the one thing she wanted more than anything else was now off limits, thanks to me.

I wonder if it has dawned on Sarah yet that, at 37, she still has the chance to meet someone else and have her family. How many hours or days would it take for that thought to creep forward? I want to sit down on the pew next to her and tell her not to waste her time worrying about how it will look, but to get on and have her children while she still has the chance. Mum is looking at me now. There are no secrets here. No private thoughts in a realm where you no longer have anything to hide.

As my eyes meet hers, I sense the sudden knowing that is becoming a regular event for me now. She wouldn't have to wait for the child – the child was already on its way.

To the left of Sarah sits my dad. In his late seventies now, but still with the same devilish air I always thought marked him out from other fathers. At 6'2 he still stands tall among most men, but his imposing height is lessened with the stoop of old age, a predicament quite at odds with his pride and desire to stay strong. His balding scalp and snow-white hair further betray his years, but otherwise he is still John Melville, the respected and now retired Edinburgh architect with an inner steel that separates him from most mere mortals. This fortitude saw him climb quickly through the ranks in his early days serving in the Royal Navy.

Whilst he had a playful and charming manner, he was a hardliner at heart and had ruled my twin brother Ben and I with an iron fist. There was always pressure on us to achieve and perform and I had danced to his tune like a captive bear. Ben, on the other hand, had turned his back on our father's idea of success and had, in protest, simply done nothing. Today, Dad holds his head high, but his eyes tell a different story.

Ben, my twin and something of a social misfit, sits to the right of Sarah. He stares purposefully at the ground but can't stop himself from stealing shifty glances at the assembled congregation around him, desperately avoiding eye contact with anyone.

He shares my father's height and slim build, but inherited my mother's angel-faced looks, still evident despite his typically unshaven appearance. I, on the other hand, had been slightly shorter than my brother but with a more solid build, suited to the rugby field.

Ben was born first but was physically the weaker of the two of us, unable to feed without a tube for weeks. I apparently never caused my mother a moment's trouble while Ben cost her many sleepless nights – from birth and right up until her death from cancer, 12 years ago at just 61.

He was a long list of nevers: never made any friends, never found his vocation, was never where he said he was, could never hold down a relationship, was never what any of us wanted him to be. He and I clashed from an early age, defying my mother's hopes for the kind of twins you read about who feel half of one whole, finish each other's sentences and cry out when the other is in pain. Instead, I would cry with laugher whenever my brother came a cropper.

But I loved him. I still love him. Today, we're both thinking how ironic it is that I – who was so full of life – was the one who died the early death.

Bob is speaking now. Welcoming the congregation to this service of remembrance. Let us pray, he says. He asks that my soul will find rest.

Where do they imagine I am now, I wonder? Gone without trace? Would they do anything differently if they knew I was right here with them? Would they want me to find rest, or stay close?

They sing my favourite hymn. Amazing Grace. I sing loudly too: 'I once was lost, but now I'm found. Was blind but now I see.'

I spot an old school friend, Michael Anderson, ten rows back and chuckle as I remember how we stole a whole salmon from the buffet at the end-of-term disco and hid it in our English teacher's drawer to rot over the summer.

How we tortured that poor woman on a daily basis when she remarried and changed her name from Bryant to Gore, delivering hours of entertainment as we sought to create new variants to call her, but never straying too far from our very favourite – Mrs Giant-Bore. It drove her crazy. I still remember her literally spitting with rage and frustration as she tried to unmask our innocence and expose us for the unruly little brats we were.

She once humiliated another boy who passed a note to a friend about a girl he fancied which she then read aloud in front of the whole class. That was a crowning moment for her. It was sweet revenge then when she fell for another of our stunts one day, seizing a note that Michael and I very obviously passed each other between our desks, eventually dropping it at one point and scrabbling around the floor to find it. She couldn't hide the delight on her face as she pounced, prising the note from between Michael's fingers.

'And what could this be, boys?' she asked with mock naivety. 'Let's find out shall we?'

She was enjoying the prospect of humiliating us so much that she didn't even pause to check the content before dramatically holding the note up high and reading loudly: 'GB has the most enormous snotter hanging out of her left nostril.'

I still laugh. It was a wonderful moment and worth the one hundred lines on the blackboard after school. I note that Mrs Giant-Bore didn't make my funeral.

So enraptured was I with this memory that I didn't notice my brother getting to his feet. I snapped back to attention to catch him taking his last few steps towards the alter, walking as slowly as a death row inmate on his way to the chair.

He attempted to rest his crumpled notes on the lectern, but his shaking hands meant he knocked them clumsily to the floor. I watched Sarah roll her eyes as he bent to pick them up before finally getting them to stay in place on the stand. He cleared his throat.

'Harry Jonathan Melville was my twin brother yet, in truth, the similarities between us were few.'

I was surprised both by the unusual note on which Ben had decided to begin his eulogy but also by the fact he seemed to be speaking with some degree of poise and purpose – despite his obvious nervousness – where usually he would appear aloof and distracted. I noticed he'd made a bit of an effort with his appearance too, looking smart in a dark navy suit he'd borrowed from my father. His hair, now greying at the front and sides (as mine had been), was clean cut and freshly washed.

As he stood awkwardly at the pulpit, he radiated some of that mysterious appeal that had marked him out so much from others in our youth. He had been quiet but intriguing, and the girls loved him – much to my annoyance.

'Harry was an achiever,' he continued, 'in business and in life. He started young, selling parking tickets to the unsuspecting drivers who tried to enter our cul-de-sac. Harry always got them to pay. They could never resist his cheeky grin as he politely asked them to part with ten pence.' Ben paused to accommodate the amused titters of the congregation before continuing.

'His entrepreneurial initiatives continued into adulthood. The rest of us could only look on in awe as he built up a staggeringly successful business empire around his online auction site, yourlot.com.'

Ben cleared his throat again before glancing up fleetingly at the people spread out along the pews before him, all listening attentively.

'His success also spilled over into his private life. Eleven years ago he met Sarah and they married three years later in this very church. On the morning of their wedding, Harry told me he was the luckiest man on earth, but the truth was that Harry created his own luck. He didn't wait to find out what life had in store for him, he knew exactly what he wanted to achieve and he set about accomplishing it with vigour.'

Ben glanced at Sarah, then looked quickly back at his notes.

'He made it look easy but nothing was ever left to chance. If he wanted something he pursued it until it became a reality. When he first met Sarah she was dating another law graduate from Edinburgh University and she told him she had no intention of ending what was a happy relationship. Where others would have heard 'no', Harry heard 'not quite yet'. From that moment on he asked her out daily, until two months later she finally gave in and agreed to a date. It was this mixture of tenacity and self-belief that marked Harry out from ordinary men.'

Ben paused again now to rearrange his notes. I could see how hard this was for him. The energy he had piled into giving his speech a strong start had given way to exhaustion.

'What life gave Harry, he gave back,' Ben forced himself on, 'setting up the Melville Youth Foundation five years ago when he was still a relatively young man himself at 39, to help disadvantaged teenagers get on a career path. He cared deeply about the futures of these young people. Their victory was his victory, their losses his own personal defeats. His outstanding contribution to the community was recognised three years ago when he was awarded an OBE by the Queen.

'He was a loving son to my mother, Anna, and father, John. And they were so proud of his achievements,'

I noticed Ben swallow hard, emotion now obviously starting to get the better of him. He raised his hand and swept it roughly across the front of his hair.

'Harry Jonathan Melville had so much more to give this world… in particular, the young people he fought so hard to help. It is on behalf of them now that I say thank you, Harry.'

With that Ben, head bowed, face crumpling, collected his notes and walked silently back to his seat having delivered a speech I would have previously thought him incapable of. This was the first of many surprises he would deliver – a man I considered my polar opposite but whom, until now, I believed I knew inside out.

CHAPTER two

I HAD ALWAYS WONDERED how Ben filled his days, and now I know. He usually gets out of bed at 8am and makes himself a cup of tea while listening to the news on the radio.

He showers, gets dressed, then takes a walk past the harbour at Newhaven, one of the city's rapidly developing coastal areas with cafes, shops and businesses sprouting up where once there were just neglected buildings and warehouses.

Often he stops to buy a Guardian newspaper and a few groceries on the way home, then, seated in his kitchen, he'll sit and fret about the state of the world while drinking another cup of tea.

He cleans obsessively. Same routine every day of spraying and wiping surfaces and putting bleach down the kitchen plughole and toilet.

At one pm precisely he has his first drink. I knew exactly what that was about. Touch a drink in the morning and you had a problem. Drinking at lunchtime though was acceptable, so he would head off down to the pub to sit with a quiet pint and read a book. Then he'd walk back to his flat past the harbour where he would often stop and rest against the tall stone wall that stood between him and the rocks below, and he would look out past the lighthouse across the water to Fife.

The sea could so often determine his mood. Choppy waters would stir his agitation and restlessness and he'd walk quickly back home where he would sit at his laptop and obsess over all the things that had and could continue to go wrong in his life. He'd fret over the lack of money in his account – even though dad was financially propping him up. He'd check the job ads again, then slam the laptop shut with the realisation that he simply couldn't face spending eight or more hours a day stuck with strangers – or with anyone. There were limited things he felt comfortable with. Going to the pub, and taking a walk past the harbour were two of only a handful of activities he enjoyed.

On the days when the sea was calm, its tranquility would radiate through Ben. He'd stand looking into the waters sometimes for half an hour or more, and in those moments of peace he would have a vision of himself as someone who could once again cope in the world, make something of himself.

In his flat, nothing was out of place. I had only actually visited him there once in the 10 years he'd owned it, but I hadn't quite appreciated at the time just how tidy it all was. Ben was certainly a mystery. A strange mix of out-of-control and totally controlling.

Forty-four years of age and now an only-child, in the not too distant future, my brother realised he would also become an orphan. That situation should have suited such a life-long loner, but somehow it left him deeply unsettled. He was a loner with a fear of being alone.

My death had hit Ben much harder than he, or I, could have ever imagined.

He'd been born first only to live in the shadow of his brother – and now I was dead where did that leave him? He felt exposed.

In the evenings he would drink more – typically beer or wine but occasionally whisky if he wanted to completely remove himself from life for a few hours. He usually fell asleep in the armchair again, eventually taking himself off to bed when he found himself still sitting upright in the early hours.

It seemed to me a miserable existence. But Ben didn't seem so much unhappy as resigned. In a strange and unsatisfying way, at peace. I now understood my brother's need for an unwavering daily routine. Change, of any description, stirred deep anxiety in him. Yet change was coming and there was no place to hide.

~

Two weeks after my death and Ben is shuffling around nervously on Sarah's doorstep, desperately hoping she'd forgotten inviting him for dinner so he could head home to his little flat and drink the bottle of red wine that was sitting on the kitchen table waiting for him.

He found it very difficult to be in new situations. He imagined her opening the door only for him to panic and have to rush past her to the bathroom to throw up.

That fear of vomiting in public was always with him. Ever since he'd started throwing up in the changing room toilets as a boy before rugby on a Saturday morning, the anxiety about doing it in front of other people had virtually left him imprisoned by his own mind.

He swallowed hard as he heard footsteps approaching the door. It opened and there she was, smiling obligingly as always, ushering him in. Ben reluctantly stepped forward and stood in her embrace for a deeply uncomfortable and very long few seconds until she let go. He had patted her back awkwardly, wishing all the time that he didn't find everything so damned difficult.

Finally, he took a seat in the living room of the plush townhouse we owned in Edinburgh's exclusive Stockbridge area, while Sarah fetched him a drink.

She returned quickly and handed him a very full glass of wine, clutching another in her left hand which was equally generously charged.

'Thank you,' he mumbled.

But she didn't move. Her eyes searching his, desperately seeking traces of her dead husband. Traces she would never find. He looked away quickly and took a swig from his glass.

'Have you seen Dad?' he asked as she took a seat in the armchair opposite him, perching formally as if conducting a job interview.

'Yes, I dropped in to see him earlier. He's doing okay. Bit tearful, but I think he's coping pretty well.'

'Good,' said Ben. This was going to be a long evening.

'How have you been feeling?' she asked with genuine concern.

'Okay.' She was looking for more detail, he could tell. 'Bit up and down. You know.'

'Of course,' she replied, glancing down at her wine before taking a large gulp of the red liquid as though it were blackcurrant juice. He noticed now the dark circles that had formed under her eyes, the frailty of her hands clasped tightly around the wine glass. Ben guessed she probably hadn't slept or eaten much in the two weeks since the funeral.

'How are you coping, Sarah?'

She stared deep into her drink again, her eyes welling up. Ben froze, hoping there wouldn't be an emotional outburst. He suppressed another wave of nausea and took a drink of wine.

'I miss him, Ben,' she said, her face twisting with pain. 'What am I supposed to do? I barely did a single thing without consulting Harry first. He handled all the bills, all the financial stuff. Now I'm supposed to just pick up when there's this glaring hole in my life.'

She was searching his face again; this time for answers he didn't have. He rarely had answers to anything. The fact she even asked angered him.

He shuffled uncomfortably in his seat as he tried to think of something suitable to say.

'Time will heal,' was the best he could manage.

But by now she was rocking on the edge of the armchair, her distress increasing by the minute – as was Ben's just watching it.

'If it's too much my coming, I'll just head home, Sarah,' he suggested hopefully.

'No,' she snapped. 'Stay here, Ben. I need to talk to you. I feel like I hardly even know you and you're – you were – Harry's twin brother. Why weren't you two closer?'

'We were just different that's all. We didn't have much in common.'

'You were brothers, born on the same day to the same mother and father. That's something in common. Harry tried time and time again to be part of your life. He wanted to involve you in his business but you knocked him back. Every time. Did you not care?'

'I cared,' Ben finally fixed her stare for a second before glancing at the door, trying to control his desperate urge to leave. 'It was complicated.'

She tilted her head back and closed her eyes as she let out a long, world-weary sigh.

'It was such a wasted opportunity, Ben,' she said, opening her eyes to fix him again. 'You'll never get that back.'

'I know,' he said, his head bowed. He supposed she was right to confront him on another one of his many failings. But it wasn't that he hadn't wanted to build a closer relationship with me, he just hadn't known where to begin. We were emotional strangers who had grown up in the same house.

'He left a will you know,' Sarah continued, studying his reaction. 'He apparently wrote it the month before he died – which is just weird.' Her voice was distant, as if she were describing another family's tragedy. 'Anyway, you're in it.'

Ben looked at her, unsure of what was coming next.

'He wants you to run his foundation, Ben. To continue his work with young people.'

Ben stared at her as she spoke, his eyes wide as saucers.

'Will you do it?' Her tone was challenging, harsh even.

He started to shake his head, thinking of all the reasons why it would just never work. After all, he had never held a job down for more than a couple of weeks, how could he help others try to make something of themselves? He had nothing to offer them: no experience, no success stories, he carried with him only a legacy of failure and disenchantment.

His eyes darted around the room as he prepared to let Sarah – and me – down again. Then he noticed for the first time a tiny picture on the mantelpiece showing the two of us, aged five, dressed in little summer sailor suits, arms locked round each other, beaming into the camera. He remembered the holiday in France where the photo was taken. We had stayed on a farm in the Loire Valley where Ben and I spent two weeks chasing each other around the barns and outhouses, taking delight in ruthlessly scaring the chickens and watching them flee in panic. In this picture there was no tension between us. We were just brothers at a time in our lives where I had no idea of my own power, and he was a stranger to panic attacks.

Ben looked away for a moment and allowed a wave of grief to wash over him before steeling himself long enough to glance back at the photo; our arms entwined and faces pressed gleefully together. Why did we let go, he wondered? What was it that forced us apart?

He closed his eyes and thought of the many days he'd stood by the harbour imagining a life more meaningful than the one he was now living.

And then Ben uttered the words that surprised even him: 'Okay, I'll do it.'

Sarah sat back in her chair, her mouth slackening as she realised he was serious.

Later that evening, back in the security of his one-bedroom flat, Ben sank another glass of wine. He felt even more agitated than usual, terrified of what lay ahead the following morning – his first visit to the Melville Centre.

Sarah had told him he would be meeting the three full-time staff who ran the centre – the very idea of which filled him with terror. Why had he agreed to it? Little did any of them know just how much it was going to take for him to walk into the building, let alone sit with strangers and have a meaningful conversation.

He glanced at his mobile phone. He could call Sarah now and tell her he wouldn't be able to make it. Then he visualised her angry, disappointed scowl and suddenly the idea of making the call became scarier than going to the meeting.

What were they expecting him to say? God forbid they'd be looking for him to make some kind of speech. And what would he say to the forty youths who came through the centre's doors each week? The whole thing was horrifying – he himself was a bigger drop-out than any unemployed 16-year-old could ever aspire to be. Wasn't that what everyone thought? He must have been out of his mind to have agreed to take on the job. A stupid emotional gesture at the height of his grief, he thought, taking another large gulp from his glass.

Then Ben remembered there was worse to come, because our father, who had always taken more than a passing interest in my work at the centre, had offered to be there 'to ease him in'. While Ben was sure Dad was simply trying to be supportive, the thought of his eagle eyes, weighing up his every move added to the pressure even further. Ben had tried to talk him out of coming when they'd spoken on the phone earlier, but Dad wouldn't hear of it. 'Nonsense,' he'd bellowed. 'The very least I can do is introduce you to the team, and I know your brother would have wanted me to be there with you on your first day.'

Together, Dad and I had been a formidable – and intimidating – double-act. In many respects, Ben felt our father had brought out the worst in me, bolstering my competitive streak and writing off my bullying as 'assertiveness'.

Ben's sense of humiliation from our treatment was never stronger than after a rugby game he was forced to play in at the age of thirteen, watched from the sidelines by both myself – a keen rugby player – and Dad. As a tall and skinny teenager, Ben was as physically unsuited to the game as he was mentally. Playing in the wings, it was the coach's hope that, with his long legs, he'd be able to charge past the other players – but in reality, the only speed he gained was in running away from the ball to avoid contact of any sort. It was cold and there were a million other places he would have rather been and he had no intention of playing well enough to get permanently selected for the team. Throughout the game, he had been aware of Dad and I heckling from the sidelines and furiously shaking our heads at him.

'Get a move on you loafer,' I'd hollered across the field, much to the amusement of Dad and several other players who were near enough to hear it. But not even his family's obvious embarrassment was enough to motivate Ben, in fact it made him more resolute in his desire to do badly.

When the game was over, Ben left the changing rooms to find Dad and I chatting with a group of other parents and pupils outside. As he approached he could hear Dad's voice booming over the others: 'Dear God, my six-year-old niece could have outplayed Ben. He looked more like an old-age-pensioner chasing a letter down the street than a rugby player chasing a ball.'

The other parents had chuckled with various degrees of amusement, but I had practically split my sides at this joke – because I knew how much it had hurt Ben.

'What a loser,' I howled, in between great gulps of laughter. But rather than correcting my crass remark, Dad had ruffled my hair in a gesture designed to portray me as the lovable rogue. I turned to see Ben stopped in his tracks just a few feet away. The hurt in his eyes wiped the smile from my face.

The rugby pitch had been my stomping ground in my youth – as my business became in adult life. Ben had made a fool of himself back then when forced to follow in my sporting footsteps, and he couldn't help but fear he was about to do it all over again as he took over the running of the Melville Centre. And there, watching from the sidelines as he had done all those years ago would be Dad.

CHAPTER three

LOOKING BACK ON IT, my decision to write a will one month before my death was indeed weird timing and I can't honestly say what compelled me to do it other than my accountant's constant nagging. 'There's too much at stake for you not to have your estate in order,' he would frequently remind me.

His words finally hit home one night as I left a fundraising event for the centre that Sarah and I had hosted. I remember being struck by the thought that if I died there'd be no one left to keep it going. Surprising that I hadn't been similarly concerned for my business but, by then, the foundation had become my major driving force in life. It was like an addiction. Help one disadvantaged kid, watch them succeed and you wanted to help them all. Turning lives around made me feel good about myself. And I liked the Harry Melville who ran that centre.

Some of the kids who came in needed a bit of career advice, others needed intensive psychological counselling to build enough self-confidence just to get through a job interview. For me, the tougher the challenge the greater the buzz.

When I finally got my solicitor and accountant together to write the will, they both looked relieved. It was simple enough to begin with. The bulk of my estate would be left to Sarah, but I made a considerable allowance for Dad to allow him to enjoy the rest of his retirement in style. The business would take care of itself as it had become a PLC three years ago. Sarah would retain a 20 per cent stake and could take on a non-executive director role, but otherwise there was nothing for her to worry about – if she chose, she would never have to work another day in her life and would still remain an extremely wealthy woman.

So that left Ben and the Melville Centre to take care of, and it seemed like the most obvious thing in the world to lump the two things together. It certainly killed two birds with one stone; I was loath to leave a large sum to Ben which could simply end up – via the off-licence – down his throat, and I needed someone who I thought would understand the whole ethos behind the place to pick up with running it. Ben had never taken much interest in my business affairs – but he'd always asked about the work of the foundation and, call it what you like, I had a very strong feeling that he had a role to play there. Pairing them together would allow me to support Ben financially, while giving him something to restore his self-respect. He would have hated a hand-out. If I'd left him a million he would have taken it as a final insult. Living off his brother's money. This way, I hoped, he'd feel like he was doing me a favour.

Of course, I hadn't imagined that less than five weeks after I'd finalised the will, my requests would be actioned. Now here I was, watching Ben squirm as he braced himself for a first day in which he'd either sink or swim.

Dad would be there to introduce him, and that, to me, was a good sign. The two of them had reached a strange understanding after years of practically viewing each other as the antichrist; Dad bemused by Ben's creative and introverted leanings, and Ben angered by Dad's seeming refusal to try to understand or accept him for who he is.

~

Ben hadn't heard his alarm in years – and now he remembered why he kept the damned thing off. The screeching, beep, beep, beep, could have been used by intelligence officers to extract information. The clock said 7.30am and he had to be at the Melville Centre for 9am so he guessed he'd better shift himself. His stomach lurched at the thought of facing all those people, but he knew he was going to have to go through with it.

Sixty percent of him desperately wanted to go, but there was a very noisy forty percent that was screaming 'NO'.

Once showered and dressed – jeans and a T-shirt would have to do – he drank the final dregs of his cup of tea and grabbed a plastic carrier bag out of the cupboard, sticking it in his jacket pocket just in case he threw up. Old habits die hard after all.

It was only a ten-minute walk, but it took Ben twenty as he deliberately dragged his heels the whole way. It was a glorious Spring day and he wished he could just head down to the harbour and dream the morning away as he usually did.

Taking a shortcut along the cobbles of Main Street and Fishmarket Square, Ben allowed himself to be transported back in time for just a few seconds to imagine the hustle and bustle of fish merchants noisily trading in bygone days. From the corner of the square, Ben could see Newhaven Lighthouse, a landmark that usually brought him strange comfort, but today only served to increase his anxiety as he realised he was nearing his destination. He turned onto the main road running along the shore towards Leith and was promptly forced to swap his imagined days of the past for the stark present as the vast multiplexes now assembled along the front consumed his vision, changing the skyline – and the future – forever.

Finally, he reached the front door of the Melville Centre, housed on a quiet residential street close to the notorious Fort estate, from where many of the young people who entered the building hailed, the others usually coming from nearby Granton and Muirhouse. The first thing he noticed was the large sign in the front window: 'If you have a dream, step inside.' Cheesy, thought Ben.

His stomach lurched again and he felt for the plastic bag in his pocket. This just wasn't for him. He'd never been able to achieve a single one of his own 'dreams' so how could he possibly tell other people how to do it?

Convinced he needed more time to think this through, he turned on his heels and was about to set off for home when he heard a voice from the entrance behind him: 'Come on in my boy. There are some people here who can't wait to meet you.'

Get ready to be disappointed, thought Ben, who smiled meekly before heading into the centre, Dad leading the way.

~

Sarah paced around the cigarette pack on the coffee table in front of her one more time. She knew if she took just one out and smoked it she'd be straight back to a 20-a-day habit, but what did she have to lose? Sure, I would have been devastated, but I wasn't there to care any more. No one cares if she has a cigarette, she thought, and so what if she dies early, what else was there now anyway? At least have some little pleasures along the way, she told herself, searching for a lighter. The stand-off didn't last long once it was located. Within seconds she was inhaling her first cigarette in eleven years. As she drew the smoke back into her lungs her body retaliated with a coughing fit. That's the warning to stop right there, she thought, but it was too late now. She took her next drag and this time her lungs submitted as she enjoyed the familiar feeling of warm smoke circulating her airways before she slowly exhaled again.

Looking around the living room, she noticed how she'd let things go. When I'd been there not a single thing was out of place – like Ben, I'm obsessively tidy and demanded a clean home. This was her little rebellion that she was supposed to enjoy. The cleaner I had employed annoyed her so much with her endless chattering that she'd paid her off a week ago, a decision she was now regretting.

One month had passed since my death, yet the day it happened is never far from Sarah's mind. She had been searching for her car keys as she prepared to head to a lunch meeting, when the doorbell rang. She knew it was bad when the policeman she found at her door wouldn't tell her anything until they had sat down. But nothing could prepare her for the pain of what followed as the poor constable tried to explain what had happened.

'Your husband was involved in a car accident earlier today on the eastbound carriageway of the M8.'

At first, Sarah's thoughts instinctively turned to figuring out what I'd been doing on the motorway between Edinburgh and Glasgow, but then she remembered I'd had a meeting in Livingston that morning and must have been on my way back into town.

'No other vehicles were involved, and it would appear from our initial investigation that your husband lost control of his vehicle and hit the barrier at the side of the road.' The officer looked expectantly at Sarah, clearly expecting an outburst of grief or at least a set of frantic questions; instead she'd stayed absolutely quiet, her eyes fixed intently on his, urging him to continue.

'I'm afraid he sustained very serious injuries in the crash and the ambulance crew, despite intensive efforts, were unable to revive him. I'm very sorry to have to inform you that he was pronounced dead at the scene of the accident at 11.15 this morning.'

She slumped forward in her seat, clutching her hair with both hands and tugged at it as hard as she could. She wanted to feel a physical pain that could block the emotional agony, but there was nothing that could counter the surge of horror that filled her in that instant.

It was a pain that continued to eat into her soul day by day, and instead of gaining some kind of peace or understanding, she was becoming more and more angry.

She wanted a glass of wine. It was only one o'clock in the afternoon but, sod it, she thought. If I can't indulge myself now when is it okay to let go a little?

She took a bottle of red from the wine rack we kept in the cupboard under the stairs. It was a merlot – I'd bought a box of six. Even that thought plunged another dagger into her heart. I'd only drunk one bottle, she despaired, but now I'd never taste that wine again. Bloody good thing too. It was so light and fruity, I might as well have been drinking Ribena. I was always trying to teach Sarah about wine, urging her to pour a little into the glass and slosh it around before taking a good moment to taste it fully. Today, she didn't pause to take in the aroma, or even to let the liquid settle in the bottom of the glass. Instead she hastily poured and then slugged back the contents before going back for a second measure. It could have been Vimto for all she cared. It was the effect and not the taste in which she was interested.

Standing at the kitchen table, wine glass in hand, she started to sob uncontrollably. It happened at least three or four times a day. Often it wasn't even a thought that triggered her crying, but more a wave of emotion that seemed to come from nowhere – like her soul had suddenly remembered. She felt alone and desperate as she poured herself a third glass of wine and lit a cigarette before slumping into a chair by the table. As she hurriedly drank, her senses dulled and she started to feel the release she had been craving; her mind now muddied and her grief diluted. Much better, she thought.

~

Ben felt so rigid with fear as he walked into the meeting room that he could hardly put one foot in front of the other. He wondered if they noticed that he'd lost all fluidity to his movement. Did he look as weird as he felt?

There was little clear floor space in the office where they'd managed to squeeze a couple of filing cabinets in along with a meeting table and chairs and a book case filled with career pamphlets and brochures from various colleges and universities. This room, like the main entranceway and recreation room he'd managed to glance around on the way past, was clean but functional in its décor with plain white walls covered in posters and notices, and dark wooden floors.

Ben managed to squeeze out a smile as he reached to shake the hands of three people who had anxiously awaited his appearance. The first to greet him, Dave, was the 28-year-old centre manager, who I always described as the 'heart and soul' of the project.

Dave had left a violent and unhappy home at fifteen and spent four years on the streets before starting work as a seller of a homeless magazine. Within a year he was one of the best sellers in Scotland, shifting twice as many copies each day as the average street trader and, as a result, was soon enlisted as a trainer. After a couple of years in the job he spotted an ad for a team leader for the Melville Foundation. We had been up and running for six months by that point and it was time for me to take a step back and find someone else to run the ship. He replied and two days later we met in a coffee shop in Leith. Thirty minutes after we sat down, I offered him the job. Becoming leader at the centre had been the hardest thing Dave had ever done. Much harder than living rough. Kids would turn up thinking it was just a place to play pool – or in the worst-case-scenario, to shoot up. Some of the states we found the toilets in will never leave either of us and for a while we doubted we'd ever get the local kids to take us seriously. But we never gave up, believing that eventually the message would get through that we meant business. It took time, but after we cracked down on drugs in the premises and laid down some hard and fast rules, things started to change.

Dave was both personally and professionally devastated by my death, believing the foundation could no longer continue without me. He was, therefore, incredibly relieved to hear I had a twin brother who was willing to pick up as the major driving force behind the centre. He had imagined Ben to be a carbon copy of me, with the same charisma and charm – and yes, ego – of his former boss. He was surprised then, if not a little concerned, to see the incredibly nervous, dishevelled and awkward character that now stood shaking in front of him.

Ben grasped Dave's hand and mumbled something incoherent that Dave took to be 'nice to meet you' before moving on to meet the next person in line who happened to be Sonja, the centre's team leader. Like Dave, she came from humble beginnings and had become a heavy drinker by the age of 16. Facing a grim future she made a decision that marked a maturity way beyond her young years, and gave up alcohol for good, went to college and got herself some qualifications. Three years ago she had been working as an administrative assistant with a youth charity when she saw an advert for a support worker job at the Melville Centre and, tired of sitting behind a desk all day, decided to apply.

She'd been impressed by my sense of purpose and ended up practically begging me for the job. Now twenty-nine, the thought of working anywhere else just didn't even occur to her. That's why my death had shaken them all up. Suddenly, their cosy, safe environment was under threat and they were going to have to fight for their future. Now, more than ever, they needed strong leadership and Sonja wasn't convinced that the terrified man who had just walked through the door would be able to give them that.

'Nice to meet you,' she said to Ben, shaking his hand while looking him up and down, barely able to hide her disappointment.

Lastly, Danny, one of the senior youth workers, introduced himself. He was a former visitor to the centre who was later recruited to do for others what had been done for him. He was only twenty-one, but was already great at handling some of the tougher kids who came in. He managed to calm even the most heated situations and often was the one to get through to the kids who were proving hard to reach.

Ben smirked awkwardly as he shook Danny's hand.

Dad gestured for them all to sit down but, once seated, a painful silence followed while they all waited for Ben to say something. Finally, Dad stepped in.

'So Ben, here's your chance to get to know the team and to put your questions to them.'

More silence.

Dave stepped in this time, helpfully adding: 'We hold a meeting like this every Monday morning which you'd be very welcome to attend.'

'I will, thanks,' said Ben.

At last he speaks, thought Sonja. What a revelation. And just as she contemplated the likelihood of another embarrassing silence, he spoke again.

'What do you need me to do?' he asked earnestly, as if he had rehearsed the line before coming to the meeting.

Sonja raised her eyebrows at the bluntness of his remark, but Dave thought it was the most pertinent thing he could have asked, so decided he would be equally straight in his answer.

'Your brother provided a significant amount of funding to this organisation and we have received an additional two million pounds through his will. That money will go a long way, but we need a longer-term plan and new sources of income to ensure we are a self-sustaining organisation.

'We've been able to get some good press coverage and support in recent years, but we can't rest on that alone. We need to be getting back out there now and raising the profile.

'Also, we have to keep moving so we need you to help us plan ahead. Some of the facilities need to be upgraded this year and we need to get more businesses on board in providing mentors and traineeships.'

Ben gulped – he hoped not audibly – at the weight of the task. After all, to date he had zero leadership experience. What use could he possibly be here? He needed to talk to Dad about finding someone else – someone who knew what they were doing.

To his horror, he realised they were all looking at him again. Waiting for him to speak. He felt for the bag in his pocket, another wave of nausea threatening to send him running from the room. He took a deep breath and managed to get another question out.

'What are the kids like who come here?'

This time it was Danny who answered.

'Most of them come from broken homes where they've had little or no encouragement from their parents. Most have been told they're no good from the day they were born. One of the boys here told me that on his first day of nursery school the teacher had

FROM the OUTSIDE

asked him his name and he'd replied 'shithead' because that's all his mother had called him. All this means you're dealing with kids who have little or no self-esteem and no sense of direction. It's our job to give that back to them.'

Ben nodded, he knew all about lack of self-esteem and direction. He should be queuing up for help here, he thought, not giving it out.

'How do you select the kids you're going to help?'

'In recent years we've had more young people interested in using the centre than we can handle so we have a waiting list now,' Sonja explained. 'We interview all the candidates who apply – and that just means all those who come in the door and ask to join – and we knock back those we don't think are serious. It's usually pretty easy to tell the ones who genuinely want to improve themselves and those who have come along to keep a parent or carer happy. Quite often the ones we say no to will reapply a few months, or even years later, when they've had the chance to do a bit more growing up.'

Ben thought she had finished but after a moment's pause she spoke again, this time with urgency. 'This is a special place. It's changed all our lives, along with those of the young people who come here. The three of us give everything we've got and we expect the same of everyone involved. That's what we tell whoever walks through the front door.'

'I see,' said Ben, smiling half-heartedly at the team.

'Nicely put,' said Dad, chuckling mischievously. He could see Ben felt completely out of his depth, and he couldn't think of anything better for him than being thrown straight in at the deep end.

CHAPTER four

AFTER A ROCKY START AT THE CENTRE, within a year we had our first major success story – a young guy who came from the worst of homes where he'd been verbally and physically abused all his life and told he would amount to nothing. This boy, Jimmy Donald, had a dream. He wanted to be an actor. He just had no idea how. When Dave told me about Jimmy I immediately asked to meet him. Two days later we came face-to-face at the centre; me clutching a book of famous monologues from which I asked Jimmy to choose one and read it to me. This was something Dave immediately guessed would be a problem. Jimmy couldn't read. So, Dave recorded one of the shorter pieces onto a cassette which Jimmy then listened to for half an hour before walking back into the room and bowling us both over with an extraordinarily raw and powerful rendition.

I told Jimmy right there and then that I would get him his first acting job within a month – and I did. I called a friend who was the director of a theatre company in Dundee and begged him to give Jimmy a part in a show he was casting. He must have been a good friend because two weeks later he cast Jimmy as an out-of-control drug addict and he went on to steal the show with his incredible performance. Six years on and he's now a star across the pond as well as in Britain, playing a lawless Chicago cop in a major US TV show.

The game changer for the centre came three years ago when Jimmy told the world, literally, through a series of TV and newspaper interviews, about how we had helped him get his first break. Interest in the story was huge and, as a result, there was a rush of journalists clamoring to write features on the work of the centre and what we were doing to help turn young lives around. As the profile of the Melville Centre grew so did its budget and it became THE fashionable project to fund and be associated with among local businesses and philanthropists. From there, it felt like we went from strength to strength.

In the days before my brother was due to start work at the centre, my pride in it and all we had achieved was turning to fear as I watched him struggle to pick up the mantle and run – or even crawl. Ben was clearly looking for the exit as he tried to come up with the perfect excuse as to why it was no longer possible for him to take on the job of running the foundation. But I felt just the smallest cause for hope when Danny told him about the young people at the centre. Because, while I had been able to talk to teenagers about success and what it was like to achieve, Ben understood all too well what it was like to fail. He wouldn't just float in and out like some untouchable being; he was real, he had made mistakes, he was someone they could relate to. Although he couldn't see it yet, this was the perfect job for him. I just hoped he would tough it out for these first few weeks and that this new challenge would be enough to force him out of the hopeless rut he'd dug himself into. It seemed a long shot, I know, but I learned long ago that there's more to my brother than meets the eye. He does, in fact, possess an inner grit that has been as much his undoing as it could be his making.

When we were boys I believed it was my life's purpose to torment Ben in whatever way I could. Usually it would involve throwing cold water over him when he was in the bath – once actually peeing on him in the same situation (I had to improvise when I couldn't find a bowl for the water). I guess I never stopped to think how that might affect him, because, in the moment that I was tormenting him, I would enjoy the power. My 'pranks' always hit the mark, and sent Ben storming into his room where he would barricade himself in while I rolled around laughing at just how predictable his response was.

But in reality, I was angry with him – and confused by his hold over Mum. Ben was slighter than me, would never fight back if provoked and shunned any form of physical exercise except walking, yet he was the mightiest by far because my mother simply adored him. She'd share little jokes with him, draw with him, read to him – and shelter him from his big bullying brother. So instead of being smart about it and trying to win her affections by staying out of trouble, I persecuted Ben all the more, and when she wasn't looking I would think nothing of shoving him into the wall, tripping him up or throwing the nearest available object at him. He always just walked away, and he never told. He was loyal like that.

One day though, he got his revenge. Dad had dropped us at school in the morning and from the moment I entered the gates everyone who walked behind me burst out laughing. After assembly I ran straight to the bathroom to try and work out what the hell was going on. Standing in the toilet cubicle I quickly removed my blazer but found nothing unusual with it. Then I took my trousers down to check if I had some kind of stain on them, and instead found two large holes where the pockets used to be. So, I'd been walking around with my bright green underpants on show. I didn't know how Ben had cut the holes without my noticing – but my routine of getting dressed quickly without opening the curtains had clearly worked in his favour. I didn't live it down for years.

And through my fury in that cubicle, one thought pervaded: So he's got guts after all. Because he was surely aware he would pay for a stunt like that.

~

Sarah heard the doorbell but there was no way she was going to answer it. Instead, she sat and nursed her cup of coffee. She'd had a shower that morning and had eaten some cornflakes so it was the closest thing she'd had to a healthy start in a few weeks. Still the rage burned inside of her and although no amount of alcohol would douse the flames, she could at least keep the fire from consuming her while she drank.

Suddenly she noticed someone at the window, banging on the glass. Ben.

'Oh God,' she thought. 'This is all I need.' He'd definitely seen her so there was no avoiding him. Reluctantly, she got to her feet and headed for the door.

He could barely disguise his shock as he stepped inside. He didn't even say hello. Just walked in quietly and took a seat in the kitchen.

'Do you want a cup of tea?' Sarah said coldly.

Ben looked around at the dirty cups and plates covering every surface and felt a rush of panic in his chest. The mess was overwhelming and he wasn't sure he'd be able to sit in it for very long.

'No,' he said politely. 'I'm fine, thanks.'

'How are you feeling?' he asked, although it was pretty obvious to him from the way she looked that she wasn't doing too well.

'Just great, Ben,' she almost hissed. 'High on life and all that it has to offer.'

'I'm sorry,' he muttered, guessing this wasn't the right moment to tell her he'd changed his mind about running the centre. It had taken him two hours to pluck up the courage to come over, and now he couldn't get the words out of his mouth.

He studied the deep, dark circles under her eyes and felt a pang of pity for the wretched creature now sitting at the table in front of him.

'Are you getting any sleep?' he ventured.

'No,' she said, shaking her head.

'Why don't you go and sit in the living room and let me make you something to eat then?' Ben suggested this partly out of concern and partly because it meant he could do something about the mess.

She stared at him blankly for a moment, trying to work out where he was coming from, but the thought of protesting exhausted her so she agreed, figuring it would at least buy her ten minutes more peace and quiet.

Left in the kitchen alone, Ben opened the fridge door to see what was in there. It didn't take him long to assess what she had, because she had nothing. There were a handful of broken crackers in a biscuit tin lying out on the counter and there was a pint of milk and a few bruised bananas within eyeshot. The cupboards were largely bare, but he found a tin of tomato soup that he thought would be ideal.

First though, he'd have to clean a pan to heat it in. The dishwasher was packed with dirty dishes so he threw in a soap tablet and put it on. Next he filled the kitchen sink with hot water, adding some washing liquid, and got started on the pile of pans, mugs and glasses that lay around him. It also didn't take him long to deduce that she'd been drinking a lot of wine these last few weeks, the empty bottles piled up in the recycling bin at the back door telling their own story. So we do have something in common after all, Ben thought.

He got stuck into the washing up, then wiped down the main surfaces before heating the soup. He put the bowl on a plate with some broken crackers and took it through to her with a cup of tea. Nudging the sitting room door open with his elbow, Ben found Sarah sitting curled up on the sofa, hugging her knees and staring at the floor, her already tiny frame reduced to little more than a skeleton. Forcing himself to look away, he put the mug of tea down then cleared a space on the coffee table in front of her to lay the bowl on. He could tell she didn't want to speak and he didn't know what to say anyway, so he decided to just clear up what he could from the table without disturbing her, then carried the rubbish through to the kitchen.

He took out some bin bags and started to fill them with the junk mail, tissues, cigarette packs and other assorted garbage that had been scattered over the last few weeks.

Seeing the place restored to some kind of order brought him the greatest sense of purpose he had felt in a long time.

He hoped Dad hadn't seen the mess, but he suspected he had and just hadn't known what to say. Being an eternal optimist, Dad would have probably thought she was having a blow-out and would come right soon enough, but Ben feared she was on a downward spiral that was already out of control.

Once he had finished in the kitchen, Ben headed back through to the living room where he was pleasantly surprised to find Sarah had actually finished the soup. When he turned to look at her she was fast asleep, sitting upright with her head lying back against the top of the sofa. Her legs, curled to the side, were almost invisible beneath her flared jeans, she had lost so much weight. The rest of her body was hidden under one of my old sweatshirts.

Ben reached behind her and gently laid her on her side, resting her head on a cushion before covering her with a throw from one of the armchairs.

He decided he should probably clear up the rest of the house too. He couldn't stand the thought of her living in such a mess. If he could get her house back into shape, it might just rub off on her emotional state.

Upstairs the guest bathroom and bedrooms were relatively untouched, but her own room and en-suite looked as though they had been ransacked. Used tissues covered the bedside tables and there were old photographs of the two of us together lying all around. By the look of them, my brother estimated her bedclothes probably hadn't been changed since the accident but he didn't want to overstep the mark so he just straightened the covers and arranged the photos in a neat pile. Once he'd cleared up, he took a heap of used towels from the bathroom downstairs to wash. He hoped she wouldn't mind him helping like this, it was the only thing he could think to do.

Sarah opened her eyes to find herself lying on the sofa covered with a blanket. She let out an embarrassed sigh with the realisation that Ben must have moved her, the intimacy an uncomfortable thought. Looking around she saw he'd tidied up too. I'd told her my brother was a bit OCD so she guessed that, for him, walking into her house today must have been like throwing a gambling addict into a casino with a pocket full of chips.

She was desperately hoping he'd left, but then she heard him unloading the dishwasher next door. She walked into the kitchen to find him putting the last cup into the cupboard – perfectly aligning it with all the others.

'Ben,' she said, sounding exasperated. 'There was really no need to do all this tidying. I'd have got around to it eventually – I'm just tired and...'

'I know.' He looked a little crushed. 'I was just trying to help.'

Sarah softened as she realised how dismissive she'd been of him lately. It couldn't have been easy being the depressed brother of a multi-millionaire entrepreneur. A golden boy if ever there was one. But her sympathy was then replaced with the thought that Ben might be actually enjoying stepping out from beneath my shadow and she felt the anger, now such a familiar friend, come rushing back to the fore.

'You're holding it together remarkably well considering your twin has just died,' she snapped, taking even herself by surprise.

Ben stared blankly back at her, but she could see she'd hurt him and immediately regretted it.

'I'll go,' he said finally, moving out to the hallway to collect his jacket.

Sarah rushed forwards, stopping just short of him.

'Ben, I'm sorry. I don't know where that came from. I've just been feeling so angry lately. I'm not trying to hurt you.'

'I'm grieving too, Sarah,' he said, before grabbing his jacket from the stand and folding it over the crook of his left arm. 'But if I fall apart again, I'll never get myself back together. I've flirted with a break-down for too long.' He looked away from her and let out a long sigh before finally returning her gaze. 'Don't think I didn't love him, Sarah. In some ways, I idolised Harry. Everything he did, from the way he dressed, the way he filled a room with his presence, the look of pride on my father's face when he spoke about him – it was all so much more than I could ever achieve so I just didn't bother.

'I've spent the entire afternoon trying to figure out what this all means and I've decided I have to start again. I need to get past my fear, otherwise he'll have died for nothing. I know I have to run that centre for him, but I can't do it on my own. I waited here to ask you if you'll help me.'

Sarah folded her arms in front of her and took a step back.

'Help you, Ben,' she said, incredulously. 'I can't even help myself right now.'

He nodded his understanding. 'Okay, then I'll help you first. I'll be back tomorrow.'

And without giving her the chance to reply, he left.

Sarah stared at the front door slammed shut by my brother just seconds earlier. She knew she couldn't keep the world at bay for much longer. Ben would be coming over again tomorrow and her friend Rosa had left about twenty messages in the last two weeks, at first begging for her to call her back and now telling her she was worried sick and would be driving through from Glasgow to see her whether she was welcome or not.

Sarah had also made another important decision. She wasn't going to return to the legal firm where she had worked part-time. She had emailed her boss earlier to tender her resignation and would take her time before deciding what to do next. Maybe she would move abroad and get away from everything that reminded her of her past. Even the good times caused her pain now – and the bad times struck her like a knife blow. They permeated her dreams, and her waking thoughts.

She turned towards the fireplace and reached for a picture of the two of us sitting in the open-top jeep at 5am on an African morning three years before, waiting to head off on our dawn safari. Our smiles were wide and open, our love strong although fraught with the jealousies and insecurities that were so often the source of the terrible rows which usually ended in us throwing ourselves into each other's arms and vowing we'd never leave.

Sarah clutched the picture tightly in her shaking hands. 'I'm sorry Harry,' she cried. 'I'm so, so sorry.'

I studied her for a while as she stood sobbing wretchedly – her shoulders shuddering and her tears splashing down onto the picture frame. Guilt and grief are a potent mix.

$\sim$

Ben rang the doorbell at 10am the next morning, but Sarah was ready for him. To his obvious surprise she was up, showered, dressed and, by the looks of the bags lining her kitchen counter, had even been to the supermarket.

'You seem brighter today,' Ben said with a slight air of suspicion.

'Yes,' she replied. 'I did a bit of thinking after you left yesterday. I realised I need to start trying to live again, even if I don't feel like it.' She smiled, unconvincingly, at him and he noticed the dark circles still visible despite the make-up she wore to try to cover them. Still, he thought, this looked like progress.

He wondered too if she would be able to resist the urge to drown her sorrows, or if, like him, she would wait for the cover of darkness to lock herself away with her self-pity and drink. He knew the blissful numbness that alcohol so reliably delivered was a hard companion to turn your back on.

He himself hadn't been able to totally deny himself the comfort offered by his old friend The Bottle, but had in recent days cut back on the time they spent together, only meeting after work, at home and in secrecy.

'Good,' he said, deciding to play along with Sarah's apparent togetherness. 'I won't hang around long then. I just brought us a couple of croissants.' He handed them to her in a paper bag. 'Thought you might be hungry.'

'Snap,' she replied, laughing as she held up another two croissants she had bought that morning.

'Great minds,' he smiled.

They sat down at the kitchen table together and Sarah poured him a coffee.

'So, why are you so worried about running the centre?' she asked candidly. Her direct manner had always left him feeling a little uncomfortable. He thought she was very like me in that sense. At times she would appear vulnerable, but there was a steeliness at her core.

'I've no idea where to begin.' He stared into his coffee. 'I want to do it, but I have no management experience whatsoever. The team I met told me I'd have to go out and persuade businesses to help fund the project, but I couldn't persuade a cat to catch a mouse. And I..,' he thought about how much he should say. He was so fed up of being the weak one. 'I have a fear of meeting people, being out in public, things like that.'

'What do you mean?' Sarah asked.

'I've been told it's, em.. an anxiety disorder basically. I'm pretty much anxious about most things.'

'I had no idea. But it makes so much sense now. I wish we'd known that earlier, Ben. I think it could have helped.. you know, with the way you and Harry were.'

'It's not something I talk about a lot,' he said, eyes fixed on his plate.

'I know you can do this, Ben. You have to fight the fear – it's controlled you long enough. And you'll finally be earning some money. It's a great opportunity for you to do something with your life.'

She could see she'd embarrassed him by mentioning money. He'd be earning £45,000 a year, although he'd accepted the job without asking what he'd be paid – a fact that had both surprised and impressed Sarah. She guessed she'd misjudged him by assuming he was lazy. These days she was beginning to see there was a lot more to Ben than she had thought. In fact, she wondered how she'd missed it all those years. His gentle calm. She had put his shyness and reluctance to join in and be part of the family down to him being a little high-minded, judging even.

But the man sitting with her now seemed the very opposite – humble, willing, utterly devoid of affectation or the desire to impress. She wished she could say the same for herself. Trying to appear perfect had been one of the major driving forces of her life – as it had mine.

'I'm here if you ever need a sounding board,' she told Ben.

'Thanks,' he replied, managing a half smile. 'It's good to be able to talk to someone about it.'

Sarah tilted her head as she took in this stranger, my brother, the man who had been a mystery for all those years but she was finally getting to know. She noticed his sculptured looks, so much more obvious now he had got rid of his stubble and stuck to being clean shaven.

Sarah had barely said goodbye to Ben, when there was another knock on her front door. Rosa can't be here already, she thought, she wasn't due for another half an hour. But, sure enough, she opened the door to find her formidable friend already pushing past her.

'Where the hell have you been?' Rosa demanded. 'I convinced myself you'd committed suicide and I was coming to find a body.'

'Well, I'm still here,' Sarah called after Rosa who had by now made her way through to the kitchen where she was removing her coat. 'Sorry to disappoint.'

'Oh, don't be so bloody ridiculous. Just make me a cup of tea can you. I've driven like a bat out of hell to get here.'

Sarah realised Rosa had put herself out. She had two very young children who she'd probably had to leave in her elderly mother's care for the day so she could make the journey from Glasgow to visit.

'Thank you for coming, Rosa. I know it can't have been easy getting away.'

'Don't be daft. It's a bloody relief just to have an excuse to get out of the house. I left my mother desperately grappling with the TV remote, while Maddie and Esther bounced up and down in front of her screaming for CBeebies, but I felt not even the faintest desire to help. Now give your old friend a hug.' Rosa outstretched her arms to embrace her former flatmate. 'And don't shut me out like that again,' she jokingly warned Sarah. The two had met at university and had been close ever since. Sarah felt her spirits lift as she relaxed into the company of a friend whose loyalty had never wavered in the near twenty years they had known each other. She even looked the same. Rosa had always carried a bit of padding, and her cheeks were permanently flushed as if duty-bound to match her name, but she had a radiant face and personality Sarah admired and adored.

They sat down with their cups of tea and smiled at each other across the kitchen table, Sarah's eyes welling up as she was finally able to let down her guard with someone she trusted.

'I miss him, Rosa.'

'I know.'

'And I'm so angry that he's gone, but I've no one to blame but him. He was speeding and lost control of his car, the police said. How could he be so bloody reckless?'

Rosa sat silently, willing her friend to continue. She was no stranger to grief herself, having been forced to deal with her father's suicide when she was just fifteen. All she had wanted to do then was talk to someone, but there was no one to listen. Her mother was too lost in her own pain and her school friends treated her like a leper for the first few months after his death, afraid that grief was catching. Today she was here to provide nothing more than a pair of ears to a friend she suspected just needed to open up and let it out.

'You've probably guessed I've been a bit down.'

Rosa nodded.

'The pain and sense of injustice that I felt when Harry died was just overwhelming. It still is. I know I have to go on, I just haven't figured out how.'

'It'll take time,'

'I guess so.'

Rosa watched Sarah fall deeper into her own thoughts, staring into oblivion and biting on her lower lip.

'I need to tell you something, Rosa. Something that's been eating me up but which I am scared to say out loud because it's so horrible.'

'Just say whatever's on your mind. That's why I'm here. You know you can tell me anything.'

Sarah nodded and took a deep breath before continuing.

'I had a fling with someone just before Harry died.'

Rosa's eyes widened in surprise.

'It was completely meaningless. Just a guy from work – Paul – who'd had a crush on me for years and didn't seem to pay any attention to the fact I was married. He was always coming on to me on work nights out and I'd usually brush him off. Then, just a few weeks before Harry died, Paul and I went to a conference in Birmingham together and I ended up spending the night with him. I guess in some subliminal way I was punishing Harry. It only happened once but I felt horrible. I'd been trying to figure out whether to tell Harry or not… but then…'

She put her head in her hands and started to sob. 'He died thinking I was a loyal, loving wife, Rosa, when in actual fact I was an unfaithful, selfish bitch.'

Rosa got to her feet and walked round to rest at Sarah's side. She placed an arm around her shoulder and whispered: 'Harry died believing the right thing then. You were a loyal, loving wife, you just slipped up and he'll never know that.'

Sarah raised her head and looked pitifully into her friend's face. 'But I know, Rosa. And it's tearing me apart.'

CHAPTER five

I HADN'T SUSPECTED AN AFFAIR – but then I was way too arrogant to ever think Sarah would cheat on me. I hadn't been able to provide her with the child she so desperately wanted, and I never really stopped to think about how difficult that must have been for her. I hadn't always been the most fantastic husband either, especially in the two years leading up to her fling. I wonder whether if she had felt able to confide in me our relationship could have ever recovered? Could I have forgiven her? I feared not. Pride would have prevented me from even thinking about what the reasons for her cheating might have been. I'd have shut her out along with my emotions.

My life was, in truth, all about me. Everything I'd ever strived for had been one big shout for attention: 'Look at me, look at what I've achieved.' That's how my business had started – with a small venture I tried my hand at as a student in an effort to impress my father.

Edinburgh University had been chock full of little rich boys and girls who were living in flats bought for them by mummy and daddy. They had been filled with old bits and pieces from home, including vases, paintings, rugs and furniture that their mothers had long gone off. Some of these unloved items were actually pretty valuable. And that's where I stepped in. I helped these cash-strapped students earn a bit of extra dosh by relieving them of the older furnishings, having agreed to a 50:50 split on whatever I got for them. Those bits and pieces that I reckoned were actually worth a bob or two I'd take to antiques dealers, and the rest I'd flog at my weekly boot sale in the university car park. These sales became legendary, with bargain-hungry customers scrapping over the old tat and the occasional genuine article. It was a perfect marketplace. And it was also the birth of the YourLot empire. Shortly after I left uni, Dad backed me in opening up my own antiques dealership. Then, when internet enterprises really started taking off, I realised I could sell an awful lot more stuff online. To begin with we simply traded antiques, but quickly opened it up to more modern pieces and then – six years ago – took the leap of allowing members to sell their own items via our site. The rest, as they say, is history. I was the eternal optimist, but not even I envisaged the level of financial success I would reap through the website. YourLot.com became a global phenomenon and I, in turn, a very rich man.

Dad was so proud. My achievements were a favourite topic of conversation for him, with my long-suffering mother taking the brunt of it in the early years. She always listened patiently and smiled encouragingly in my direction, but I could have been a billionaire ten times over and it wouldn't have made any difference. Material wealth never impressed her. She was only ever interested in our inner wealth; namely the talents she thought my brother had in abundance but never used.

Mum didn't live to see the height of my success, but she saw the depths of my personal failings. As did Ben. Whenever I was in his presence my achievements became as weightless as air and my determination to prove myself as solid as stone.

~

Ben took a deep breath as he prepared to enter his first Monday morning team meeting. Pushing the door to the office open, he found three faces staring at him expectantly from their seats behind the meeting table. This time he'd be more assertive he told himself. So he forced himself to look straight into the eyes of his new employees as he entered the room, but in doing so failed to spot the umbrella at his feet which sent him stumbling around the doorway like a circus clown. Once he'd regained his balance he returned his gaze to the three faces in front of him realising pretty quickly that it was too late to salvage his dignity. They were already desperately trying, and failing, to stifle their laughter.

'I guess that's what you call an entrance,' said Ben, managing a smile. At this they all fell about laughing, but at least they were laughing with him, he hoped.

Ben sat down and reminded himself that he had to remain in control. He pressed on with the statement he had planned, clasping his hands tightly as he spoke so they wouldn't see them shaking.

'I want to meet as many of the kids as I can this week.'

'No problem,' said Dave.

'I need to spend this week getting to know the place and everything that goes on here. Then, next Monday we'll talk about how we move forward. If you have any ideas then that will be your opportunity to raise them, and I'll bring a few of my own too. Everyone okay with that?'

'Absolutely,' said Sonja, at last looking at him with something he thought could just pass for respect. He noticed for the first time that behind the tough facade, she actually had a nice, round, kindly face – a face that was comforting to look at.

Ben smiled at his colleagues and hoped this fleeting feeling of belonging might last.

He was about to tell them the meeting was over when Sonja cleared her throat. 'Ben, we…eh, we're not quite sure what to do with Harry's stuff.'

'What stuff?'

'Eh… that filing cabinet behind you is full of his paperwork and files. We didn't want to go through it without talking to you first.'

'I see,' said Ben, turning to look at the cabinet in question behind him. 'Why don't you give me the key and I'll go through it this afternoon.'

Sonja's relief was palpable. Clearly, she wasn't relishing the idea of working her way through my secrets. Personally, I thought that showed a rather disappointing lack of adventurism, but then I always was a nosey sod. Ben was certainly afraid of what he'd find in a locked cabinet belonging to his heedless twin. And there was a secret within that cabinet, one I longed to be uncovered but would only be done by the most astute of minds. Just as well then, that it was my brother unlocking it.

Ben waited until the staff had left the office before turning to open the filing cabinet with the small key Sonja had handed him moments earlier. He had no idea why he felt so apprehensive when all he was likely to find were a few bits of accountancy work. He pulled open the drawer to see – as he expected – a well-organised row of hanging folders, all carefully named and in alphabetical order: Accounts, Annual Report, Donations, Letters Received, Maintenance, Staff. Ben immediately reached for the Letters file to see what kind of correspondence I had kept. He soon found the file would have been more aptly named Thank Yous, as it contained note after note from young people who we had worked with and/or their parents all eulogising about the centre – and me. I can't lie.

Ben read a few and smiled before carefully returning the cards and letters to their folder. He worked his way to the back of the cabinet where he noticed a solitary untitled file. He suspected the tag had been knocked off as the folder looked old and slightly worn. Lifting it out of the cabinet, he retrieved from inside four sheets of folded and crumpled paper. He opened the first to discover a stunningly detailed pencil sketch of an elderly man with a bulbous nose who looked like he'd been sinking a few pints over the course of a long afternoon in the pub. The skin was mottled but his eyes were smiling through an alcoholic haze. Ben hastily opened the other sheets and pored over each piece of work; all featured single, character-filled subjects by the same artist who signed only his first name, Luke.

Ben folded each of the sheets of paper carefully and filed them away again, unsure whether they should be kept or thrown in the bin. That was a decision he would save for another day. He knew all about Luke. I had spoken of him several times and he remembered what I'd told him all too clearly; the good, the bad, and the very, very ugly.

~

Sarah perched on the edge of the bath as she waited for the small plastic stick in her hand to reveal her future.

Then she gasped, clasping her hand to her face as it delivered its verdict. 'Pregnant'.

'Oh shit,' she said aloud. Immediately, she thought of all the days and nights she'd spent these last few weeks drowning her sorrows and smoking.

She hadn't been careful with Paul Davis but never imagined – never really imagined – that she'd be pregnant. She thought the tiredness and nausea she'd been feeling these last few weeks was grief. She had barely noticed missing her period until the fog started to lift and she began piecing her symptoms together.

She dropped the test stick and put her head in her hands. 'Why now?' she begged out loud. How the hell was she going to explain this to Ben and Dad?

But as she gripped the edge of the bath, imagining their angry, confused faces, her anguish began to give way to something else. There was a child growing inside her, the very thing she had been longing for, and the one and only person who might just be able to wipe away the ever-present stain of grief from her heart.

And before she knew it, she couldn't suppress her joy at achieving the very thing she had so desperately wanted – even though the truth would surely devastate my family.

~

Two days later and Ben was standing to attention in the recreation room waiting to meet the first of a few new recruits, Jason Weir. Ben's first impression of Jason was that he looked like a guy you wouldn't want to meet down a dark alley. He wasn't tall, but he was well built and there was a hardness about him, though he was smartly turned out in jeans and a navy bomber jacket. He tried to take a guess at what career this 20-year-old might be looking to pursue – he'd clearly made an effort with his appearance – but he just wasn't someone you could easily categorise.

Extending a hand towards the youth, he introduced himself, adding, 'You must be Jason.'

'That's right, aye,' Jason replied, looking Ben up and down with more than a degree of suspicion before returning the handshake.

'When did you join the centre?' Ben asked.

'Couple of weeks ago.'

'What is it that you'd like to do?'

'Just get into something where I can use my talent. I want to make something of myself but I don't know how to get started,' he said with unexpected candour. 'I've got no qualifications.'

'Right,' Ben replied, already feeling out of his depth. 'What line of work would you like to get into?'

'I want to be an artist,' said Jason, fixing him straight in the eye as if to say – 'and what you going to do about it?'

Jason must have noticed Ben squint as he processed this last piece of information. He hadn't seen that one coming. This young man was such a curious mix of rough but polished, from his accent, distinctly Scottish yet clearly spoken, down to his stylish suede ankle boots.

'Do you draw or paint?' Ben finally asked.

'Draw. I've got some sketches with me,' Jason offered, producing a notepad from his pocket. He handed it to Ben who quickly opened it, intrigued to see what Jason would class as art.

Inside he found a series of drawings so detailed they almost looked like black and white photos, but done entirely in ballpoint pen. Ben thought most of the people and animals Jason had drawn were probably based on pictures. He was struck by one of a middle-aged man with a cigarette hanging out of his mouth, holding a pint and wearing a, 'come and have a go if you think you're hard enough', kind of look on his face. The other was of a child, bawling his eyes out, dressed in a Batman suit that he clearly didn't want to wear. Each one was so detailed you felt like you were in the picture, not just looking at it. Incredibly, the drawings brought the subjects to life more masterfully than a camera ever could.

Jason without doubt had a serious talent.

'What do your teachers say about your abilities?'

'I've not really been to school since I was fifteen. They used to say I was quite good.'

'Quite good,' said Ben incredulously. 'I've never seen anything like this. You are seriously gifted.'

Jason turned an instant shade of purple at this compliment.

'I'm going to get you the materials you need to produce ten pieces of work, Jason, and when you're finished we're going to display them at a special exhibition here at the centre and invite everyone we can possibly think of who could help you.'

Ben thought he could see Jason's chest physically puff out with pride at this suggestion.

'No bother,' he said with the most delighted smile Ben had ever seen. Once Ben became aware of himself again he realised he was beaming too.

Ben left the centre that night bursting with enthusiasm. He had been shocked by both the talent and the ambition some of these young people had – many from backgrounds that were challenging to say the least. After he met with Jason, he talked to a girl called Gemma, who he found sitting with Sonja filling in an application form for college.

'What are you applying for?' he had asked.

'Telford College,' she replied. 'I'm going to sit some Higher exams and see if I can go on to study nursing.'

'Excellent,' said Ben. Genuinely impressed. 'You're in good hands with Sonja advising you,' he added, wondering if she could tell he was just sucking up. Somehow he felt he had yet to win Sonja over. She still seemed a little suspicious although he wasn't sure why.

Sonja smiled back at him as if to say, 'you'll have to do a lot better than that to convince me you're up to the job'.

Ben sensed it was time to move on, before he made the situation worse. He would wait until the next team meeting to discuss his plans for Jason. He thought he could ask Sarah to help too as he was sure she'd mentioned she knew Emily DiRollo who owned a big gallery in town. It would be fantastic if Sarah could persuade Emily to take a look at Jason's drawings. He was sure she'd want to snap them up. He decided to head over to Sarah's on the way home and talk to her, hoping he wouldn't find her drunk if he was dropping in unexpected. He realised he was hardly in a position to judge when he'd spent the last twenty five years completely out of it. It seemed strange that he was suddenly the responsible one.

He wondered how long he could continue feeling this good and resolved to keep moving so the pin couldn't catch up with him and burst his bubble.

~

As Ben rang the doorbell, he stiffened at the thought of what could be about to greet him. The lights were on so he knew Sarah was in, but it didn't look like she was going to answer. He imagined her slumped on the sofa, half asleep, wine glass half-tipped over as she lost awareness, but just as he was about to turn on his heels the door opened.

Sarah stood smiling in front of him, dressed immaculately in white jeans and an expensive-looking jumper with her hair swept cleanly back into a pony-tail. She looked as relaxed and stunning as she once always did and, clearly, she wasn't drunk.

'Come in,' she said, gesturing towards the living room. 'It's nice to see you.'

For the first time, Ben thought she sounded like she meant it.

'It's good to see you looking so well.'

'I'm feeling good,' she said, still smiling. 'Can I get you something to drink? Glass of wine, cup of tea?'

'A glass of wine would be bloody marvellous,' Ben said, realising he sounded a little too enthusiastic. He'd been desperate for a drink since lunchtime.

'No problem. You go and take a seat and I'll be back in a minute.'

Ben sat down, his mind ticking over as he tried to figure out what could have cheered Sarah up so much. He knew her mother, Angela, had travelled up from Cumbria to stay last week so maybe that had been a bit of a turning point.

When she appeared back in the room with his glass of wine, he asked: 'Did your mum enjoy her visit?'

'I think she did – and it was so nice to see her again. She wants me to go and stay with her and Dad for a week next month so I think I might just do that.'

'Great,' said Ben. 'It's nice to see you looking so happy again. Are you not joining me in a drink?'

'There's a reason for that,' Sarah said quickly, her voice hardening.

Ben shuffled in his seat, hardly daring to ask in case she'd met someone else in a fit of grief-induced madness. But she'd laid down the gauntlet so he supposed he'd have to follow up.

'What's the reason?'

'I'm pregnant.'

A mixture of relief and overwhelming joy rushed through Ben as he began to absorb that statement. He leapt to his feet, but she held her hand out as if to keep him at bay.

'Ben, it's not Harry's,' she snapped.

This statement gave him such a jolt he toppled back onto the sofa. His brain went to jelly as he tried to figure out what that meant. Then he realised she must be referring to the fertility treatment I had mentioned to him. Another wave of relief swept in as he reassured her: 'That's okay, Sarah. Just because it's a donor it doesn't change the fact this is Harry's baby – because it's the baby Harry wanted.'

Sarah studied Ben's hope-filled face with a mixture of something that looked like horror and pity.

Then her features softened again; her smile returning as quickly as it had left a few moments earlier.

'That's right,' she said. 'It was a donor.'

'Sarah,' said Ben, his eyes filling with tears as he rushed towards her. 'I can't believe you were afraid to tell me that.'

'I know. It was silly.'

He threw his arms around her and they fell into a natural embrace for the first time ever.

'Dad will be thrilled,' said Ben. 'And I'll be an uncle. When's it due?'

'November. It seems ages away.'

'Oh wow. This is amazing news.'

Sarah could only watch in silence as Ben got lost in his excitement.

'I wonder if it'll be a boy?' he mused out loud. 'I don't care either way. But it's just what we need isn't it, Sarah? After these dark, dark weeks, suddenly some sunshine.'

Sarah stuck her hands awkwardly into her pockets and nodded.

What a funny fish she was with all her mood swings and strange notions, Ben thought. He imagined he'd never work her out, but he was just so happy that the very thing I would have wanted for her was actually happening.

Dad broke down at the other end of the phone line as Ben told him about the pregnancy. After a long discussion, he and Sarah had agreed not to mention the 'donor' – as my brother so innocently had come to call him – as it would simply confuse the issue for

Dad. After all, Ben felt this was the child that Sarah and I had tried for and, therefore, I was theoretically still the father so there was no need to complicate things further by explaining the science.

When he heard how overcome our father was though, Ben did have a moment where he wondered if they should have told him the full story.

'That's so wonderful,' Dad sobbed. 'God has given us back what he has taken.'

Ben winced again. But he had to rationalise this. Dad would be the grandfather of what would have been my child, so why was he feeling weird about this?

'I'll let you speak to Sarah,' he said, passing the buck as quickly as he handed over the phone.

He listened for a moment as Sarah laughed with Dad, sharing his joy.

'I know, I can't believe it,' she kept saying. 'I'm so happy.'

Ben suddenly felt a little light-headed – the mix of emotions, that ill-fitted pairing of grief and excitement, had almost caused his brain to fuse. He walked through to the kitchen and poured himself a glass of water, gulping it down quickly and letting the coolness of the liquid suppress the heat of the situation.

Later that night and finally alone, Sarah lay back on the pillow and took a long, deep breath, exhaling all the weirdness of the day. She had fully meant to tell Ben about the baby's real father but, when it actually came to the moment, seeing the joy on his face, she just couldn't do it. When he jumped to the conclusion that she and I had opted to use a donor it gave her the perfect solution to a very major problem. And in a way, she reasoned, we had used a donor. It may not have been in the conventional way but, biologically, it was no different to plucking a test tube out of a sperm bank. She did have flashes of guilt when she thought of Paul, the real father, and how he would never know he had this child. But she told herself he'd probably rather not know. He was a single guy in his thirties who didn't want to be lumbered with the responsibilities of parenthood without having actively decided to become a father. The worst guilt came when she thought of Dad and Ben. They were so elated. It was like she'd turned the light back on in their dark worlds. She knew that feeling well. The light had just been switched back on for her too. How unthinkable then it would be to plunge them back into the abyss from which they'd all just crawled out.

CHAPTER six

I SET UP THE MELVILLE FOUNDATION after an encounter with a relentlessly cheerful Big Issue seller, who based himself outside my local Tesco store. When one day my curiosity got the better of me, it resulted in one of the most interesting conversations I'd ever had. It was a freezing January morning, complete with driving winds and sleet, when I dashed from my car towards the store, hoping to pick up a packet of Beechams powders – I had a stinking cold. Although he'd been standing at the doorway every time I'd visited the store in the last four years, I still couldn't believe he'd turned out in such terrible weather. And today, like every other, he stood happily smiling and bidding a good day to every customer who walked past him. As I approached within a few feet of him, I was about to offer my standard greeting, 'Hiya mate', when instead, I found myself asking: 'Why are you here?'

'Sorry pal?' he squinted behind smiling eyes, still eager to please.

'Why are you standing out here on this bloody awful morning?'

'I come here every day, except Sundays.'

'Don't you even make an exception on a day like this – how many copies are you going to sell today after all?'

'More than you'd think. Bad weather can be good for business when you're homeless,' he chuckled. I liked his style.

'Do you mind me asking what brought you here; why you're selling the Big Issue?'

'I was in care most of my life and went straight onto the streets at sixteen. I got this gig not long after that.'

And then I posed the question I'd been itching to ask all along.

'So what would you really like to be doing?'

For the first time since we started speaking, his eyes left mine and his face turned serious as he thought for a while.

'Actually, I'd like to be a social worker. It's a powerful job, that. And there's too many people doing it that don't have a bloody clue what they're talking about. They destroy families because it's easier than keeping them together.'

'Families like yours?'

'Aye, like mine, pal. Like mine.'

It was the briefest of exchanges but it set me on what became an endless quest to help people like him accomplish what they were capable of in life; to help them live and not just survive. It had often troubled me that just because of my privileged background, I had a passport to opportunity, when people just a few blocks away were sentenced to a lifetime's struggle. Who decides who gets to make something of themselves and who remains in squalor? And what would happen if I decided to reshuffle the pack and deal a new hand?

~

Ben walked to work with a definite spring in his step. He'd spent all night imagining life as an uncle. After all, it hadn't escaped him that he would be the immediate father figure. He envisaged afternoons in the park, visits to the zoo, the ice cream parlour just down the road.

He couldn't wipe the smile off his face at the thought. Whether it was a boy or a girl he didn't care, he just couldn't wait. Ben's elation had taken him by surprise, but he was enjoying every minute. It almost felt like a new lease of life. There was so much happening right now, so much to celebrate. He couldn't help but marvel at the way things had turned around for him, but it was equally perplexing to realise these positive changes had so closely followed my death.

Ben's desire to be a big part of his niece or nephew's life had also helped cement the changes he was making to improve his health. He had significantly reduced his drinking to just a few beers in the evening, and some days nothing at all, and he had even begun eating salads lately. It had taken the death of his twin for Ben to realise he should at least try to preserve his own life. Such a dark and painful event had jolted him back to reality – and he couldn't deny that he had never felt happier now he suddenly had so much to live for.

What a crash back down to earth then when he reached the Melville Centre and opened the door to the staff room only to find Sonja in tears at the meeting table. He was trying to make a split-second decision on whether to walk back out and give her some privacy or go in and try to comfort her. But when she looked up at him, her cheeks streaked with tears, he knew it was too late to back away.

'What's wrong?' he asked, wishing it had been anyone but Sonja he'd found in this state. After all, she knew how to make him feel generally useless at the best of times, let alone when she was in need of a tower of strength.

'Nothing'. She shook her head as if that ended the matter.

'Look, you may not know me well but it could help to talk. I'm more than happy to listen.'

She looked him up and down with the usual degree of suspicion before deciding on her response.

'One of the girls here, Gemma, has just told me she's pregnant,' she explained.

Ben took the opportunity to sit down while she was in the frame of mind to talk.

'She's seventeen-years-old and had just got her life on track and a college place sorted when this happens. She's just thrown away everything we've worked so hard for.' Sonja shook her head while Ben searched for the right words of encouragement for his new colleague.

He remembered Gemma. He had talked to her while she was filling her application form out with Sonja a couple of weeks ago.

'That's really frustrating,' he said.

'It's not this situation in itself that has got me down. It's just that we invest so much of ourselves in these young people. When good things happen for them it's just as exciting as it happening to you. And when it goes wrong, you're devastated. I can't seem to separate myself from it all.'

'I don't think you should,' Ben interrupted. 'If you separated yourself from it then you wouldn't care, and that's what makes this place different – the fact that people care.'

'Do you care?' she asked, turning to face him directly.

'Well,' Ben said, ready to deliver a defensive answer. But then he paused to truly ask himself the question.

'Look, Sonja, I know I'm not my brother. I'm not confident and inspiring. I know you can probably tell I'm nervous right now. But all I can say is that every night after working here, I go home and think about the young people I've met that day. All the drama in their lives. Some of them have come from the worst of backgrounds, the kind of homes where you think they wouldn't stand a chance, yet they come in here because they just want to make a better life for themselves. I look at some of them and I know exactly what they mean when they talk about not being good enough and feeling foolish for even daring to believe they could have a good career. That's how I felt when I walked through these doors. It's how I feel right now. But – and I know I may not have a lot of experience – I want very much to try and make this work. And, with you and the rest of the team behind me, I think we will.'

Sonja tilted her head as she considered what he'd said, and then, for the first time in his company, she broke into a smile.

I think I've just made a friend, thought Ben, smiling back.

~

Sarah slowly selected the contact from her mobile and hit dial. She had put off making the call for weeks but she knew she had to do it. Emily DiRollo was an intimidating character at the best of times, so the thought of having to ask her a favour made her stomach lurch in trepidation. It didn't help either that Emily loved to remind Sarah she had once dated me way back when we were teenagers. To Sarah, this seemed like Emily's little power card which she would dangle in front of her each time they spoke, just so she could watch her squirm.

Still, she had promised Ben and, with everything he was putting into the centre, she felt she owed him one.

Emily was a client of the legal practice where she used to work. She was a sharp operator which, combined with her knowledge of the art world and eye for great pieces of work, had pushed her right to the top of her game. Her Edinburgh gallery was renowned throughout the city, and the wider art world.

The phone was ringing now and within seconds Emily answered.

'Sarah, how are you?'

'I'm fine, thank you..' She was about to launch into her prepared dialogue when Emily interrupted her.

'I was so sorry to hear about your husband,' she said, her voice genuinely full of concern. 'You must have been through hell.'

'It's been a pretty difficult few months, yes. Thank you for asking though.' Not wishing to linger on the subject, Sarah moved quickly on. 'I wanted to ask you a bit of a favour.'

'Oh yes?' Emily replied.

'You may be aware that Harry started up the Melville Foundation through which he ran a centre to help disadvantaged young people.'

'I'm more than aware of it. I have donated towards it in the past.'

Sarah couldn't help but bristle at this little snippet of information. I hadn't mentioned Emily's donations. To Sarah, this seemed to hint at an ongoing connection between her late husband and the woman at the other end of the phone.

Sarah took a deep breath before continuing. 'I wasn't aware of that, Emily. But thank you for your generosity. Harry's twin brother, Ben, is now running the centre and he is currently helping a twenty-year-old called Jason Weir who is a rather exceptional artist.'

'I see.'

'He has produced a series of portraits of his family and friends using the only resource he had – a ballpoint pen – to create incredibly detailed pictures which appear, at first sight, almost as photographic prints.'

'Interesting,' Emily added. Sarah could tell she was going to make her work for this.

'We wondered if you would mind taking a look at them?'

'I would be happy to do that, Sarah, but may I ask for what purpose?'

Sarah swallowed hard as she tried to figure out how she could subtly suggest Emily might sell the pictures in her gallery or at least point Jason in the direction of another gallery owner or agent who could help.

'Well, we would value an expert opinion on his talent and also some advice on where he can go from here. Coming from a housing estate in Leith, he doesn't have many contacts in the art world.'

'No,' said Emily. 'I can appreciate that. Bring a selection into the gallery on Friday will you. Shall we say around eleven?'

'Yes, that would be fine, Emily. And thank you – again.'

Sarah slung her mobile phone into her handbag, before shaking her head and letting out a long sigh at the thought she was now beholden to a woman she held little positive feeling towards.

~

Ben had been ecstatic when Sarah told him of Friday's meeting, but standing in front of DiRollo's gallery on the Royal Mile, she wasn't feeling quite so overjoyed. She hadn't felt so self-conscious since my funeral, when it had seemed the eyes of the world were upon her in what was undoubtedly her darkest hour. She checked over the outfit she had so carefully chosen for an unusually warm early Summer's day in Edinburgh that included a new silk wrap-over blouse – she figured she could let the ties out as her stomach got bigger – and white maternity jeans she had bought only the week before. Her bump was barely noticeable to others, but she could see it and loved checking it whenever she got undressed. Unusually for her, she'd also recently treated herself to a very expensive pair of Alexander McQueen black suede 'sneakers', as the sales lady had described them, figuring she would need a sturdy pair of stylish but comfortable shoes.

One of the things I had come to admire most about my wife was that, despite being married to a very wealthy man, she would never accept money from me and insisted on paying her own way. She could have easily given up work years ago, but insisted on staying at the law firm, despite the pressure she was often under. 'I just don't want to be a kept woman,' she would say, joking that she'd only turn to drink and drugs if she didn't have a job to keep her out of trouble. As a result, although she dressed well, she rarely bought designer clothes yet often looked like the most expensively-dressed woman in the room.

She was also incredibly hard on herself, and looking over her outfit for a final time, she decided the shoes were the wrong choice for today's meeting, and made her look like she was trying a bit too hard.

She imagined Emily's critical eyes casting over her feet, and let out an audible sigh before ringing the buzzer on the intercom outside the gallery.

A young, attractive girl – dressed in black skinny jeans and a black vest top – came to the door to let her in.

'Are you Mrs Melville?' she asked politely.

'Yes.'

'Just come through. Emily's in her office at the back.'

Sarah walked obligingly behind the girl, taking in the impressive array of canvases lining the whitewashed walls. The studio, with its unvarnished wooden floor and glossy black doors, was minimalist and well maintained, not unlike Emily, Sarah observed.

Suddenly, the meagre pieces of drawing paper Sarah clutched in a folder in her hands felt a little trivial, although she kept reminding herself that it was Jason's abilities on trial, not hers.

The assistant knocked on Emily's office door.

'Sarah Melville is here to see you.'

'Ah, wonderful,' Emily said, sitting behind a glass desk that was completely bare apart from a laptop and mobile phone. 'Do come in, Sarah.' She stood up and walked around the desk to kiss Sarah on each cheek.

'Please,' she said, pointing to a very expensive-looking black leather armchair. Sarah sat down and took a moment to digest Emily's small, but beautifully assembled office, with its own collection of modern art works. Emily herself appeared as demure as always in a fantastically chic purple silk blouse and a pencil-cut calf-length black skirt with black patent ankle boots.

'What a wonderful office,' Sarah said. 'I wouldn't mind working in these surroundings myself.'

'Perk of the job,' Emily smiled, sweeping back her cropped bob on one side to tuck her hair behind her ear. 'Do you have the drawings in there?' She pointed to the folder Sarah was clutching to her torso.

'Yes. Would you like to see them now?' Sarah asked, aware that Emily seldom made time for small talk when there was business to be done. Her cut-to-the point style had become legendary in the firm of solicitors where Sarah had worked. There were grown men with over thirty years in the legal profession behind them who were terrified of the woman sitting across the desk from her.

'Please.'

Sarah opened the folder and plucked the handful of drawings out before surrendering them to Emily who pounced on them like a hungry viper.

She took several minutes to carefully scan each one without giving away any hint of what she was thinking.

Finally, she looked up at Sarah.

'This Jason Weir is a very gifted boy indeed,' she said, 'and I would very much like to meet him.'

'I'm sure he'd be delighted,' Sarah gushed.

'I've only seen talent of this magnitude in someone without tutoring once before – and that was from Harry Melville.'

Sarah stared at her blankly for a moment trying to control her slackening jaw.

'My Harry?' she asked.

'Your Harry, yes.' Emily replied, smirking in what Sarah felt was a patronising way. 'You'll probably be aware we dated when we were younger.'

'Yes,' Sarah snapped, unable to conceal her astonishment at both the fact Emily had brought that up within seconds of their conversation starting, and seemed to be claiming I had a talent for art which she'd never even heard about.

'I wasn't aware he had any artistic ability.'

'How funny,' Emily raised her eyebrows, clearly amused. 'I went to St Hillary's for girls and, as you'll know, he was at Glendinning for boys, and once or twice a year they threw us all in the same room together and called it a school dance. We only dated for a year or so, but in that time he used to draw me the most incredible sketches. It was really rather romantic. I was staggered that he didn't go to art school.'

'I find that remarkable,' said Sarah. 'I've never even seen him doodle.'

'Gosh. That really is a shame.' An uncomfortable silence fell between them before Emily spoke again. 'Well, Sarah, let's make sure another young man's talent doesn't go to waste now shall we? Will you bring Jason with you next time?'

'Yes, of course' Sarah replied, trying to remain collected. 'I expect Harry's brother Ben might like to join us too if you wouldn't mind?'

'The more the merrier,' said Emily. And with that, Sarah knew she was dismissed.

Ben grabbed his mobile as soon as it started to ring, excitedly confirming, 'It's Sarah', to Dave and Sonja who had been sitting with him in the meeting room waiting for her to call.

'Sarah, hi. How did it go?'

'Well,' she said, her voice sounding strangely tense and flat. 'She loved the drawings and wants to meet Jason. I said we'd take him in to see her.'

'Oh,' Ben paused.

'I thought you'd want to be there,' Sarah interjected with a hint of accusation.

'Yes, of course. Sorry. That's fantastic,' he replied with all the confidence he could muster, giving the thumbs up to Dave and Sonja who beamed enthusiastically from their chairs.

'Did she say where she thought we could go from here?'

'No, I…,' she hesitated. 'I got a bit distracted when she started reminiscing about dating Harry before informing me that he had been an incredibly gifted artist who had clearly missed his vocation in life. Did you know he had a talent for art, Ben?'

Ben's face fell. He recognised immediately what she was talking about but didn't want the others to notice the shift in conversation.

'I didn't but I've got Dave and Sonja here, Sarah. So we'll talk later, okay?'

'Alright,' she sighed. 'But I'm just starting to think I didn't know my husband as well as I thought I did and I don't like it.'

～

Four days later, Sarah, Ben and a very nervous Jason Weir sat side-by-side in three leather chairs neatly arranged opposite Emily DiRollo, who they were waiting to be addressed by from the other side of her desk. Ben shuffled in his seat, feeling more than a little anxious himself. He hadn't seen Emily in about thirty years, and she was just as intimidating as she had been back then. He stifled the thought of being sick, reminding himself that it never actually happened even when the waves of nausea seemed so real.

Noticing Emily still wore that classic sharp bob, he was suddenly transported back to when she was my girlfriend.

I'd been pretty possessive of her all the time we dated and had never brought her home to meet Mum and Dad. Ben rightly assumed that because Emily was so posh I was afraid our comfortably-sized home wouldn't live up to her standards. Emily had lived in what can only be described as a mansion in the city's highly-prestigious Hermitage area. Sitting across from her all these years later, Ben noticed she hadn't lost either her class or the dazzling effect of her beautiful sky blue eyes which cut through you like a Samurai sword. Ben wondered how it was possible to fear a woman and desire her at the same time, but these were certainly the two feelings stirring in him that afternoon. The third was guilt, at having avoided Sarah's phone calls for the last few days, always telling her he was with someone and couldn't talk properly, and only stopping long enough to arrange today's meeting. He just didn't know what to say about the drawings. Now, as Emily leaned forward in her chair to offer her personal condolences, he realised both she and Sarah would likely learn the truth sooner rather than later and an uncomfortable spotlight would be thrust on him.

'I was so very sorry to hear about Harry's death, Ben,' Emily's face was flushed with concern. 'It's bad enough to lose a sibling, let alone a twin.'

'Thank you,' Ben replied awkwardly. 'Sarah's probably told you we've been through the wringer, but we're just trying to focus on the future and, in particular, keeping his work at the centre going.'

'Well, I am glad to hear that, and if this young man is anything to go by, you are unearthing some great talent.' She nodded towards Jason who instantly turned a deep shade of crimson.

'So, I have a proposal for you, Jason.' Emily fixed the youngster square in the eyes as she leaned forward, folding her hands in front of her.

'If I provide the materials and the working space – which will be my own studio upstairs – I would like you to produce larger versions of two of your drawings that I've selected which I will then exhibit in this gallery.'

Ben and Sarah gasped then quickly turned to congratulate a now beetroot-coloured Jason, who looked like he wanted to both jump for joy and bury himself under the carpet simultaneously.

'Well done, Jason,' said Ben, patting him on the back.

'Thank you so much,' Sarah said to Emily.

'It's my pleasure to help such a promising young talent.' Emily spoke with such previously-unheard warmth that Sarah decided there may just be a glimmer of a human being in there after all. Their last meeting had left her feeling very threatened by the woman Sarah regarded as the Anna Wintour of the art world – or of the Scottish art world at least.

'I wanted to show you both something before you go,' Emily announced, looking a little pensive.

'I hope these won't upset you,' she added as she produced a series of sketches and paintings from her top drawer. 'I have kept them at home all these years as I couldn't bear to throw them away. They're so magnificent don't you think?'

Sarah looked down at the art work. A couple of pieces were clearly of Emily herself in her teenage years; her trademark bob on the go even then. Head tossed back and laughing gaily, her face radiated the flush of young love. Sarah fought the stabs of jealousy as she shifted her attentions to a pencil drawing of a rose; the shading and detail bringing to life the symbolic flower in all its glory.

She looked up at Emily, her eyes now full of tears. 'Harry's?' she asked.

'No,' Ben cut in abruptly. 'They're mine.'

'Why didn't you tell me before?' Sarah berated Ben as they walked down the High Street towards her car, Jason trundling along behind feeling like a spare part, but not caring an ounce. He was still on the biggest high of his life.

'I found it all a bit embarrassing really,' said Ben, aware this answer was unlikely to satisfy Sarah.

'A bit embarrassing? I've just spent the week wondering why my dead husband failed to share what could have been his greatest passion with me, including several nights lying awake trying to work out just what I did so wrong that he never showed me any of his art work. You could have saved me that anguish in an instant.'

'I'm sorry, Sarah. It's difficult to explain.' Ben hung his head. 'I didn't want Emily to know they were mine for obvious reasons. It's now pretty clear I had a teenage crush on her. I haven't drawn or painted anything for many years because it's just a painful reminder of my failure to do anything with the only talent I ever seemed to have. Suddenly having it all brought up again was just.. difficult.'

They stopped next to Sarah's BMW convertible and Jason gladly hopped in the back, leaving them to continue their verbal spat on the street.

'Ben, you've got to start communicating. You can't keep living in your own little world, only coming out for a few minutes here and there to help the kids at the centre.

'Emily's right. Like Jason, you have an extraordinary talent and it's not too late to do something about it, but you can't offer these kids real advice until you fulfill your own potential.'

Ben sighed. He knew what she was saying made sense. In fact, he didn't really know where he'd been for the last thirty years. How had he allowed all that time to pass him by?

Sarah felt a tug of guilt as she watched the anguish spread across Ben's face. She was growing fonder by the day of him, strangely drawn to the gentleness of his manner and his totally unassuming nature. How ironic, she thought, that after all these years of being cast as the bad apple of the family, Ben was actually turning out to be extremely gifted. And how painful for him that it was a talent his family refused to support.

She put her hand out and touched Ben's arm. 'Let's take Jason home and we can go for a coffee.'

Ben smiled gratefully, although he still felt as though his insides were hanging out after his teenage drawings and boyish crush were spread across the table for all to see.

Along with them, came the hurtful memories of our father ripping some of his best work up at the kitchen table during a row over Ben's future and telling him to get a proper job. But instead of obeying Dad's demands to find a sensible career, he had done the worst thing of all; nothing.

~

Emily stared again at the sketches before her as if, now armed with the truth as to the identity of the real artist, they should somehow appear different to her. She had treasured these drawings for thirty years and still, as she gazed at them, they brought back the same old emotions of pure admiration for the person who had put pencil to paper. Piecing it all together, the fact that I had tricked her should have come as no surprise. After all, I was never able to sketch in front of her, and went out of my way to prevent her from visiting our home where, of course, she would have discovered the truth. It was a pretty crude con, but at that stage, although formidable, she was more trusting. Back then, she took me at face value. As she did when we met years later.

Looking at the sketches, her one source of comfort which was growing in strength with every passing moment, was that the real artist was still alive – as was his talent. Emily realised too that, as with many artists, Ben would not be an easy person to reach, but she had the hook – Jason – through which she could keep him in sight and try to persuade him to pick up his sketch pad again.

~

As Jason began work on the drawings Emily had requested, Ben and the rest of the team at the Melville Centre planned their campaign to attract the local press to an exhibition of both Jason's new work and his original sketches. All involved were aware that this was their big chance to attract some publicity and, in turn, the donations which were so vital to the centre's future.

Ben hoped to persuade Emily to come along to the launch party for the exhibition and pose for photographs with Jason. He didn't know how she'd respond after the bombshell he had dropped at their last meeting and feared she'd feel she had been made a fool of.

As he sat in the staff office mulling over the possibilities, he realised there was only one way to find out where they now stood with her, so he picked up the phone.

'Good afternoon, Di Rollo's Gallery.'

'Hi. Can I speak to Emily please?'

'Who's calling?'

'Ben Melville.'

'One moment,' the assistant said. He heard the holding tone and wondered if, presented with the option, Emily would refuse his call.

'Hello Ben.' Her voice was instantly recognisable with that ring of pure Edinburgh establishment.

'Hello Emily,' he decided to avoid chit-chat and press on. 'Hope I haven't disturbed you.'

'Not at all. How can I help?'

'I wanted to personally invite you to our launch party for Jason's exhibition. That's assuming you're happy with the pieces he's doing for you?' Ben asked, desperately trying to sound relaxed.

'I'd love to,' she replied. 'I've had the chance to look in on him a couple of times and I'm very pleased with his work so far.'

'Wonderful,' said Ben. 'Would you mind also if we invited a couple of press photographers along to record the occasion. We are aware this would be a good opportunity to highlight the work of the centre.'

'No problem at all.'

Ben couldn't believe how easy it had been to enlist her help so he thought it wise to wind up the call in case he said something to change her mind.

'Thank you so much.' He was just about to say goodbye when she abruptly cut in.

'Do you still draw, Ben?' He detected a softness and familiarity in her voice that immediately threw him off-guard.

'No. Not for some time now.'

'What a waste.' She paused. 'I'd very much like to see some more of your work if that would be possible? Perhaps you could take

FROM the OUTSIDE

some pieces along to Jason's exhibition?' Ben deduced from her tone that his compliance on this would help ensure her continued cooperation.

'I don't know, Emily. I'm not sure where they are.'

'I did something for you, Ben. Please do this for me.'

'Alright,' he said. 'I'll take whatever I can find with me for you to look at.'

'Excellent,' she paused. 'I'll look forward to seeing you.' He heard the phone click and she was gone.

Later, as Ben walked to Sarah's house on what had turned out to be a beautiful evening, he played the conversation with Emily over again in his mind. The fondness with which she spoke about his art work, the vulnerability she allowed to creep through that had made him feel they were in some way connected. Could someone like Emily possibly be interested in him, he wondered? It had been a few years since he'd had any kind of romantic involvement, but he couldn't help but think there was something in her tone which was more than just professional interest. Ben laughed to himself as he realised he was probably delusional – no doubt a mid-life crisis, he thought, that had made him believe women were starting to throw themselves at him.

Rounding the corner to Sarah's street his thoughts changed to figuring out why his sister-in-law had invited him over for an evening meal. At the time, she simply said, 'It would be nice to catch up'. Ben imagined she was having an issue with her laptop again, or had a leak that needed fixing. It had never even entered his mind that Sarah could actually enjoy his company – could want to be around him. To Ben, Sarah was still so closely connected with me that he hadn't noticed her migrate towards him. He hadn't thought about how relaxed he had become in her company, or how big a part of his life she was now. Sarah was still up there on her untouchable throne in his eyes.

He stopped at her front door and rang the bell. She answered within a few seconds and Ben immediately noticed she had started wearing make-up again. She must be feeling better, he thought, reasoning that this would also account for the change in her behaviour towards him lately. She was becoming much easier to deal with – helpful, caring almost.

'Hi,' she said breezily. 'Come in. Dinner's ready.'

He noticed her little bump as she turned away to lead him to the kitchen. He guessed she was probably wearing maternity trousers already as he could see an elastic expanse of material at her waist, supporting her stomach. He wondered how long she'd waited to wear trousers like these. Her joy at being pregnant was so obvious and so charming that he allowed himself to feel another little buzz of excitement at the thought of being a special uncle to this child.

'How's my little niece or nephew doing?' he asked brightly.

'Just fine. I've even started feeling some flutters of movement.'

'That's fantastic,' he said, throwing his jacket over the back of a kitchen chair and sitting himself down at the table. 'I can't wait to meet whoever's in there,' he said pointing towards her swollen stomach.

'Well, Uncle Ben, you've got a few months to wait yet, but it'll be worth it. Would you like a glass of wine? I'm afraid I can't join you but I can watch enviously.'

Ben felt tempted, but his reduced drinking was beginning to pay dividend – his mood and confidence had improved, as had his energy levels – and he knew it wouldn't take much to throw him off track. 'Nah, don't open a bottle on my account. A glass of water is fine. I'm trying not to drink much in the week.'

'I can see the difference in you, you know – since you've cut back. You look much brighter and more youthful.'

Ben wasn't aware she'd ever really known about his heavy drinking, but he guessed it must have been obvious.

'I'm feeling pretty good,' he replied cautiously. 'It's nice to be busy.'

He watched as she carefully dished the risotto she had prepared for them, sprinkling what looked like flat-leaf parsley over it, before she topped it with grated parmesan.

'This looks great,' he said, inhaling the aroma as she put his plate down in front of him.

'My signature dish, aka the only thing I can cook without messing it up,' she smirked, taking her seat at the table directly opposite him.

'I wanted to ask you something, Ben?'

Here we go, he thought as he waited for Sarah to assign him his task for the evening.

'Should I have worn my overalls?' he quipped.

'No, nothing like that,' she glanced down at her plate nervously, before fixing on him again. 'I wanted to ask if my baby can call you Daddy?'

Ben heard his fork hit the table.

CHAPTER seven

EMILY HAD SHOWN next to no enthusiasm when I first asked her out. Instead she sniggered, 'I don't think so', after I cornered her outside the girls' toilets at an under-18s disco. But her haughtiness just reeled me in further so I asked one of my friends to do some investigative work and find out what her interests were. When I discovered Emily had a love of art, I realised I was in luck – because I had talent on tap in the shape of my brother.

So I wooed Emily with a series of drawings – along with a smattering of watercolour paintings – I knew would impress even the toughest critic. To my surprise, it was easy to persuade Ben to provide the artwork. I'd approached him cautiously in his room one evening with a view to bribing him. I'd seen him smoking down the lane a few nights earlier so I had plenty of ammunition. But, incredibly, he agreed to help without even the slightest threat being uttered. I didn't even have to tell him what to draw – he did the lot himself. Course, I didn't realise then that he had a bit of a crush on Emily himself, but his creations absolutely did the trick. I penned a different note on the back of each one, posting them individually to her home and eventually including my telephone number with the fifth. She called that same evening, sounding very nervous, and asked me outright if I was the artist. 'Of course', I replied proudly. 'I hope they didn't disappoint', I added, smirking to myself.

'A gift like yours could never disappoint', she said. And that was that; we were inseparable for over a year until, that is, I decided to take up with Becky Rutherford, a junior tennis champion who netted almost as many boyfriends as she did trophies.

When Emily and I met at a fundraising event two years ago, she asked me if I was still painting and drawing. She appeared to know everything about me – as if she'd charted my every move since we left school. I told her I still sketched the odd thing now and then, but generally didn't have much time for art any more. 'How terribly sad,' she said, looking both concerned and perplexed in equal measure.

Clearly, she had never forgotten the first major talent she had spotted – but the rest of us did. Ben's was a gift that was at first neglected and then buried. What part in that did I play, I wondered? Had I, along with our father, worn Ben's self-confidence down until there was nothing left?

~

It proved to be a restless night as Ben tried to sort through the day's events. First Emily opening the lid on his unfulfilled promise – something that had caused him years of angst – and now Sarah effectively asking him if he wanted to be a father to what would have been his brother's child. He had asked – diplomatically he hoped – for some time to think about it, but it had taken him all night to reach a decision. It was quite a leap from being an uncle to 'Daddy' as she had put it. But she had certainly thought it through, carefully setting out how this didn't mean she was asking him to live with them – although she thought she could use some extra support in the early days – but just wanted him to be the official 'first man' in the child's life. Looking at it like that, Ben thought it made sense. He had also concluded that I would have wanted my son or daughter to have a constant male figure in their life after recalling how I once told him how sorry I felt for a boy in my class at school whose father had died of cancer. 'He's only got his mother now,' I'd told Ben, astonished such a thing could happen. 'I can't imagine losing someone so young. Everyone should live until they're old,' I had added naively.

And as soon as Ben considered what life would be like if he didn't take on this new role, instead watching from the sidelines as he had always done, his decision was easy. He batted away his concerns about what would happen not if, but when Sarah found a new partner – a thought he found strangely troubling – and focused on what was best for the child. He would tell Sarah tomorrow that he would become the baby's father-figure and they could see in time whether calling him 'Daddy' felt right. With that decision he swallowed the nagging anxiety about what would happen if, further down the line, she changed her mind.

The next morning Ben headed into the centre early to start tidying up the recreation room, which was soon to host Jason's showcase event. But when he arrived outside the entrance he found Jason curled up in the doorway fast asleep. Ben wondered how long he had been there.

'Jason,' he said, shaking him gently.

'Sorry pal,' a groggy Jason muttered, peeking up at Ben through one half-opened eye, the other still jammed shut.

'How long have you been here?'

'All night,' said Jason, stretching his arms above his head and yawning before rising to his feet. 'My dad threw me out when I told him about getting my pictures shown in the gallery.'

'Why?' asked Ben, although he suspected he already knew. He had been down this road once before.

'He says drawing is no job for a man, and if he ever caught me in a gallery showing off a bunch of pansy pictures he'd not let me back in the house.'

'And what do you think, Jason?'

'I think I'm homeless.'

~

Standing outside the sprawl of flats in one of Edinburgh's most notorious housing estates, Ben wondered if it had been such a good idea to offer to try and talk Jason's dad round after all. So much of the area had been regenerated that this long, wretched-looking building stuck out as an obvious eyesore seated at the top of a hill off the main road running along the shore to Leith. Ben smiled to himself as he imagined how an unsuspecting passer-by could be ambling along, past the array of advertising agencies, architects offices, bars and restaurants, thinking what a thoroughly vibrant area this was then, taking a wrong turn, be met with this imposing sight. The building was not pretty - not for the stranger looking at it, and particularly not for the people living in it.

Things didn't improve much inside, and Ben took a deep breath before climbing the stairs to the fourth floor where Jason's family lived. Stopping at the top of the steps, he leaned against the wall for a few seconds until he got his breath back. He vowed to himself that he would join a gym some time soon. Once reasonably composed again he started down the hallway until he found the door he was looking for.

He knocked tentatively.

'Who is it?' A gruff voice bellowed from the other side.

'It's Ben Melville from the Melville Youth Centre,' Ben answered in what he feared sounded like the pitch of a five-year-old girl. He swallowed hard as he heard keys being jostled, wrestling panic thoughts of being sick on the doorstep. The door opened.

'Aye?' The gruff voice had a face, and it wasn't attractive. A short and stout man blocked the doorway, dressed in a stained green T-shirt and black tracksuit bottoms.

Ben swallowed again before attempting small talk.

'I don't know how you manage these stairs every day – nearly killed me.' He laughed nervously at his own joke while the man he presumed to be Gary Weir remained poker faced.

'I dinnae take the stairs,' he grunted. 'I send the wife oot instead.'

Ben laughed a little too loudly and wished he could make a hasty retreat.

Instead, he held out his hand towards the man who, surprisingly, shook it.

'Ben Melville.'

'Gary Weir. Whit stupit ideas have ye been puttin' intae ma son's heid aboot drawing?'

'Can I come in?' asked Ben nervously.

Gary stood back from the door and pointed towards a dark room at the end of a very short hallway which was crowded with shoes and boxes. Next to the door, coats had been haphazardly flung over a stand that could only be identified by its base. Ben cautiously entered the flat before stepping into what was a tiny room by anyone's standards. It housed a two-seater sofa squeezed against the back wall covered in newspaper and children's toys, and an arm chair that looked like it belonged in the tip. A TV on the far side of the room screened a mid-morning chat show which, by the very high volume, Gary had clearly been watching.

'Sit doon.' Jason's dad jabbed his middle finger towards the sofa while he sat himself down in his armchair. Ben attempted to clear himself a space to sit on without drawing attention to the fact he was doing it. But he need not have gone to the effort. When he was finally seated he noticed Gary's eyes were still firmly fixed on the TV where a warring couple were squaring up to each other while the over-animated presenter pretended to attempt to defuse the situation, without defusing it. Ben wondered why they didn't just replace this crap with WWF wrestling and be done with it.

He cleared his throat before addressing Gary whose attention he felt would be difficult to hold.

'Jason told me this morning that you'd had an argument about his ambition to become an artist.'

'It wisnae an argument,' Gary clarified in his unique style. 'I telt him nae son ae mine wis gonnae make a livin' fae drawin' stupit pictures. If he's that much ae an artist why doesn't he pick up a brush and paint some walls? It would be a hell ae a lot mare use.'

'I understand this may not be what you had in mind for Jason,' Ben wasn't quite sure where he was going with this, 'but I have to tell you that he's not just some two-bit street artist. He has an exceptional talent which has already been noticed by the leading gallery owner in Scotland.'

Gary fleetingly drew his eyes from the brawling on the TV to look at Ben.

'That right,' he said, clearly unimpressed.

Ben cleared his throat and decided to alter his tactics.

'I was like your son once, Gary. I loved to draw and I was good at it but, like you, my father thought it was no job for a man so he stopped me from taking it any further. It's taken me almost thirty years to get over my anger and disappointment at being prevented from doing the one thing I loved – and that's thirty wasted years too.'

Gary was looking right at him now so Ben knew this was going to have to be his best shot.

'Jason respects you and he'll do what you tell him to. But he's got a chance here to make something of his life and to be someone. The art world is not for the weak. Real artists work damn hard and have to fight their way through the thousands of others masquerading as talented painters and sculptors, to get their work noticed and be taken seriously. Jason is already half-way there. He has the support of someone who knows the business and can get his work out there. This is his chance. He'll never forgive you if you don't let him grab it and he'll spend the rest of his life hating you for it.'

'Ye finished?' barked Gary, his cheeks glowing red with rage.

'Yes,' said Ben, unsure of what was coming next.

'Good. Cos ye've got a bloody cheek comin' in here and tryin' tae tell me whit tae think. You ever thought how the other folk round here are gonnae start treatin' that lad when they hear he's an 'artist'?' Gary sounded out the word in an overtly camp, theatrical accent.

'He'll no stand a snowball's chance in hell ae walkin' doon the street without gettin' the absolute piss taken oot ae him – or worse. And I'll tell ye somethin' else. The last few years have no been easy for ma boy. He's had nothin' but shite tae get through and he's just startin' tae sort himsel' oot. He doesnae need tae be drawin' attention tae himsel' right noo. So just keep yer nose oot ae things ye dinnae have the first idea aboot and go back tae helpin' some wee lassie get a supermarket job.' With that, Gary turned his attention back to the TV and left Ben to see himself out.

Jason could tell from the look on Ben's face that his attempt to talk his dad around hadn't been successful.

Ben pulled up a stool and sat down in front of Jason who he found slouched in an arm chair in the recreation room sketching something in a notepad and looking very demoralised.

'I tried,' Ben shrugged before offering an apologetic smile.

'I knew he'd throw you out,' said Jason. 'My mum's gonna be devastated. She's only just got me back home.'

'Why, where were you before?'

'I went a wee bit off the rails for a couple of years and I wasn't around much. Staying with mates and that,' Jason said, his eyes fixed to the floor.

'Were you in trouble, Jason?'

'Sort of.' Jason shuffled in his seat and transferred his gaze to the window. 'I'd rather not talk about it, eh.'

'I understand,' said Ben. 'Your dad might come around yet, Jason.'

'No. He's a stubborn old bastard. He'll sit it out.'

'Well, I've got a very comfy sofa that's yours until you work things out, or get on your feet. Whichever comes first.'

'Cheers pal,' said Jason, still looking utterly dejected. 'That would be great. I won't stay for long.'

'No problem,' Ben smiled, though inwardly he was less than thrilled about the idea of flat sharing. He'd lived alone for over 20 years and wasn't quite sure how this was going to work out.

'I'd better get over to the studio now before Emily comes looking for me.' Jason got to his feet.

'Is she a hard taskmaster?' Ben smiled.

'Aye.' said Jason. 'But at least she cares, eh.'

～

Sarah admired her growing bump as she stood sideways on in front of the mirror, her sweater pulled up to reveal the curve of her tummy. People were starting to guess now – and one of the staff in Waitrose the other day had even asked if she needed help carrying her bags to the car. People were so much sweeter when you're expecting, she thought. Why can't they always be like that?

There had been no one more considerate towards her needs than Ben, who was never more than a phone call away and seemed genuinely happy just to fuss around her and make sure she was alright. He'd agreed to come to her twenty-week scan and, after Sarah had given his name to the hospital ahead of the appointment, they had both laughed as they predicted the radiographer would ask for Mr and Mrs Melville in the waiting room. How very convenient that was, she thought. She wouldn't have to explain anything to the hospital staff. They could just wrongly assume that she was a happily married mother-to-be, expecting a child in the most uncomplicated of situations.

Sarah didn't want to have to tell anyone her baby's father was dead; that she was a single parent. Most of all she didn't want to have to break that sorry story to her child. And that was where Ben came in. He would make up for my absence, filling the void that had been created with such abrupt finality just three months earlier.

She thought of how her view of Ben had changed beyond recognition now, to the point where she couldn't even remember what he was like before my death. She couldn't help but feel too, that it was wonderful to have someone around who had time to listen to her, to ask how her day had gone and how she was feeling. I had always been in a hurry. In truth I probably thought she should be grateful to be the wife of someone so successful, and I'd get frustrated when she complained about how little time I spent at home.

'Where do you think all this comes from, Sarah?' she recalled me snapping at her one day. 'New Town houses don't come cheap – and neither does the Veuve Clicquot you like to dish out to your friends,' I'd added, fixing her with a steely glare and a raised eyebrow. Then, just to make sure I'd drummed home my point –

purely to rid myself of any sense of guilt – I threw in: 'You may think you're Miss Independent, but you'd soon feel the pinch if you had to pay the bills.'

Sarah winced at the memory. She felt horribly guilty thinking any negative thoughts about me now, but the truth was we had become distant and our marriage was beginning to show the kind of cracks that couldn't just be papered over. In short, I was neglecting her.

She realised, with not a small degree of shame, that the night with Paul had been a subconscious toe in the water – and a desperate cry to me that unless things changed, our marriage wouldn't survive. She'd even considered dropping clues by leaving incriminating emails open on her laptop. A small part of her had wanted me to find Paul's messages, get hideously angry and threaten to rip his head off before forbidding her from even returning to the office. But instead, all that followed her unfulfilling night with Paul, was an even louder silence between us. She deleted his messages in which he pleaded to see her again. She knew there was no point leaving them open on her laptop, as I simply wouldn't have noticed.

Sarah checked my picture on her bedside table again. It was her favourite of me. I was relaxed and smiling warmly up at her and, in that moment, she missed me terribly. The old me. The me she had married but later lost.

There had been those darker hours during which she'd wondered if my early death had actually been for the best. She couldn't imagine having to tell me she was carrying someone else's baby. It would have broken us. But what she still couldn't figure out, was whether she had wanted to break us.

And all I could be certain of was that I had failed her.

CHAPTER eight

THINGS AT THE CENTRE hadn't always gone well, and there were times I wondered why I'd even bothered starting the thing up in the first place. The very worst of times though had happened early on. One Spring morning, just weeks after we'd opened the centre, I dropped in to pick up some files first thing before any of the staff arrived. I was just on my way out again when the front door swung open and a shaven-headed, hollow-eyed, gaunt-faced youth walked into the office as though he were staff, slung himself into a chair in front of me and propped his feet up on the meeting table. His skin was covered in a fiery acne that was hard to take your eyes off. I sensed this boy, though only sixteen, was trouble from the start, but still I chose to believe him when he said he was there to straighten himself out. 'I'm frae Muirhouse, eh. It's not a walk in the park growing up there, but I want tae sort myself out and make ma mum and da proud.'

'Well, we'll help you in whatever way we can,' I'd said. 'What's your name?'

'Luke.' He was laughing now. 'You'll no forget it either.'

And he was right. I didn't.

From that point on, Luke had arrived at the centre on an almost daily basis; telling the staff he was there to try and work out what he wanted to do with his life, although whenever a suggestion was put to him he would always bat it away with the same line: 'Naw, that's no for me, man.'

Sensing that Luke was using the centre for some alternative reason, one of our earliest youth workers, Tony, confronted him one day and asked: 'Are you really looking for career help, Luke, or do you just want a place to hang out for a few hours each day?'

At that, according to Tony, Luke had reared up, clearly rattled by the truth, and after hurling a wooden chair across the room began shouting, 'You've no idea man. You shouldn'ae be in a job like this if you cannae even be nice tae the kids who come in here. You're the one who's wasting time. You're wasting ma time.' By chance, I happened to walk in the front door, just in time to find Luke closing in on Tony in the recreation room, shouting: 'What's your fucking problem? Think you're better than me? You're a fucking nobody.'

'What's going on here, Luke?' I intervened.

'He's calling me a fucking liar,' Luke bellowed, jabbing his finger in Tony's direction.

I turned to Tony, looking for answers.

'He doesn't seem interested in finding a career. I was just trying to get to the bottom of it that's all.' Tony shrugged, white with terror from his ordeal.

'You go into the office, Tony. I'd like to speak to Luke.'

He didn't stop to argue, and made quickly for the door.

'Why are you here, Luke?' I made sure to stare him directly in the eyes as I spoke – a kind of primitive action that I sensed would in some way impress or intimidate my opponent. Hopefully both.

'I'm here tae find a job. What d'you think?' Luke was pacing the room now, agitated and looking as though he could charge again.

'I'm glad to hear that,' I said, trying to placate him. 'Where we going wrong then?'

'You're just no coming up with anything I'm interested in, that's all.'

'And what do you think you'd be interested in?'

Luke stopped pacing for a moment while he dug his right hand into his trouser pocket. I backed swiftly away and prepared my defence tactics if he came at me with a knife. But it wasn't a weapon Luke was pulling out, but a piece of paper. He unfolded it quickly before thrusting it in my hands. So taken aback was I by its contents that it took me several moments to digest what I was actually looking at; an extremely skillful black pencil drawing of an old man whose world-weary and alcohol-worn features gave an instant life history.

'Where did you get this?' I asked suspiciously.

'I drew it,' Luke said, unable to look me in the eye. 'Just dinnae make a big issue out of it.'

'What d'you mean?'

'I dinnae want people around here knowing I draw.'

'But you do want to take this further, is that right?'

'Aye,' Luke replied. Head still bowed. 'If you think I'm any good.'

'I do, Luke, think you're good. Seriously good.'

~

Sarah and Ben sat nervously in the reception of the clinic, waiting to be called for her scan. Even though Sarah had been scanned at twelve weeks and assured everything was normal, she still felt apprehensive after reading about some of the conditions they were seeking to rule out at this stage. All she wanted to do was speed through the next twenty weeks so she could meet her – hopefully – happy, healthy baby.

Ben repeatedly cleared his throat and shuffled in the seat next to her. After what seemed like the hundredth time he'd done it, she finally snapped.

'What's wrong with you?' she asked, spinning round swiftly to look at him.

Ben shrugged, bewildered by her aggressive questioning. 'I'm a little nervous that's all.'

She turned away from him again to check for signs of a midwife or radiographer coming but, irritatingly for her, Ben carried on talking.

'We've got this launch night coming up as well and we don't have a bloody clue where to begin when it comes to inviting newspaper journalists along, and what we'll do with them when they get there.'

'You'll be fine,' Sarah replied dismissively. All she could think about right now was the scan. Looking at her, Ben could see she was distracted – and more than a little uptight, so he decided to drop the subject.

Just a few seconds later, the radiographer appeared clutching her file and – as Sarah had predicted – asked for: 'Mr and Mrs Melville.'

Ben stood up and gave Sarah a goofy grin that she assumed was meant to be reassuring.

They walked briskly to catch up with the radiographer who introduced herself as Karen whilst holding the door open to the room where the scan would be carried out.

Once they were inside and Sarah was settled on the treatment chair, Karen set about putting the cold gel on her patient's tummy before beginning the ultrasound.

Sarah and Ben watched with a mixture of amazement and confusion as they saw various body parts flash before them on the radiographer's screen.

'What are we looking at now?' asked Ben.

'You should just about be able to make out the baby's head,' said Karen, 'right here.'

Sure enough, the curves of a forehead and a tiny nose and mouth came into view. Continuing with the scan she reassured them, 'The heartbeat is still strong.'

Before he'd had even a chance to control himself, the tears started to flow down Ben's face as he saw this new life before him. He fought in equal measure his raw feelings of grief for a brother whose heart would never beat again and who wouldn't have the opportunity to meet his child; and the pure joy too, of seeing this little person who would soon change their lives forever.

'It's nice to see a dad let the emotions out,' Karen smiled, clearly impressed with what must have appeared to be the ultimate modern man.

He noticed Sarah glaring coldly at him now with a look that said she understood exactly what he was thinking, but there was no room for sadness and mourning around her child.

She turned her head back to the screen once Ben had begun to show signs of regaining his composure.

Suddenly, he felt like a fraud sitting in the seat that I should have been filling. He tried to listen carefully as Karen pointed out every little detail of his niece or nephew's tiny anatomy, but he couldn't take any of it in. He was using every ounce of his energy to suppress the overwhelming sadness that was threatening to spill out of him. He wanted to shout at the top of his voice and run from the room, but instead he sat in silent agony.

Slowly, he became conscious of a debate between Sarah and Karen.

'I'm very sure of my dates,' Sarah was saying.

'Well, there's not much in it, but I think because of the measurements we should move the due date back a little, just by a week.'

'Fine,' Sarah bristled. 'I don't suppose it matters anyway,' she added while the radiographer altered the date on the front of her file.

Once outside the room, Sarah and Ben walked in silence along the corridor until Sarah finally stopped him as they neared the exit.

'You're not here to replace Harry,' she said, fixing him again with that icy stare. 'But I do need you to represent him. You're the closest thing this child has got to its father and we need you.'

'I know that,' he said defensively. 'I'm not going anywhere.'

'Good,' Sarah said stiffly. 'I need to know we can rely on you – and you're not going to go all.. flaky on us again.'

She turned away and continued walking, leaving Ben to follow a few steps behind and wonder just what had turned her mood so suddenly.

For the first time in over three months, Ben bought a bottle of whisky on the way home and he was looking forward to drinking it. Over and over again as he walked, he played out the same thought – that he must have been fooling himself if he believed he could run a youth centre inspiring young people to fulfill their potential when he'd done absolutely nothing with his own life. And this bizarre situation where Sarah was trying to shoehorn him into becoming me was taking its toll. Not that it wouldn't have been tempting to play the part of her husband. Ben had long wondered what it would be like to be married to a woman as vibrant and beautiful as Sarah. She had intrigued him from the first day he met her, when I'd suggested we all take Dad for a meal out. Ben had been desperately struggling with his grief over Mum's death. She had been his rock, always there to support and guide him. Somehow being with Dad and I made his sense of loss even worse, because we were so closely associated with her.

For Ben, at least having another person there to fill that all-important fourth chair made the idea of dinner together more bearable.

Sarah had been late – because of a client meeting that had overrun. Ben had been sitting facing the entrance on the other side of the table from Dad and I. He was in the middle of telling us about a bad fall he'd seen an elderly neighbour have that day when the door had flung open and a slight but striking woman rushed in from the street, all bags and work files and flustered.

Ben knew before I even got the chance to tell him that this was my girlfriend. I always landed prize catches, and Sarah was surely the greatest prize of them all.

'God, I'm so sorry I'm late. I just couldn't get away,' she'd announced dramatically.

'Don't worry about it young lady,' Dad said standing up and looking altogether much brighter. 'You must be Sarah.'

'Yes,' she said through flushed cheeks. She held out her hand to Dad who gave it a lingering shake. He always was a flirt. Then she had turned to my brother.

'And you must be Ben,' she smiled.

'Pleased to meet you,' he'd replied, making minimal eye contact as he followed Dad in shaking her hand.

With that she dropped her assortment of legal folders to the floor and threw herself into the evening with gusto, delighting John with tales of her obnoxious clients and colleagues – all of whom were invariably classed as overpaid fools. Ben had listened and laughed, and from time to time stole a look in my direction to find me vaguely amused, but ultimately distracted. Because, as Ben saw that night, although I was clearly very fond of my new girlfriend, I was not quite as captivated as he was.

As Ben quickly paced the streets towards home, he played mind games with himself in which he pretended there was a choice over whether he would drink the bottle of whisky or not. He could just have a small glass to relax, he reasoned, though a louder voice told him that one would lead to many more.

By the time he reached his flat, his pulse was racing at the thought of that first drink. He pulled the keys out of his pocket and struggled to get them in the lock, his saliva glands in overdrive with anticipation. As soon as the door opened he made a dash for the kitchen, but was stopped in his tracks by a voice from the living room.

'Alright mate. How was the scan?'

'Oh shit', he thought. He'd completely forgotten that Jason was staying with him. He could hardly fill his face with whisky in front of a youth he was supposed to be setting a good example to. He stuffed the bottle in a cupboard before turning to face Jason who was entering the kitchen behind him.

'The scan?' said Ben, as if he'd had trouble hearing Jason.

'Aye. Was everything okay?'

'Oh yes,' Ben tried to sound relaxed. 'Everything's good. Thanks for asking.'

'No bother. The footie's on in a minute if you want to watch the game?'

'Great idea,' said Ben, who was starting to feel restored by the thought of watching a good game. 'You sit down and I'll make us something to eat.'

Ben thought if he'd just told Jason he'd won the Lottery the young lad couldn't have looked happier than at that moment. He stopped only to say two words – 'You beauty' – before speeding back through to the sitting room.

Alone again, Ben opened the cupboard door, picked up the bottle of whisky, unscrewed the lid, took a deep breath and poured the liquid down the sink.

~

Sarah tried to stifle her laughter as Rosa crawled around the floor after her fifteen-month-old daughter, Esther, who refused to lie still to have her nappy changed. Looking at Rosa trying to stick down the seal with one hand, whilst attempting to keep Esther in one place with the other was like watching someone trying to tag an eel.

'Just you wait,' panted Rosa as she finally got the second nappy seal stuck down, 'this will be you soon and I'll be the one looking on smugly'.

'At least you're not bitter,' laughed Sarah.

Seeing her old friend was always a real tonic and worth the car journey through to Glasgow. Rosa's house was just like the one Sarah had grown up in; large but homely and full of love.

Exhausted from her nappy-changing ordeal, and with Esther and her elder sister Maddie now happily watching children's TV, Rosa threw herself back onto the sofa, savouring every second of rest she was granted.

'So, what news do you bring me from old Edinburgh?'

'Well,' Sarah started hesitantly. 'The other day I asked Ben if my baby could call him Daddy. Do you think that's weird?'

Rosa's eyes bulged. 'Umm... yes.'

'It's just I can't stand the thought of my child growing up

without a father and Ben, being so close to Harry, would be so perfect.'

'You can't just bring on a substitute, Sarah. Life doesn't work like that.'

'I know, Rosa. That wasn't what I meant. It's just that I would like Ben to be a father-figure to my child because I think he's a genuinely good person.'

Rosa squinted her eyes and looked suspiciously at her friend. 'Are you attracted to him?', she demanded, lunging forward to grab a handful of chocolate fingers which she hastily began munching on.

'I'm... drawn to him as a person.'

'Do you actually want to BE with Ben in the fullest sense?'

'Well.. that wasn't what I meant.. I mean, I don't know, Rosa. My head is just swimming right now. I don't know what's going on.' Sarah curled into the sofa to sit in an almost foetal position.

'Oh Sarah, love. I think you need to give your mind a break right now. Don't go doing anything rash. Just give yourself a bit of time to work out fantasy from reality. Right now, you're trying to fix things that can't be fixed in an instant.'

'I suppose you're right,' Sarah sighed. 'I don't know where all this has come from. Do you think I should talk to Ben about it?'

'No,' Rosa spat the word out quicker than a piece of gristle. 'Just let things lie for a while. Ben is the uncle of your child. He won't be going anywhere, but this is no time to get yourself into something you can't get out of.'

'Oh, Rosa. I'm sorry to put all this on you. I'm a total mess.'

'You're not a mess, Sarah. You are pregnant and grieving. Not a good mix.'

Sarah's voice broke and she started to sob. 'I just wish I didn't have to go through this on my own. I'm so damn lonely.

Everything has happened so fast. Harry dies and before I can even process that I find out I'm pregnant.'

'Don't cry, Sarah. I'll always be here for you. You must remember you're not alone. You have so many people who love and care for you.'

'Thank you,' Sarah whispered through her tears.

CHAPTER nine

AFTER SHOWING ME HIS DRAWINGS, Luke grew in confidence – not a thing he'd appeared to lack in the first place – and began treating the centre even more like a home from home. He would usually make himself a cup of tea using the facilities provided in the small kitchen next door, before settling down to read the papers, provided for visitors to the centre. The staff noticed that Luke's presence had also had a negative impact on the number of young people coming through the centre's doors. It seemed his reputation had gone before him and there was no-one willing to come within a one-hundred-metre radius.

This, of course, suited Luke fine as he now had the centre almost entirely to himself.

The final crunch came one morning when Tony used the toilet only a few minutes after Luke and noticed a peculiar smell in the room – or one that you wouldn't usually associate with going to the loo anyway. A hunch caused him to look inside the sanitary bin – not a place someone would usually voluntarily check – only to find several scrunched up pieces of tinfoil inside. Afraid to challenge Luke alone, Tony had called me on my mobile.

'I think Luke's doing smack in the toilets.'

'What?'

'I smelt something funny so I looked in the bin and I found bits of tinfoil. Unless he's decided to take up hairdressing, I can't think of any other reason for it.'

'What do you want to do?' I knew the answer before I'd even

asked the question but I was going through the motions, stalling for time while I tried to work out what I wanted to do.

'We need to ask him to leave. Can you come over?'

'I should be able to get there in the next half an hour. So just leave him where he is for now until I arrive.'

I got to the centre about forty minutes later only to find Luke snoring loudly in the armchair. My blood boiled at the thought of how much he'd taken us for a ride these last few weeks while I'd been calling around colleges to ask about art courses, desperately trying to find somewhere that would take a talented boy with no qualifications to his name.

'Luke,' I said loudly, causing him to open his eyes momentarily before closing them again.

'Luke,' I bellowed this time and he sat up startled.

'Easy man,' he snapped. 'What's yer problem?'

'You're my problem. I want you to leave this centre now. We don't allow drugs in here and never will.'

'What ye talkin' about ye loony. I've no taken any drugs.'

'We've got good reason to believe you've been taking drugs and that's enough for me. I want you out of here now.'

Luke slowly got to his feet, eyeballing me all the time while he calculated his next move.

'What about ma drawins'?' he asked finally.

'I'm not prepared to help you any longer,' I replied. 'I'll take you to a doctor or look into drug rehabilitation options for you, but you're not coming back to the centre in the state you're in right now.' It hurt to turn away a boy with such obvious talent, but there was nothing we could do for a junkie.

He studied me for a moment, trying to work out if I could be cracked with an emotional plea, but I stepped back from him and pointed towards the front door.

Luke shuffled slowly forward before coming to a stop at my right side and leaning in to my face.

'You're a rich bastard using young folk like me tae make yourself feel better. You dinnae actually care about us. If ye did, ye'd remember everyone deserves a chance, eh.'

I experienced another surge of rage at his sheer audacity in questioning my judgment. 'I decide who deserves a chance here. Now get out and don't come back unless you're clean.'

'Fuck you,' he spat into my face, before shoving me and stomping out, slamming the front door behind him. As I stood staring into the empty space he had just filled, I was left with a crushing sense of guilt – and of unfinished business.

~

There was a mixture of anxiety and excitement in the air at the Monday morning team meeting as Ben sat down with Dave, Danny and Sonja to discuss the imminent launch party for Jason's exhibition. First on the list of things to discuss was whether or not to invite the press – the main hesitation being they didn't know whether any of them would turn up.

'Do you think we should send them an invitation in the post or email them?' Sonja asked before answering her own question: 'Maybe we should just give the Evening News a call first and ask them if they'd be interested in coming along?'

'And who's going to do that?' Dave asked, terrified they might suggest him.

Silence fell. Ben suspected this was going to be a long meeting. Just as he was about to volunteer himself for the task of calling journalists – one which he wasn't relishing – there was a knock at the door. The four colleagues looked at each other, silently acknowledging that nobody was expecting the interruption. Ben was just about to shout, 'Come in', when Sarah popped her head round and announced: 'Make way for the cavalry.'

They then watched in amazement as Sarah led two very polished and professional looking women into the room.

'This is Lizzie and Cara from TwoPlus PR and they're here to organise our launch party.' Sarah said smugly, drawing up three chairs for each of them to sit down at.

Ben caught the eyes of his co-workers just in time to spot the slightly bemused but nonetheless impressed smiles spread across their faces at the same time as his own.

'You couldn't be more welcome,' said Ben.

'It was like the blind leading the blind in here a minute ago,' added Sonja, cheerfully. 'We were about to draw straws for who should phone the Evening News.'

'No need for that,' Lizzie informed them. 'We're going to see to it that this event gets the maximum amount of exposure.'

Ben wondered how Sarah had managed to swing this one, but he suspected she would be paying for it out of her own pocket. Just when he had begun to wonder what he was getting himself into by agreeing to co-parent with her, she had shown what a dependable person she really was.

'So,' Lizzie continued. 'Sarah has briefed us on the event and the plan is that we'll write a press release for your approval this week which will be sent out to all local and national news outlets. We'll then follow up with each of them by phone.' Now in full professional flight, she added: 'We're aiming to get newspaper, digital and broadcast media there so we should create an overflow room where we can entertain other guests while the press do their interviews with Jason, Emily and Ben with the exhibition pieces as a backdrop.'

Ben was quietly marveling at Lizzie's efficiency as she continued her briefing when he registered his name being mentioned alongside the words 'do the press interviews'. His heart sank, but he knew he would have to pull it together enough to put himself in the spotlight for an evening and publically represent the centre – and all that I and the rest of the team had worked hard to create. He felt the stir of anxiety in his stomach which was starting to lurch. Six months ago he would have fled from this situation, but just as the idea of making his excuses flickered for a fleeting second, a voice warned him: 'Don't even think about it.' Ben visibly flinched. I could see he was struggling to work out what had just happened. The voice had been inside his head, but it was not his own.

'Are you okay?' Sarah asked, concerned by his suddenly startled face. Soon all eyes around the table were on him.

'Yes,' he replied. 'I just think Harry would be pleased with our plans.' And everyone smiled again.

The following two weeks were a blur for Ben and the rest of the team at the Melville Centre as they worked towards the launch. Every one of their new young recruits was seconded to help prepare. The recreation room had to be emptied and the walls painted, ready for Jason's two main pieces to be mounted on the main wall facing the door. The wall running along the back of the room already hosted a collection of Jason's best sketches – most of them on paper torn from old jotters, a couple were even drawn on loo roll. It didn't matter, Ben thought, because this incredible collection of work only served to further authenticate the purity of Jason's talent that would be on show tonight for the first time.

The office would be used to serve drinks and food, so it too had to be painted and rearranged, with additional tables brought in and pushed to the back of the walls to create standing room.

Ben had barely seen Jason in the last fortnight. He spent most of his time down at the studio, perfecting the large drawings he was preparing for this exhibition – and ultimately for Emily to sell in her gallery. This afternoon, Sarah was collecting Jason from the studio to help him bring his finished drawings down to the centre to be mounted on the walls. He had framed them with Emily that morning and she had declared herself very satisfied with the finished result. Ben couldn't wait to see them.

He also wanted to thank Sarah who had completely saved the day over the launch by bringing in the PR firm and arranging caterers for the event. At their team meeting on Monday, Lizzie had told them they were expecting three newspaper journalists, a couple of magazine writers, a news agency reporter and four photographers. They were expecting a TV crew from Scottish Television and, incredibly, another from Sky News. All, seemingly, had been sold on the idea of a boy from one of Edinburgh's roughest estates, bowling over the art world with his extraordinary gift. A great story indeed, Ben thought.

Suddenly, Sonja burst loudly into the room behind him. She had started work at 7am that morning and had barely taken a break for a cup of tea since.

'That's the caterers arrived,' she said breathlessly, 'so they'll be setting up next door in a minute.' She was about to bustle out of the office again when she turned back towards Ben, adding: 'Oh, and I think I saw Sarah's car pull up behind their van.'

'I'll go and check,' said Ben, hastily making his way to the front door. He opened it just in time to let three, heavily-laden caterers in followed by Sarah and Jason. They were happily smiling and chatting as they made their way towards the centre, each carrying a large picture frame, wrapped in brown paper. Ben felt like a child on Christmas Day. He wanted to grab the frames from them and rip off the wrapping so he could see what lay underneath.

'You're here,' he called, unable to contain his excitement.

'Yes,' Sarah replied cheerily, 'and we've made it without dropping the frames too, despite having to carry them almost the length of the Royal Mile to my car.'

'Well done, but are you sure you're okay?' Ben asked Sarah anxiously before quickly prising the frame from her. 'You shouldn't be lifting large objects.'

'I'm fine,' she laughed, placing a reassuring hand on his shoulder. 'You're such a worrier.'

Once back in the recreation room, he laid the frame down on the bare wooden floor and slowly peeled off the brown paper cover. The first drawing was even more breathtaking than he could have imagined. It was a simple head-shot of Jason's father which Ben guessed had been sketched without Gary's knowledge one night as he sat watching his beloved reality TV shows. Jason's drawing in black ink managed to capture almost every year of Gary's life in its detail, each line on his worn face telling its own story. It was absolutely magnificent. He wondered what Gary himself would have thought of it.

Jason laid the second frame next to the one Ben was admiring and set about removing the covering paper.

'This picture of your father is incredible, Jason,' Ben said quietly.

'Cheers pal.'

Ben turned now to look at the second picture which he soon discovered to be equally breathtaking. The subject this time was a toddler who appeared to be wandering aimlessly around with his arms outstretched desperately looking for attention; his grubby pyjamas and ruffled hair telling their own story of hardship and neglect. Ben suspected the picture reflected Jason's own childhood

– one in which he fought for his parents to notice his talents, only to be met with derision and a total lack of understanding from Gary. It suddenly struck Ben that though he and Jason had come from such different homes, their experience in this respect had been so similar.

'Stunning,' he said, turning to look at the young artist only to find he was already heading off with Sarah to decide where to hang the frames.

Ben watched as they pointed and nodded in agreement before Jason hammered the first nail into place on the wall, with Sarah standing at the other side of the room ready to advise on height and the evenness of the hang. Ben and Jason lifted the first picture together and positioned it over the nail, maneuvering it left and then slightly right until Sarah was happy it was straight. They did the same for the second, before all three of them stood back by the door to take in the display in its full glory. Within moments they were joined by Sonja, Dave and a couple of the other kids who had been helping out that day. For a minute, no one said anything. They simply stood, silently consuming a talent that was about to have its rightful moment. Finally, Sonja broke the spell to utter just one word: 'Brilliant.'

An hour later and the preparations had reached fever-pitch. Lizzie and her assistant had arrived to oversee the final touches. She had a list of all attendees – including some of the great and the good of the Scottish art world, as she had put it – and a separate list of all the press that were expected. Ben had changed into his one and only suit jacket and shirt, paired with dark blue jeans. Sarah had been home to change and had arrived back wearing a chic, black, floaty dress which Ben guessed must have been another new maternity outfit.

He had just finished being briefed by Lizzie – she had instructed him to personally greet every guest – when he felt someone tapping his shoulder. He was already feeling quite harassed and wasn't relishing receiving another set of orders when he turned to find it was Emily who was trying to get his attention.

'Hi,' she said casually. 'Lizzie advised me to get here early so here I am.'

'Yes, she's good at giving advice,' Ben muttered in a conspiratorial tone, raising his eyes to the ceiling to embellish his point.

'I consider myself warned,' she smiled.

'I think she'll want to make sure that you'll only say nice things about the centre,' Ben suggested. 'Not tell the world it's now being run by a hopeless fool who's never held down a proper job in his life.'

'Ah, but you have other talents,' said Emily wryly. 'Speaking of which, did you bring the pictures you promised me?'

'Yes,' Ben replied, a mix of anxiety and embarrassment flashing across his face. 'They're in a drawer in the office so I'll show you later if you can stick around?'

'I'd be delighted.'

'Ah, Emily,' a high-pitched voice boomed over the room. Ben and Emily turned to see Lizzie waving over in their direction. 'Let's have a quick chat.'

'Looks like I'm under orders,' Emily whispered to Ben. 'Catch up later.'

Ben turned to find Jason standing alone next to his collection of art work looking totally petrified.

'You alright?' Ben asked.

'Aye, just a wee bit nervous. I'm not used to all this fuss.'

'I know. And if it's any consolation I'm shitting myself too. I had

to resist the urge to down half a bottle of whisky before I came out.'
The two laughed together, releasing some of the tension that had
built up over the day.

But before they had time to counsel each other any further,
the first of the evening's guests arrived. It was Dad. Ben had
completely forgotten he was coming, but he was pleased to see the
old fellow nonetheless – and grateful to finally have his support.
The irony that Dad was attending an event to celebrate a young
artist's work, when he prevented his own son from pursuing such
a career, would not be lost on either of them, but Ben wasn't going
to throw it in his face. There was too much water under the bridge
now.

'Hello Dad,' he said warmly. 'Come and meet Jason, the star of
the show.' Ben gently guided our father towards the artist who was
standing sheepishly next to his work.

'Ah,' Dad exclaimed as if he had just made a major discovery.
'So this is the fellow everyone's talking about.'

Jason blushed as Dad made an obvious display of taking in the
collection of work in front of him.

'Very impressive too,' he said, although Ben could tell that Dad's
mind would have already turned to acquiring his first drink. A
lover of culture he wasn't. When asked, he would take great delight
in devilishly announcing to whoever would listen that, 'Golf and
wine are my only interests these days, along with women, who are
sadly no longer interested in me.'

The old man's eyes roamed the room until he'd spotted his target
– the waitress. He shuffled in her direction until he caught her eye,
then offered a warm smile to the teenage girl who carried a tray
full of champagne. 'Wouldn't say no to a glass of fizz,' he grinned
and she dutifully provided him with a drink. Ben couldn't help but
smirk as Dad thanked the girl with the same line he had used in

such situations for as long we could remember: 'Much obliged, my dear. Much obliged.'

As the waitress turned to offer drinks to the assembled few, Ben gladly accepted a glass of Dutch courage.

Several other guests were now arriving and Ben could see Lizzie seeking him out to begin his meet and greet.

The first two guests he introduced himself to turned out to be the centre's biggest donors – a transport tycoon and his wife. Ben thanked them kindly for their support before Lizzie whisked him away to meet a couple of local politicians who he could tell were itching to be associated with this triumph over adversity story.

One, whose portliness matched his pomposity, even suggested: 'If you would like a little back-up for your media interviews, I'd be glad to help out.'

'I'll keep that in mind,' Ben replied diplomatically.

He toured the room for the next half an hour, meeting an impressive selection of art enthusiasts and supporters of the centre. Then the moment he had dreaded arrived as he spotted a TV cameraman setting up in the corner of the recreation room. Lizzie was ushering the guests away from the camera to continue their conversations, so that they could begin the interview. He noticed another girl standing on her own with a microphone and pack that suggested she was a radio reporter. Then there were two young guys with Dictaphones who he took to be press reporters and a photographer who had already started taking shots of Jason's work. Just when he thought that was it, he noticed another camera crew in the hallway. What had Lizzie said to get all this press interest? When she said it was 'silly season' in news terms, she wasn't kidding.

Lizzie turned her attention to the waiting reporters.

'Okay, we'll do the broadcast interviews first as they've got tighter deadlines,' she told them.

Ben flinched at the thought of his face being beamed across the country as he struggled to find words. He imagined what the viewers would make of him stammering and stumbling, before the reporter then turned to Jason with his tendency to mumble under pressure. It didn't bode well.

He turned to see a young, blonde TV reporter delivering her piece to camera, setting the scene of – to cut a long story short – the boy from an estate who could draw.

Staring earnestly into the camera as she began her pre-recorded piece, she explained:

'Twenty-year-old Jason Weir left school four years ago without a single qualification but with one big dream. Just three months ago he came here to the Melville Centre in Edinburgh hoping someone could help him develop his artistic talent further. He brought with him a selection of some of the sketches and drawings you can see behind me now.

'The director of the centre, Ben Melville, was so impressed with what he saw that he arranged a meeting with the renowned gallery owner Emily DiRollo, who immediately commissioned two pieces for sale. Today, as the young artist puts his work on public display for the first time, the rest of the world gets to see just what all the fuss is about.'

She stopped there and asked to interview Jason first before Emily. There was no mention of Ben – to his great relief – but just as he contemplated going to find another glass of champagne, one of the newspaper reporters stepped forward.

'Ben, can I ask you a few questions?'

'Fire away,' said Ben. Trying, as usual, to appear calm.

Ben could hear Jason muttering away in the background while both Lizzie and the TV reporter were animatedly trying to placate him about something.

Ben turned back to the reporter who was already half-way through his first question.

'What made you realise Jason's drawings were special?'

'It doesn't take an expert to see that he has an incredible talent. It just leapt out at me as soon as he showed me his drawings.'

The reporter continued with his list of carefully thought-out questions, which Ben tried as hard as possible to give him sensible answers to, but half-way through another rambling reply he noticed Lizzie frantically waving at him.

'I'm so sorry. You'll need to excuse me,' Ben said, moving quickly across to the corner of the room where Jason had retreated to as the angry-looking TV reporter stood in front of him with her hands on her hips.

'What's the problem?' Ben asked Lizzie.

'Jason's refusing to do any TV interviews or press pictures.'

'Has he said why?'

'He just says he can't bear being on camera,' Lizzie said, her cheeks flushed with stress. 'Please can you talk to him?'

'Well, I can try.'

Ben tapped the TV reporter on the shoulder and asked to speak to Jason alone.

'Why don't you want to do the interviews?'

'I'll just look an idiot. You should have told me I'd be on TV.'

'I'm sorry, Jason. I thought we'd mentioned it. We must have just got caught up with all the planning. I really thought you knew.'

'No, and I'm not doing it.'

Ben looked away for a moment while he tried to figure out a good reason why Jason should change his mind. He realised he'd messed up by not warning him, but he couldn't imagine why he wouldn't want to take the chance to promote his work.

Just as he was about to have one last try at talking Jason round,

Ben spotted a dishevelled-looking man standing awkwardly in the doorway. Gary Weir. He'd come to see his son. Ben noticed too that he'd even tried to assemble together something that looked like a suit – only the trouser legs were too short and the jacket too tight. But his ridiculous attire only served to endear Jason's father to Ben as he considered what a fish out of water he must feel like.

'Oh no, this isn't good,' Jason said as he saw his father approaching.

'Give him the benefit of the doubt,' said Ben. 'Looks like he's here to support you, not cause trouble. Wait here a minute and I'll talk to him.'

Ben moved quickly to intercept Gary before he got in earshot of Jason.

'Thanks for coming,' he said, offering his hand which Gary eyeballed suspiciously first before shaking.

'The missus telt me to come,' he said, by way of explanation. 'She's on her way from the bingo.'

'Well, I'm very glad you did because I've got a bit of situation I'm hoping you'll help me with.'

Ben realised there was every chance Gary would turn down his request for help, but he thought it was worth a shot.

'We've got press reporters here who want to speak to Jason but he's not happy to talk to them. If he gets a reputation as someone who won't communicate with the press, he can kiss the chance of any good publicity goodbye,' Ben told Gary. 'He'll have to learn to speak to them, so he's as well to start now.'

Gary looked over at his son for a moment as he weighed the situation up.

'Jason,' he called quietly, gesturing with his head for him to come over.

His son turned around and Ben noticed the two TV cameramen and the news photographer swing into action as they captured the young artist rush over to greet his father.

'Dad, I didn't think you'd come,' Jason said.

Gary ran his eyes over the pictures on the wall.

'You did all these son?' His gaze resting on the portrait of his own face.

'Aye.' Jason looked almost ashamed.

'He's an ugly bastard.' Gary nodded towards his own portrait, laughing.

The ice broken, Jason finally relaxed for the first time that evening.

'Does this mean I can sleep in my own bed tonight?' he asked, cheekily.

'If ye hurry up and get me a drink. I'm gasping here,' Gary snapped back. 'Now what's this they're telling me about you no doin' interviews?'

'You know I can't do them, Dad.'

'Son, ye cannae hide forever. This is yer chance. Get on and take it for God's sake.'

The TV reporter had moved to stand right behind Jason again, refusing to let her target out of her sight. Jason edged towards Gary, standing so close that only his father could hear.

'What made you change your mind about this, Dad?'

'If this is what's gonnae keep ye on the straight and narrow then I'm no gonnae stand in yer way son. Now get on and speak tae that bloody lassie behind ye before she pisses hersel' will ye?'

Jason sighed and turned slowly to look at the reporter: 'What is it you want to ask me then?'

Ben smiled with a mixture of relief and pride as he watched Jason give the TV interview. He looked nervous and uncomfortable as he carefully tried to answer each question, but he did it and that was all that mattered.

'Can you say a few words to our guests now, Ben?' Lizzie was asking.

Ben had hoped she'd forgotten his promise to address the guests, but he supposed he'd better get on with it, grateful he'd at least swigged a glass of champagne back taking the edge off his nerves. Still, the nausea, there every time he felt out of his comfort zone, was making itself known. 'Will you tell everyone to gather round?' Ben took a deep breath and exhaled sharply. 'No problem,' Lizzie replied, ever efficient.

Once all the guests were assembled in front of him and obediently followed Lizzie's request that they give their attention to Ben for a few moments, he began his speech.

'Firstly, I'd like to thank all of you for coming tonight. There are more people here than we ever imagined and we're so grateful.' Ben was surprising even himself at how confident he sounded in spite of his nerves. Considering he was being filmed by several guests and the reporters on their phones, along with the two TV crews, he knew he couldn't mess it up.

'Thank you too, to those of you who have so faithfully supported the Melville Centre over the years. We sadly miss its founder, my brother Harry, but we intend to continue its work and keep on helping the young people in this community.'

He stopped to acknowledge the unexpected round of applause for his last comment before continuing.

'As you have all seen tonight, Jason Weir is an exceptionally talented young man. He came to this centre with a dream and we had a duty to help him fulfil it – to help Jason become a professional artist. Today marks the start of that future. Jason is an example to us all that it shouldn't matter where you come from, it's what you do that should take you places. Now I hope that any kid in this community who has a goal or ambition and doesn't know how to go about achieving it, will come to our door and ask for help.'

He paused again to acknowledge another round of applause, relief creeping in that he was nearing the end of the script he'd learned by heart.

'Just before we let you go this evening, I'd like to say a final thanks to Emily DiRollo for her support of Jason and his talent, and for her help in getting him started on what we hope will be a long and successful career.'

Emily smiled graciously as the guests again applauded. Then, when the crowd began to disperse, she made her way towards Ben.

'Great speech. You're such a dark horse,' she said, appearing genuinely impressed. 'Now, will you show me your work?' she demanded with mock impatience.

'I don't want to disappoint you,' Ben replied, unsure of what she was expecting to see.

'Just show me,' she smiled.

Sarah and Lizzie were leading the clean-up operation in the office and with so much noise and activity around them, it was easy for Ben and Emily to feel invisible in the corner.

Ben reached into the cabinet and pulled out a handful of the drawings and paintings he had brought with him. He'd stuffed most of his artwork in a box when he finished school and hadn't opened it since – until this morning, when he had dug it out of his storage cupboard and selected a few of what he felt were his better pieces.

'Here,' he said, handing them over to her.

Emily perched on the side of a table, her back turned away from the rest of the room as she slowly picked her way through the collection in her hands. Her expression, as always when she studied pieces of art, gave nothing away. As Ben watched her, he thought she looked as though she could have been reading a newspaper; until just a flicker of a smile made its way across her face. Ben cast his eyes to the floor, not wishing to be caught looking at her.

'These are lovely,' she whispered, partly to herself.

'Thank you,' said Ben, unsure of what to say next.

He looked down again at the pile of papers in her hand. Among them, a mixture of watercolour paintings in which he'd always picked an abstract object out amidst the landscape: a single boat making its way out of the harbour at Newhaven; a bird standing over its nest looking at two broken eggs inside; a child running from a play park. Alongside them were several sketches he had done of family and friends. But Emily had paused longest on a sketch that Ben drew of me on the beach when we were teenagers. We were walking the dog together under Dad's orders.

I remembered the day well. I'd been regaling him with tales of my antics the night before at a rugby do while throwing the ball for the dog, Ben sitting on the sand quietly sketching me as I talked. The beach was the one place we liked to go together, the lapping waters calming the growing tensions between us.

Funnily enough, I had never seen the final drawing until now.

Ben wondered if the solitary tear making its way down Emily's cheek was for the art or the subject.

'You must paint again, Ben,' Emily said slowly as if to accentuate the importance of what she was saying.

'These bring back a lot of memories,' he said. 'Good and bad.'

'You threw away a tremendous gift and it's time to reclaim it. I could sell these landscapes over and over again. I'm talking as an art lover *and* a businesswoman here.'

Ben studied Emily's earnest face, so serene he thought. He wanted to reach out and stroke her shiny brown hair that lay so perfectly straight, just resting on her shoulders. Not a thing out of place.

'Tell you what. I'll pick up the paintbrush again, if you let me take you out to dinner to thank you for everything you've done tonight,' he grinned.

Emily returned his smile, shyly folding her hair back behind her ears.

'There's no need to thank me, but dinner would be wonderful,' she said, her cheeks flushing.

Suddenly, Ben was aware of someone tugging on his left sleeve and turned to find Sarah standing behind him.

'I'm just heading off now, Ben. Could I have a quick word?'

'Yes, of course,' he said to Sarah before turning back to Emily. 'Meet you at the front door in five minutes.'

'No problem,' Emily replied.

Ben followed Sarah into the corridor where she stopped just outside the toilet door.

'Everything alright?' Ben asked, concerned Sarah may be feeling unwell.

'Everything's fine. I just wanted to check you thought tonight went okay?'

'Oh, yes. I'm delighted. And thank you for all your help.'

'You're welcome,' Sarah smiled. 'Did Emily enjoy herself?'

'Yes, I think so.'

'You two seem to be getting on very well.'

Ben cleared his throat. 'Yes, she's a nice lady.'

'Did I hear you say you're going to dinner with her now?'

'Yes.' He scratched the back of his head nervously. 'Would you like to come too?'

'No, I'm very tired. And three's a crowd,' she said sharply.

Sarah wrapped her throw tightly around her and headed out into the cool evening. The haar from the sea, so common at the shore in Edinburgh in summer, had worked its way inland taking the temperature plunging down with it. As she walked to her car alone she folded her arms across her chest in an effort to block out the chill and the thought she could be losing Ben. Worse still, it would be to a woman who now seemed to have laid claim to the only two men she'd ever loved.

CHAPTER ten

LIFE AT THE CENTRE QUICKLY RETURNED to normal again after our difficult house guest had left. Within a few months I had pretty much forgotten about the whole messy ordeal with Luke, although if I was ever walking near his estate I would quicken my pace for fear of running into him – or him running into me. I wasn't really afraid of him on a physical level – I was much bigger in height and frame – but I was aware he was volatile and unpredictable and that made me very uneasy. I also hated what he represented: failure. Mine and his.

He was only sixteen years old and already his life had been engulfed by drugs – that wasn't necessarily his fault, I knew, but there was something around the hopelessness of his situation that left me cold. I only backed winners. I tried to feel sympathy for him, but in reality his weakness just made me angry. So I hoped we'd never meet again and then I could go on believing that I was a good man who could help any young person who wanted it; whatever their ambition.

But fate had other ideas.

One night in mid-December I'd stayed behind late at the centre to help clear up after a Christmas party we'd thrown for staff and volunteers. Sarah had gone on ahead because she had a lot of work she had to get on with. After we were finished I waved Dave, who at that point had only recently joined the centre, and Tony off and I was just locking up when I heard footsteps behind. I didn't need to turn around because I already sensed who it was.

'Hiya Harry,' he laughed, mockingly it seemed to me. 'How you doing pal? Have ye had a wee party here then and didnae invite me?'

'What do you want, Luke?' I turned to see him staggering in front of me, clearly boozed-up or drugged-up or both.

'You're a mess, Luke. Get out of my face.' I tried to shove past him then, but he lost his balance and stumbled.

There was a scuffle, I had him backed into a doorway and felt like I was getting the better of him before I felt a blow just beneath my ribs. I stumbled backwards and remember only watching him turn and run.

Turns out he'd stabbed me in the stomach. Fortunately, someone had seen me panic stricken and covered in blood and called an ambulance. The police said it was a young man who sounded fraught and wouldn't leave his name. I lost a lot of blood, so his phone call was timely – I could have bled to death otherwise.

The police pressed me for a name, but I couldn't bring myself to give Luke up so I told them I didn't know my attacker. I just told them that a youth had approached me and demanded cash and when I refused to hand any over he stabbed me. With no weapon and no witness I'd supposed there probably wouldn't have been enough evidence to charge Luke anyway. Either way, I didn't want to get involved in a trial. Once it became known that one of the young people I'd tried to help had turned on me like that, I felt sure it would have reflected badly on the centre – and, yes, me too. Negative press was not something I wanted to entertain, not after I'd worked so hard to build an untarnished reputation as Scotland's ultimate philanthropist.

I learned pretty quickly after he stabbed me that he'd left Muirhouse and had moved away from the city. That suited me fine. I didn't have to fear facing him again, and I didn't have to feel guilty about him either.

The only person I decided to confide in about Luke was Ben, figuring that being an artist himself, he would appreciate my decision not to turn the teenager over to the police. But Ben felt precisely the opposite. In fact, he spent over two hours in the pub with me one evening trying to talk me into reporting him. He was horrified that Luke was free to walk the streets after sticking a knife into me.

'Firstly, he could do this to someone else who might not be as lucky as you were to escape with your life,' he'd argued. 'Secondly, if he is a drug addict he might even be better off in prison where they could help him kick his habit.'

But nothing Ben said would change my mind. My conscience wouldn't cope with Luke in prison, so I stayed quiet and liked myself better for it.

~

To Ben's relief, Emily made the easiest of dinner partners. Away from her work she was relaxed, warm, open and interested.

She had suggested the little bistro on the shore Ben had walked past many times but never actually eaten in. Inside, the atmosphere was intimate and cosy but the restaurant was busy enough to allow diners to forget themselves among the crowd. Sitting at a table in the furthest corner of the dining room, Ben felt surprisingly at home with his companion. Their initial conversation about favourite places to eat had seemed effortless and, after ordering their food, Ben even felt comfortable enough to ask Emily about her private life.

His opportunity came just after she finished telling him a story about eating out during a holiday in South Africa in which she made several references to 'we'.

'Did you go with your partner?' he tried to ask nonchalantly.

'Yes,' she replied and Ben worked hard to disguise the disappointment he feared must have been obvious, before Emily added. 'But we separated at the beginning of the year.'

'Sorry to hear that,' he offered half-heartedly, pleased to hear she was single.

After a moment's pause, Emily asked: 'Are you in a relationship?'

'No. I've never been very good at them,' he smiled. 'But I remain hopeful.'

'I know what you mean,' she laughed.

The waitress arrived with their starters of goat's cheese salad for Ben and calamari for Emily, and they stopped talking as they watched her serve the dishes and top up their wine. Alone again, Ben was just about to ask Emily whether she had any holidays planned for this year, when she abruptly cut in.

'Why did you stop?' Although Emily's question had come completely out of context, Ben didn't need to ask what she meant.

He thought for a moment, taking time to construct what would be an honest, yet hugely simplified answer. 'I lost my heart for it when my dad stopped me from going to art school. I was very angry. I think I've probably been punishing myself about it for some time. But I felt if I couldn't be a professional artist, I didn't want to be a professional anything.'

She offered him a consolatory smile.

'And, if I'm really honest,' continued Ben. 'I'm still pissed off with my dad for always branding Harry the talented one and me the one who struggled, when at one stage, I really felt I had a gift.'

Emily paused for a moment, gauging how far to go with her response.

'For what it's worth, Ben. I think your talent easily equals Harry's achievements – and I think he probably realised how good you were... are. Being an opportunist – in the most positive sense of the word – that's why he tried to pass your drawings off as his.'

'Maybe,' Ben replied, but inwardly reminded himself that it was our father who had seemed most threatened by his talent – and he who had put his foot down over art school.

Why Ben had not had the guts to go ahead anyway he still couldn't figure out. It just seemed at the time as though you had to have your parents' permission to do anything. The thought of pushing on against Dad's will had just never occurred to Ben. After years of bitterness, he was also starting to wonder whether it really mattered that much anymore; because for the first time in his life, he was actually beginning to feel like someone – not just a weird outsider with nothing much to offer society. He smiled warmly at Emily and wondered what she would have made of him if she'd met him a year earlier.

'When I said that I would paint again, I meant it. I've actually been thinking about it for a while – I've even bought a sketch pad and brushes. I've been dying to paint Newhaven Harbour again for years so this week I'm going to do it.'

'Wonderful,' Emily gushed, looking genuinely pleased. Ben noticed her cheeks had flushed with the wine and she seemed almost a completely different person to the emotional brick wall sitting behind the desk at the gallery.

'I want to see it as soon as you've finished,' she added, with mock severity.

The evening sped past as Ben made Emily talk him through her rise from art student to prominent figure on the Scottish cultural scene. In turn, Ben recalled for her the countless dead-end jobs he had attempted to hold down – and the numerous comedic tales that explained his early exit from each one.

It was only when the waitress kept asking: 'Will there be anything else?', that they became aware of the time and asked for the bill.

Outside the restaurant, Ben helped Emily flag down a cab.

'You sure I can't drop you off on the way?' she asked, concerned that he insisted on walking home so late.

'No thanks. I always walk.'

An uncomfortable silence followed while they each tried to work out how to end the evening.

'I had a wonderful time,' Ben said before kissing Emily on the cheek.

'Me too,' Emily replied.

'Well, let's do it again soon.'

'Love to.'

Ben waved as the cab pulled away from the pavement. And watching the vehicle head further down the street he wondered where he and Emily were destined to go from here.

My brother walked with an extra spring in his step as he headed out the next morning into the warm sunshine. He felt like a teenager again, bemused and embarrassed by the flurry of butterflies in his stomach every time he thought about Emily. He found it hard to believe she could feel the same way, but he was sure he would have been able to read the signs if she wasn't interested. As it was Saturday, he decided to wait until Monday before he called to ask her out again, calculating that a two-day gap would seem keen but not desperate. Today, he had agreed to go with Sarah to buy a cot and 'travel system' – it seemed pram was too simple a description these days – for the baby. He also thought it would be a good opportunity to spend a bit more time with Sarah as she had appeared pretty agitated over the last week, something Ben had attributed to the pressure of helping organise Jason's launch evening. He had agreed to call for her at 10am, but rounding the corner into her street he glanced at his watch and realised he was ten minutes early. Still, he thought, he could just make himself a cup of tea in the kitchen if she wasn't ready.

Standing on Sarah's doorstep, Ben was just about to ring the bell when he heard raised voices from inside her hallway.

'There's nothing to discuss,' he heard Sarah say sternly. 'This is my child and I don't need you to be involved. Get on with your life and forget about this.'

'Forget this?' a man, whose voice Ben didn't recognise, replied incredulously. 'How can I forget my own child?' Ben's mind began to race as he tried to work out what was happening. It then struck him that the sperm donor must have changed his mind and wanted parental rights. Surely that's illegal, Ben thought as he rang the doorbell several times in quick succession so as to sharply interrupt the conversation. Sarah answered, but instead of looking grateful, Ben thought she seemed stunned and more than a little put out to see him standing there.

'Ben,' she began, sounding panicked. 'Can you just wait there a moment? I'm just with someone at the minute.'

But that 'someone' was behind her now, and Ben was immediately struck by his aggressive posture. He looked to be in his late thirties, but was already balding at the front. He was tanned and appeared physically very fit, Ben noted, not relishing the idea of a struggle of any sort with this angry stranger.

'Who the hell are you?' the man demanded.

'I was just going to ask you the same.' Ben said, trying to appear unshaken.

'Paul Davis. A former colleague of Sarah's and father of this baby.' He pointed to her stomach. 'You?'

Ben felt as though he'd been punched in the stomach. 'I'm Ben Melville, Harry's brother,' he replied, his voice already deflated and confused.

Paul climbed down a little when he realised who Ben was and took a more conciliatory tone. 'Let's all go into the living room and talk this through shall we? I don't think this is a conversation we should be having on the doorstep.'

'I have nothing to say to him,' Sarah hissed in Paul's direction, but Ben was already heading inside towards the front room.

With Paul pacing around still clearly agitated, Ben tried to calm the situation.

'Sit down, Paul,' he said, gesturing towards an armchair. While Paul took a seat, Sarah hovered in the doorway looking fiercely uncomfortable. Unsure now of whether to sit or stand, Ben opted to perch on an arm of the sofa, turning to address Paul.

'I'm not sure how you got involved as a donor, but in your profession you must be aware that there are legally binding terms in these arrangements that I don't think you're in a position to challenge. You can't just turn up on Sarah's doorstep demanding a parental role?'

Paul stared back blankly at him for a moment, before replying: 'What do you mean 'donor'? I didn't offer to be a donor.'

Ben looked at Sarah for back-up but she was standing with her head down and, apparently, refusing to join in the discussion.

'What are you then?' Ben asked with a creeping awareness that he was about to receive another blow.

'Her lover, Ben,' Paul sneered.

'You're not,' Sarah bit back.

'I didn't pay a visit to the sperm bank,' he continued undeterred, 'Sarah and I had sex, 24 weeks ago to be precise. About the same number of weeks that she's pregnant, get it?'

Ben closed his eyes, as if trying to shut out everything he was seeing and hearing, but when he opened them, the stranger was still there and Sarah hadn't corrected a word he said.

'Is this man the father of your baby?' Ben asked Sarah quietly, the numbness of his spirit reflected in his voice.

'I don't know,' she said shaking her head, still unable or unwilling to look up.

'So, there was no donor?'

'No, Ben,' she whispered, putting her hand up to her face as if to conceal herself from the situation; a mixture of frustration, guilt and fear, leaving her exposed and desperate. 'You just assumed I meant a donor because Harry had said we'd been having fertility treatment.'

'But you didn't correct me,' Ben stood up, rage taking hold and causing his hands to violently shake as he pointed his finger menacingly at her.

'No,' Sarah sobbed, before abruptly leaving the room and running upstairs.

Ben turned to look at Paul who by now was also on his feet.

'It's my baby,' he said, his face now only inches from Ben's. 'She'd already told me your brother was infertile.'

'Get out,' Ben shouted, his fury exploding at the man in front of him who had managed to tear up their lives in just a few words.

That he'd had the gall to even mention my name was enough to make Ben want to punch him, but to mock my infertility was despicable to my twin, still loyal in spite of everything.

'You'll be hearing from me,' Paul said, leaning menacingly into Ben's face before making for the front door.

Ben could hear Sarah's loud and wretched sobs as he headed up the stairs, eventually finding her lying face down on her bed.

But although he dug deep to find some sympathy for her, it was blocked by pure anger for what he saw as a spoilt woman crying not because of what she'd done, but because her betrayal had been exposed.

Sarah looked up at Ben pitifully, her cheeks streaked with mascara, then moved slowly to bring herself to a sitting position on the bed.

'Please, Ben,' she pleaded. 'I didn't mean to lie. But once you'd jumped to the wrong conclusion I didn't have the heart to correct you. And I didn't see what good it would do anyway.'

'It might just have given me the opportunity to have a think about whether I wanted to be misled into agreeing to jointly parent a child I now seem to have no familial connection to whatsoever,' Ben seethed. 'And, let's face it, that's exactly the reason you chose not to tell me; because it didn't fit with your little plan. But what I really want to know is what the hell would you have told Harry had he not conveniently died before discovering his partner of over 10 years was knocked up with another man's baby?' His angry stare tore into Sarah, demanding a response she knew he would never be satisfied with.

'I would have told him the truth,' she gasped, trying to stifle her sobs.

'Course you would have,' Ben sneered. 'Well, now that there's another daddy on scene, I'll just head off.' He turned to leave but Sarah jumped off the bed in pursuit.

'Ben,' she shouted, grabbing for his arm. 'I need you.' She paused, her eyes desperately imploring him in the hope of finding a crack in his armour. 'I can't do this on my own.'

'Well, you're just going to have to,' he replied, shaking off her grip.

Ben's mobile rang as he reached the end of Sarah's street, but when he saw it was his sister-in-law he quickly rejected the call. Two minutes later, still on his angry march home, his phone rang again. This time it was Emily's mobile number that flashed up on the display screen. Ben stopped momentarily as he contemplated answering, but decided he couldn't speak to anyone right now. His pain and rage completely consumed him, and when he passed the off licence he could control his urge no longer. He went inside and plucked a bottle of Scotch off the shelf before handing over the money to the disinterested young cashier who continued her call on her mobile phone as she rang Ben's sale through. Setting off again on his walk home, his pace quickened even further as he rounded the final corner towards his flat. Bounding up the stairs, he felt a distinct sense of déjà vu as he thought back to a few weeks earlier when he had nursed the same intentions, only to be inadvertently thwarted by Jason's presence. This time there was no one to throw him off course and once inside the shelter of his own kitchen, he sank his first glass rapidly and waited for the warmth to hit his stomach before radiating through him, melting his rage and torment. He poured another, sat down on a chair by his kitchen window and stared blankly into the street outside. But no amount of liquid could wash this pain away. Sarah had stolen what was to be his living link to his twin. He had known that by using a donor the child wouldn't have genetically been mine, but it would have been the child that I wanted and had supported Sarah in creating. Now, some stranger was going to walk in and take that from him – probably his last chance to be a parent.

The tears started to roll now as he thought of how Sarah had cheated on me – and they were quickly followed by an endless stream of questions. How many times, he wondered? Had I known? Had I carried a crushing sadness to the grave knowing that, because of my infertility, my wife had decided to put it about with random work colleague? Ben decided Sarah was not the person he thought she was; the person he had been growing closer to and steadily more and more protective of. She had betrayed us, and there was no going back.

Ben woke to the sound of loud banging on his front door. He glanced at the clock on his oven which read 15:14. It dawned on him, as he tasted the stale whisky in his mouth, that he must have fallen asleep at the table where his head still rested.

Whoever was knocking at the door was not giving up. Ben slowly got to his feet, suddenly aware of the pounding in his head; his mouth feeling like he'd gargled a sack of sand. Once he reached the door he stopped for a minute, leaning his hand against it in an attempt to regain some composure. When the banging started again he opened up to find Jason standing on his doorstep, eyeing him suspiciously.

'What's going on?' he demanded.

'I fell asleep.'

'I could see that from the street,' Jason said. 'You were flat out on the kitchen table.'

'Sorry. Must have been tired,' Ben offered meekly.

'You're stinking of drink. You told me you'd given it up?'

'I have… had.' Ben corrected, rubbing his head to try and soothe the pain. 'Come in.'

Jason stomped into the kitchen and saw the half-empty bottle.

'You've let yerself down, Ben.'

'It's just a blip, Jason. I had a very bad morning.'

'Bad morning?' Jason scoffed. 'You wouldn't know a bad morning if it came up and smacked you in the face. Try living in my home for a week. You'd soon know a bad morning then.'

'Why are you here?' Ben asked bluntly, now full of nausea and remorse in equal measures.

'My mum's thrown my dad out again cos he was out drinking till four in the morning and got in to a fight on the way home. She's spent the rest of the day crying her eyes out so I came here to get out of her way.'

'Sorry to hear that, Jason.' Ben inched himself down onto the kitchen chair again, pushing the whisky bottle away to let Jason know he was finished with it.

'That's not the only reason I came though,' Jason said dramatically.

'Oh?'

'Emily sold one of my drawings today – for one thousand big ones.'

'Bloody hell, Jason.' Ben was on his feet now, hugging his young friend. 'That's unbelievable. Congratulations.'

'She thinks she'll sell more no bother so I'm using the money to put a deposit down on a wee flat to rent – two doors down from you. So, we're neighbours, pal.' He added with a great big beam on his face.

'I'm delighted for you Jason.'

'Aye, well, I'd be delighted if you'd throw that bottle away. Drink and drugs have been the bloody enemy of my family for years so don't you go wasting your life with it and all.'

'Understood,' said Ben, suitably chastised.

'Any chance of a bite to eat?' Jason asked cheekily.

'Come on,' said Ben, laughing. 'Let's go down the chippie. I'm starving too.'

~

Emily paced her living room floor, unsure whether she felt so panic stricken because Ben had rejected her call or by the fact she had let it get to her so much. Had she read the situation wrong? She thought Ben seemed so keen the other night, but then she never really had been any good at reading other people's body language.

She couldn't figure out how men were capable of appearing totally smitten one minute, and totally disinterested the next. Now she'd made a fool of herself by taking the chance on calling him to invite him over for dinner, and he didn't even answer. After Ben rejected her call, she had spent the first couple of hours convinced he would ring her back at any moment, but as the day crept on and morning became afternoon, she feared she had been unceremoniously dumped before she'd even been picked up. He was probably just trying to keep her sweet for Jason's benefit, she thought, reminding herself that it wouldn't be the first time she'd been used. And people wondered why she'd developed such a tough exterior in business. The truth was she was actually a sensitive soul who took everything way too personally so had decided long ago to pull up the emotional drawbridge and retreat. But in Ben, she really believed she had met a kindred spirit, so she'd dropped her guard.

She checked the clock on the mantelpiece one final time. It was now six o'clock in the evening – eight hours since she'd called him. Admitting defeat, she headed for the kitchen to look out something for dinner, but as soon as she stepped into the hallway, she heard her mobile ring. She swung around and ran back into the living room, unable to remember where she had left it. She ran from one side of the room to the other, the ring getting louder somewhere in the middle. Suddenly she spotted it tucked behind a book on her coffee table. She pounced, noticing instantly that it was Ben's number.

'Hello,' she answered breathlessly.

'Emily?' Ben asked, as if someone else could have been answering.

'Yes, hi Ben. How are you?'

'I'm fine. I'm sorry I've taken a while to get back to you. It's a very long story which I would like to tell you if you have some time this weekend.'

'Yes,' she tried to sound aloof then blew it by adding: 'I have time now in fact. Do you want to come over?'

'What's your address?'

'28 Novar Crescent.'

'I'm on my way.'

Emily hung up and sighed a breath of relief.

CHAPTER eleven

THE SENSE OF FAILURE that went hand in hand with my fertility problems ironically coincided with the period in which my earnings peaked and my ego reached epic heights. I fear the mix of power and low self-esteem were a dangerous combination that wreaked havoc with my moods, causing me to swing from enormous highs to dark and volatile lows. During the highs I might splash out on another antique sports car to join the collection I hid away in a lock-up on an industrial estate, choosing only to drive them around at night so as not to appear a hypocrite. They were my one major indulgence after I very publicly vowed, during a TV interview about the opening of the Melville Centre, to shun a life of excess in favour of social responsibility.

During the lows I became increasingly paranoid, believing that everyone was out to rip me off and dwelling on the view that I did so much for others, but no one seemed to do anything for me. I frequently bemoaned this situation to Sarah who started out trying to rationalise with me, but later chose just to roll her eyes and walk away as soon as I began one of my rants.

So, I opted to stoke up my self-esteem by pouring all my compassion and energy into my charitable foundation and I lapped up the media coverage my increasing acts of generosity were winning across both the regional and national press.

My father ended up framing a two-page interview I did with a Scottish broadsheet - which has taken pride of place in his living room ever since. 'Local Hero', read the headline. I still remember the enormous rush I felt listening to my dad recite the article aloud; I can hear the pride in his voice to this day, can see the beaming smile spread across his face. And this was his favourite section in the article, which he confided to me that he'd read over and over again:

'While most multimillionaires would save their spending power for luxury yachts and private jets, Harry Melville instead chooses to invest in some of the nation's least-supported assets; young people. Yet Melville remains distinctly modest about his efforts, insisting he is merely doing what many others would do in his position: 'I'm not a saint,' he explains. 'I just can't live with my head in the sands of some exclusive beach club. There are many, many teenagers and young adults who need support and a sense of direction. Their potential is endless as is my determination to help them. I am doing what I can and what I believe we are supposed to do as human beings.'

~

Ben reached Emily's doorstep within thirty minutes, having power-walked the route from his flat that would usually have taken him almost double the time. He was both anxious to see her and desperate to talk. He knew it was strange that someone he had known for so short a period of time should become his chosen confidante for something so deeply personal. But he had been unable to fight the overwhelming urge to share his pain and anguish with someone. Until today, that someone would have been Sarah. Now she was the root of his problems. In one moment in his eyes she had changed from being the victim of a cruel twist of fate, to the perpetrator of a treacherous, vengeful crime.

As soon as Emily opened the door Ben reached out and embraced her, an automatic response that, had he given it a second thought, he would never have gone through with. Instinctively she held him tight. She was aware, without words, that he was suffering – and that he had come to the right place.

~

Sarah must have tried Ben's mobile more than ten times on the day he had walked into her argument with Paul, but he never answered, a fact for which she was partially grateful as she had no idea what she could say to him to turn the situation around. She flinched as she recalled the look of sheer hate in his eyes before he had turned and walked out of her front door. The shock of finding he'd been lied to on such a major scale along with his outrage at discovering she had cheated on his brother had shattered their blooming friendship and Sarah knew there was nothing she could say to regain Ben's trust. She had blown it.

The pain of losing Ben was almost as bad as her grief over my death. He had restored her faith in life. Just when she thought the world was a dark place with no cause for hope, Ben had come along with his unassuming ways and his gentle kindness, and, suddenly, it had all seemed bearable again. There had been a future.

She lay her head back down on the pillow again and sobbed for everything she had lost. She only had herself to blame she guessed, so why did she feel so let down by life? Then another appalling prospect entered her mind. She prayed that Ben wouldn't tell Dad about her affair. Because if he found out it would surely kill him.

~

FROM the OUTSIDE

Ben couldn't work out whether it was weirder to wake up in someone else's bedroom or to wake up next to that someone else. He hadn't gone to Emily's the night before with the intention of sleeping with her, but after staying up talking together until one in the morning, it was a natural progression. Intimacy with Emily was easy and there was no embarrassment. A silent understanding had instead united them – as it did now that dawn had broken once again, throwing light on their new status as lovers. He noticed Emily smiling at him and he kissed her softly on the forehead then edged closer to her so she could nestle into him before falling back to sleep.

Alone with his thoughts again, he soon started mulling over the situation with his sister-in-law. He hated what Sarah had done to him on every level but still he feared for her. How would she cope on her own with what seemed destined to turn into a battle over paternity rights with Paul? He knew the events of yesterday would have left her bereft and, though she undoubtedly deserved to suffer for the pain she had caused, he couldn't escape the anxiety that gnawed away at him every time he thought of her alone and broken-hearted. He worried most for her unborn child. He hoped Sarah was eating. That she wouldn't just give up as she had in the early days after my death. Emily had told him she thought Sarah deserved forgiveness but Ben didn't agree. He knew I hadn't exactly been a saint, and there had been times where I'd treated Sarah badly, but in Ben's mind she had gone for the jugular and hurt me in the worst way possible. He felt hot tears start to well up at the thought, yet another wave of repressed sorrow over his loss. The last thing I had ever seemed to Ben was vulnerable, yet now all he wanted to do was protect me – and my memory.

Emily woke to the sound of Ben's stifled sobs.

'What's wrong?' she asked, sitting up to comfort him.

'I'm just sad and frustrated. I'm thinking about Harry again. I don't know what he'd want me to do right now?'

'What do you mean?'

'I don't know whether he'd want me to bite the bullet and keep in touch with Sarah for the sake of the child, or whether he'd want me to cut her off in punishment for her betrayal.'

'You need to do what you think is right, Ben. And you don't need to make your mind up in a hurry. Just give this time, okay?'

Ben nodded and let out a deep sigh. As he regained his composure he was embarrassed that he kept putting his problems on Emily. He felt weak again. He wanted to have a drink but he didn't want to go back to where he'd come from.

Emily pulled him closer and he turned to embrace her tightly. Just hold on, he told himself, hold on.

The following day at the gallery, Emily had just finished a phone call with Mark Weiss and could hardly contain her rapture. He owned the largest and most influential gallery in New York, with other galleries on the east and west coasts of the US, and he had just requested two pieces from Jason to show in New York. If they sold well, he hinted he might be interested in doing an exhibition at some stage. Emily had emailed a few contacts in London and New York with pictures of some of Jason's most recent work and the response had been amazingly positive considering they had not seen his drawings in the flesh and were purely trusting her judgment. An influential gallery owner in Fitzrovria, central London, had also agreed to take three of his pictures after she saw a piece on the TV news about Jason at the time of the launch.

Emily hurriedly dialled the young artist's number to tell him the good news.

'Hi Emily,' he answered.

'Jason, there's another art gallery requested two of your drawings – this time in New York,' she gushed.

'You're joking,' he laughed, sounding genuinely bemused.

'I'm a hundred percent genuine, and I've barely got started yet,' she beamed, savouring the moment. 'So I guess you're going to be busy for the next few weeks.'

'Aye. I'll have to kick my dad out the living room so I can get on with my work.'

'I take it he likes your new flat then?' Emily joked.

'He's never out of it. My mum's delighted.'

She laughed at the idea of Gary holding court in Jason's flat while his mother lapped up the freedom that his absence brought.

'Well, if you could let me have the new drawings by the end of the month I'll do the rest.'

'No bother,' said Jason, 'and thanks for everything you're doing for me.'

'You're very welcome, Jason. After all, I'm a businesswoman and, frankly, you're good business.'

'Right,' said Jason, suddenly reminded that this Samaritan who had stepped in to help him wasn't just doing so out of the kindness of her own heart.

∼

Ben had woken early and decided he was going to make the most of the summer sunshine. Now, seated on the cold, unwelcoming harbour steps, he mentally recorded the moment he began to draw again. His plan was to make some sketches then take them home to work from as the basis for his first painting in nearly thirty years. He had taken a few days off from working at the centre so he could dedicate some proper time to this task – and allow himself to take stock of all that happened since my death. Everything had moved so fast in the last few months that Ben just needed to be still for a while.

Sketching came back to him as easily as riding a bike. He put his pencil to paper and drew as though he had never stopped. This time though, there was no sense of pointlessness to his work, he cherished each outline he created as if it were his first. He would take them home and start working on a couple of paintings – and if he never sold one in his life he wouldn't care. It just felt so good to be doing something he loved without any judgment or expectation. Emily had promised to push his work in the gallery, but that wasn't the reason he was sitting on the harbour wall today. He had picked up his pencils and drawing pad again because this was part – not all – of his existence. If it was taken away from him again tomorrow he could still find fulfillment in life so he would never have to face that fear again.

His new-found strength was partly due to the events of the previous evening when he had visited Dad. His intention had been to tell him about Sarah's baby, but when he found him sitting peacefully in his cosy living room, painstakingly poring over the crossword, Ben couldn't bear to break the news. Instead he'd sat with Dad, helping him complete his puzzle and talking to him about life at the centre. He explained that Dave had decided to move on to a new role with another youth charity, with Sonja set to fill his shoes as manager. He spoke of the plans Sonja had set out to him for developing the centre, including launching a dedicated day each week where they would host teenage mothers and their babies to offer them guidance on parenting, and also to nurture their career ambitions and self-confidence. Ben had thought it was a wonderful idea. Although he feared, in practice, they wouldn't be able to make it work in the small amount of space they had available to them. Yet, he promised Sonja he would look into the idea, unable to dash the hopes of a woman so committed to helping young people that she would sell her soul to do it. He remembered reading somewhere that those who dedicated their lives to others were in fact earthly angels. Ben had chuckled at the romanticism of that statement when he read it at the time, but listening to Sonja and watching her at work, he often wondered whether there might actually be some truth in it. Her only reward in life was helping others, yet she was totally fulfilled.

Buoyed by that pleasant thought, Ben thought it was time to try and bridge a gap between him and Dad by finally raising the issue of his refusal to let him go to art school.

As they sat sipping their cups of tea, Ben posed the question he'd been trying to ask for twenty-seven years: 'Dad. Why did you stop me from becoming an artist?'

Dad stared back at him, momentarily stunned and somewhat confused.

'I didn't stop you,' he finally mumbled, attempting to instantly dismiss this line of questioning, but Ben persisted.

'You did, Dad. I asked to go to art school and you said no.'

'Well, I probably considered it a bit of a waste of time, Ben. You don't go very far in life by painting pictures.'

'You do if you have talent. I was talented you know.'

'I realised,' John said coldly, some of the steel Ben remembered from his youth returning to his voice.

'My teacher told me she had practically begged you to allow me to go to art school, but you refused. I just want to know why?'

'But what does it matter now, Ben? It was a long time ago.'

'It was all I wanted to do, Dad. Did you know that? When you took that dream from me I had nothing left. I've spent nearly thirty years just drifting, wondering what could have been.'

'You were always a drifter, Ben. Your brother was a doer and you were a dreamer.'

Ben felt as emotionally crushed by that comment as he had when he'd first heard it from his father all those years ago.

'I just wanted to find out why, Dad. That's all. I think you owe me an answer.'

'Because I didn't want you to spend your days struggling to make ends meet while you sat doodling on a piece of paper,' Dad snapped. His old, croaky voice now steady and strong. 'I knew you had a talent, Ben. Even a fool could see that. But art is not a career – it's an indulgence.'

'And God forbid you would have indulged me, Dad.'

'It was for your own good.'

Ben watched in alarm as our elderly father turned red in the face, infuriated to be challenged on his decision.

I drew closer to Ben, urging him not to react – not to run. They were words he couldn't hear but which I desperately hoped he could feel.

My brother wanted so much to tell Dad he'd ruined his life but, instead, he paused for a moment, reasoning with himself that he had to take his own share of the blame for letting others dictate what he could and couldn't do. And for the first time, he realised too that in some ways he was relieved our father had stopped him from going to art school, because if he'd tried he might have failed – and it was failure that he feared the most. Staring now at the man he'd spent so many years blaming for his misery, Ben felt a wave of love and sympathy for him. He reached forward and took Dad's hand.

'It doesn't matter now, Dad. I'm just glad you're still around for me.'

Dad's eyes filled with tears as he reached out to his only living son, fondly squeezing his shoulder.

'I know I never said it, Ben, but I always knew you would make something of yourself. You have talents that you're only now beginning to realise. But I saw them when you were just a boy. You understand and empathise with others in a way not many of us do. Your sensitivity is your strength.' Dad smiled warmly, flashing the set of stained and crooked teeth that he was so proud to have hung on to for eight decades.

'I can still see you and Harry running around this living room in your pyjamas. Harry jumping up and down for attention and you, happy to indulge him, happy to please.

'I often hoped you'd go into business together – and now in a way you have. Just not in the way I'd imagined.'

Dad's eyes were moist, his gaze somewhere else as though he were looking at a film playing out before him. Ben placed a hand on his shoulder and the two sat together in silence lost in their own thoughts, united in grief.

~

Her busy day at the gallery meant Emily was running late for Ben who was coming over for dinner. They had passed a milestone a couple of weeks ago when she had given him a key to her flat, where he increasingly spent most of his time. Ben often cooked for her, but tonight she had promised to make something for him.

She felt a little rush of happiness as she looked up at her windows from the street to see the lights were already on. Once inside, the enticing smells drifting from the kitchen told her Ben had started the dinner which, to her relief, meant she'd be able to just flop down at the kitchen table and relax while he cooked.

Ben popped his head around the kitchen door as she hung her jacket up on the coat stand in the hallway.

'Hope you don't mind,' he said breezily. 'I was starving so I thought I'd crack on with dinner.'

'Mind,' she exclaimed. 'I'm bloody delighted,' she smiled, throwing her arms around his neck and kissing him hard on the lips. She couldn't believe how much her life had changed in the space of a few weeks. She had resigned herself to a life of living alone and now Ben had come along and filled a void she barely realised existed. Their relationship was loving, comfortable and respectful – and she was so happy.

'I have something for you,' Ben said, pointing towards the kitchen table.

There she saw an ornate and enlarged pencil drawing of the rose that I had once passed off to her as my own work all those years ago.

At the bottom of the picture Ben had written: 'To Emily. The genuine article, just like you. Ben.'

She picked the paper up to admire the stunning detail in the drawing that was a mirror image of the one she had been given as a teenager.

'It's beautiful, Ben,' she said. 'Thank you.' She paused to look again at the picture in her hand before gently placing it back down on the table.

Turning to Ben, her eyes now serious, she said: 'You must give me some of your work so that I can sell it. You could make something out of this.'

He stepped away from the pots on the oven hob and crossed the kitchen to sit next to her for a moment.

'I want to do this for the love, Emily. Not for the money. Taking time off has given me the chance to think. Events had just taken me over and I didn't know whether I was working at the centre simply because I'd been asked to do it, or because I actually

FROM the OUTSIDE

wanted to do it.' He stroked her brow, soothing the frown that had etched its way across it as Emily struggled to understand his reasoning.

'I want to dedicate my professional life to the centre, Emily,' he continued. 'It will be the blank canvas on which I hope to create many masterpieces.'

Emily opened her mouth to challenge him before thinking better of it. Instead she simply shrugged. 'Whatever makes you happy, I guess. Besides, I've got some really good news for you,' she flashed him a smile. 'I've been talking to a gallery in New York and, today, they agreed to take some of Jason's drawings.'

'Wow. That's incredible,' Ben gushed, grasping Emily's arms in his excitement. 'And it's so quick. Jason will be beside himself. You've done so much for him, Emily, I just can't thank you enough.'

'Don't thank me, Ben,' she said, folding her arms around his waist. 'You spotted his potential, I'm just doing my job.'

'You're a clever girl,' he teased. 'And just a pussycat really underneath it all.'

'Why? What did you think I was?'

'A tigress,' he laughed. 'And one who would eat me for dinner.'

'You'd better get on with feeding me then, hadn't you,' she said with mock impatience. 'I'm starving.'

~

In the weeks that followed, Ben continued to spend most of his time at Emily's place, their relationship settled and happy. But just when he should have been feeling as though life was finally going his way, his contentment was punctured by the thought of Sarah struggling on her own. Ben tried to put her from his mind, but he knew he'd be fooling himself if he thought he could just cut her off. It would upset Dad if the family was broken up – and he would demand an explanation.

Setting off from Emily's one Monday morning, his intention to head straight to the centre, he passed a lady who was pushing a pram and decided it was time to make a detour. Though he didn't know if he could ever forgive her, he had come to believe that staying in touch with Sarah is what I would have wanted him to do. Deep inside, it was what he wanted too.

He guessed Sarah would still be in bed – it was only just after 8am – so he rapped loudly on the front door several times after she failed to answer the buzzer. He felt a twinge of guilt at the idea of her alone, confused and probably now afraid of what she would find on her front doorstep at this hour.

A couple of minutes later he heard her open the inside door and ask, 'Who is it?'

'It's Ben,' he replied, trying not to sound in any way aggressive.

He heard her keys in the main lock before she opened the door and stood wearily before him, a large dressing gown wrapped around her swollen stomach. Even with her pale face and dark circles under her eyes that told the story of her night, Ben thought Sarah still looked graceful – she had a beauty that not even the rigours of pregnancy and grief could taint.

'Do you want to come in?' she asked meekly.

'Please,' Ben said before following her through to the kitchen. He stood quietly and watched as she filled the kettle with water and collected a couple of mugs from the cupboard before he embarked on the speech he had rehearsed several times in his mind.

'I came to say that, even though I'm very angry about the fact you deceived me – and Harry – I don't want you to go through this alone.'

She looked up at him briefly to acknowledge what he had said before continuing to prepare their coffee, leaving Ben to carry on.

'I've done a lot of soul searching and I finally asked myself what Harry would have wanted me to do. I don't have any doubt that he'd want to see me help you, Sarah. So that's why I'm here.'

She handed his coffee to him and he sat down at the table, waiting for her to do the same. She was taking her time to prepare her reply, clearly afraid that one false move could blow the uneasy truce open again.

'Thank you, Ben,' her voice low and tired. 'I didn't expect you to come back but I'm glad you did,' she let out a long sigh and glanced up at the ceiling trying, unsuccessfully, to hold back the tears, before her eyes came to rest on his again. 'I'm sorry I let you down. There's nothing I can do to change what I did or make it right. I suppose.. I had my reasons,' she faltered, 'but I have no excuses. What's done is done. We have to look at who we are now. I'm alone, Ben, and I'm terrified that I've lost you. When you walked out, I realised you're all I've got left – you and this baby.'

Sarah let out a gasp as she struggled to hold back the sobs that were now impossible to control.

'I know I messed up, Ben. But I did love Harry,' she swallowed hard, trying to regain her breath. 'It wasn't always easy being married to him. He was so focused on his work or the centre, so busy. I felt like I was just hanging around in his shadow, an unworthy recipient of his affection or rather a worthy recipient of a lack of it as things ended up.'

'Don't upset yourself...' Ben started to say before Sarah cut him off again, her floodgates now opened.

'And he had a lot of anger sometimes. It was... difficult. He would look at me sometimes with...' She kept her eyes fixed on the window. Though there was so much more she wanted to say, and so much more she wanted to confide in him, she realised he didn't need to hear it. And she didn't know how to say it. He didn't need to hurt any more than he already did so she cut the story short.

'I guess in part because of this, I hit back in the end.' She was calm again, but distant. 'I was angry because I'd been denied the chance to fulfil my dream of being a mother, when he got everything he ever set his heart on.'

Ben sipped his coffee, not wishing to interrupt what he realised she needed to get out.

'I wish to God I hadn't slept with Paul. It leaves me cold every time I think about it,' she said, biting her lip. 'But I just can't pretend that I'm not happy to be having this baby. What I fear most now is having to share it with that man. I've worked with Paul for eight years and once he decides he wants something, he doesn't let go.'

'Well, what are his rights?'

'Legally none unless he can prove his paternity and he can't do that unless the baby is DNA tested.'

'Can he force you to do the test?'

'Probably, yes. This is Paul we're talking about. He eats, sleeps and breathes the law. And if he can't find some suitable angle on his case, then he'll just keep on and on at me until I relent. I've already had a letter from him demanding we discuss access before the baby's born. He says he wants to be at the hospital for the birth.' Her pitch got higher and her breathing more irregular until she spoke in a tearful staccato.

'I can't think of anything worse than having that jerk loitering around in the corridor while I'm going through labour – and then rushing in to take my baby from me.'

'Wait a minute,' Ben cut in. 'Let's just think about this. If he doesn't have any formal rights until his paternity is proved then he can't just turn up at the hospital and expect to be able to see the baby.'

'But he's already demanded that the test be carried out on the baby the day it's born. I'm not going to be able to hold him off for long.'

Ben sighed. 'Well, I guess all you can do is write back to him and say that while you're willing to co-operate on the paternity test, you are not prepared to give him any access to the child until his parental status is proved. You could even say that is as much for his protection as the child's.'

'But the problem is he knows Harry and I were unable to conceive together so his argument is, realistically, unless I've slept with someone else only he can be the father. If that's not the case I need to prove Harry wasn't infertile.'

'Can you do that?'

Sarah paused before saying, quietly: 'No.'

'Still, Sarah,' Ben continued trying to sound positive. 'It sounds like he can't force you to do anything until you get the test results back so just send him the letter telling him he'll have to wait. It's only a few weeks after all.'

'I just can't bear to hand my baby over to that man. Not even for a minute.' She started to cry again causing Ben to bristle when he considered she had brought this situation entirely on herself.

Unable to let it pass, he blurted: 'Why did you sleep with him then?'

Sarah paused, shocked by Ben's sudden change in tone.

'I've just told you, Ben. I was in a bad place – and I didn't think for one minute I'd end up in some paternity battle with a guy I had down as being the most die-hard bachelor in Britain. I thought he'd run a mile if he thought the baby could even remotely be his. But I misjudged him,' she sighed.

'Well, what's done is done,' Ben said. 'Let's worry about access after we've got the results back. At least it buys you a few days of peace after you've had the baby.'

'Yeah,' Sarah sneered. 'And then Paul's going to be all over me like a hot rash.'

'Don't worry. You'll get through this. Just tell me what I can do to help you now?'

'Just be my baby's uncle, no matter what.' She looked at him pleadingly.

'I can do that,' Ben said, swallowing his discomfort as he sought to reassure her with a warm smile.

'I know it sounds corny. But you're the only man, apart from my father, that I've ever felt truly comfortable with. I feel like you understand me.'

'There's a lot to understand,' he smirked, surprised by her disclosure, but flattered.

'I know,' she smiled nervously, before studying his face for a few moments. 'Are you very happy with Emily?'

'Well…yes,' Ben replied, unsure of why she was asking.

'I think she's very lucky to have found someone like you. I just hope she knows it.'

'Thank you,' he looked away awkwardly. 'I think I'm the lucky one.'

Sarah shook her head. 'You've underestimated yourself all your life, Ben. I always thought there was more to you than met the eye, but now I see who you are, I know I'll never meet a man as good as you.'

Ben almost laughed at first, thinking she must be joking in some way. But her face was so sombre as she fought back tears, he realised she was absolutely serious.

CHAPTER twelve

BEN HAD NEVER REALLY been aware of his good looks – or of his effect on women – but I was. While I was the outgoing, muscular one who reeled the girls in, within a few weeks of dating me their attentions would usually turn to Ben, drawn to his sultry, brooding looks and apparent lack of interest in any other living soul.

'Your brother's very quiet isn't he?'

'Yes.'

'Does he have a girlfriend?'

'No.'

'I'm surprised. He's quite good-looking really, isn't he?'

'I suppose so.'

'Why don't we invite him along to the party tomorrow?'

'He won't want to go.'

'But, he might…'

'He won't, okay.'

There were jealousies between us in our teens and adult years, too many jealousies, but Ben and I had our moments of closeness too.

On one of those happier times, we had gone for a rare drink together just after Sarah and I had first started seriously quarreling. I hadn't discussed my fertility problems much with Ben but I guess he must have either sussed that something was wrong because of the length of time Sarah and I had been married and childless, or Dad may have mentioned something to him. He never once asked what was happening, always opting instead for small talk and idle chat about football or politics. He never enquired about my business but often asked about the Melville Centre. I liked that about him.

Sitting in the pub together that evening, we'd just chewed over the Hearts/Hibs derby, when he said something to me I'll never forget.

'It's not your fault you know, Harry.'

'What's not my fault?'

'The baby thing. Some things are just not meant to be.'

My mind raced for a moment, anger rising at the thought Sarah might have told him about our problems. But, for once, I managed to control my paranoia and reason with myself that, ultimately, my brother was on my side and had a right to be involved in my life.

'I don't think Sarah sees it that way,' I said finally.

'You do so much for other people, Harry. I just think that maybe you're not supposed to be distracted from that, you know? I think it's probably fate.'

I looked at Ben for what seemed like a long time and – equally rarely – he held my gaze. That single remark helped me more than anything any counsellor or doctor could have told me. It also compounded my guilt in knowing that although I helped endless strangers on a daily basis, I had done nothing to aid my own brother. I had competed with Ben for so many years that it just wasn't in me to give him the helping hand he so needed. Perhaps he would have been too proud to take it anyway, but I could, and should, have tried.

～

September had given way to autumn showers and Ben was battling the elements as he embarked on his morning walk to the centre. It took him even longer these days now that he left from Emily's New Town apartment and, as the driving rain struck him angrily in the face, he remembered what mum used to say when she sent him out to school on stormy mornings: 'There's no such thing as bad weather, only the wrong clothing.' Today he was kitted out in his waterproof jacket, but this was most certainly bad weather. Still, he smiled to himself that at least his hood was keeping his hair dry as he passed rain-drenched strangers who had naively wandered out without even an umbrella, only to be met moments later by a monumental downpour.

This morning – as with every Monday morning – he was chairing the staff meeting with Sonja, Danny and their latest recruit, Stephen, who had joined them following Dave's departure. Ben felt a little apprehensive, as he knew the subject of the mother's group was going to come up again and, having looked at next year's budget, he just didn't see how they would be able to accommodate the crèche that Sonja had in mind. They had to make sure the money Harry had left the centre would last as long as possible, and while he fully agreed it was a fantastic idea to allow the young mothers to focus on their skills workshops while their children were cared for nearby, it would involve recruiting additional skilled staff and, realistically, they didn't even have the necessary space. The only option would be a costly extension.

He arrived at the centre slightly late so headed immediately for the office, only to find our father sitting at the meeting table, apparently waiting to see him.

'Dad,' Ben exclaimed, slightly taken aback. 'What you doing here at this early hour?'

'I wanted to have a wee chat with you,' he said sagely, adding, 'I see you walked.'

'My jeans are soaking,' Ben replied, pulling at the wet denim that was clinging to his legs before removing his jacket and hanging it up to dry. 'I also have a team meeting in ten minutes, so I can't spare you too much time I'm afraid.'

'This won't take long.' Dad nodded at the chair next to him, urging Ben to sit down which he dutifully did.

'I've been thinking about the chat we had a few weeks ago,' he began. 'I was most impressed with your commitment to this centre, Ben, and I want to do what I can to help.'

Ben immediately had visions of his father volunteering to coach some of their young visitors and thought he should head him off at the pass: 'Really Dad, we're fully staffed here. It's very kind…' But Dad was quick to interrupt.

'So I've brought you this,' he handed Ben a small white envelope which my brother eyed suspiciously before peeling it open. Inside he found a cheque for the sum of two hundred thousand pounds. Ben gasped before checking Dad's face for any trace of laughter that would suggest this was a joke. But he was serious.

'There's no use this money burning a hole in my pocket. I want you to use it here. This is for you… and for Harry,' he added.

Several seconds passed as Ben searched for the right words.

'Thank you,' was all he could get past the lump in his throat. 'It'll be put to good use.'

'Oh I know it will,' said Dad, with a wry smile.

Ben wanted the centre's new team leader to be the first one to hear the news, so when she handily walked into the hallway just after he had said goodbye to Dad at the front door, he grabbed the moment. She was carrying a tray full of cups of tea for the team meeting so he spoke softly to avoid giving her a fright.

'Sonja. Have you got a minute?

'Of course,' she smiled. 'I'll just put the tray down in the meeting room and I'll come right back.'

Ben headed into the office and waited patiently for his co-worker, desperate to share the good news with her. True to her word, she appeared just a few moments later and took a seat at the table in front of him.

'What's up?' she asked.

'Well,' he was going to drag this one out. 'I wanted to let you know I'm really pleased with how you've picked up with running this place and just to say that I really appreciate all you're doing.'

'Thank you,' said Sonja looking genuinely pleased.

'So, I thought a pay rise to match your promotion would be in order.'

'But, you've already given me a rise,' Sonja loyally protested.

'A thousand pounds a year is not much of a rise, Sonja. We now have sufficient funds to pay you an extra four thousand.'

Sonja's eyes bulged as she took in the news.

'Well, that's gonna help with my wedding,' she giggled.

'Wedding?' Ben frowned. 'I didn't know you were getting married.'

'I was going to tell you this morning. Martin and I have set a date for August next year. And you're invited of course – and Emily.' She couldn't hide her embarrassment at mentioning Emily's name. Ben had never spoken of their relationship to her so he would no doubt guess that Jason had spread the good word.

'Well, it's a double celebration then,' Ben smiled. 'I thought you'd also be interested to know that I'm going to ask an architect to come in and have a look at the building and let us know if he thinks we can build into the outdoor space at the back to create room to house our crèche.'

Sonja's smile now shone even brighter than when he'd told her of her pay rise.

'That's fantastic, Ben. Thank you. I thought we didn't have any room in the budget for an expansion?'

'We do now,' Ben grinned.

~

Sarah arrived first at the restaurant, giving her name to the friendly Australian waitress who greeted her before leading her to a table upstairs by the window. She looked down at the street below while she waited for her dining companion and remembered the last time she'd been here – with me. She felt a tugging in her chest as she recalled how we'd enjoyed a leisurely lunch over a bottle of wine, with me regaling her with tales of the dastardly 'boardroom bores' who blighted my existence. I loved nothing more than to take a knock at the stuffed shirts who lined the executive board of YourLot and took themselves pathetically seriously. I could only watch in dismay as they puffed up like peacocks whenever it was their turn to present on their area of the business. That was one of the sad things about success. You started off as a one-man show, then hired a few friends to join you, but there is only so long that you can hold off the inevitable march of accountants, marketing executives and business strategists, and before you know it, you don't even recognise the organisation you single-handedly founded.

Sitting at the lunch table, staring into space, Sarah reflected on how sad it was that those very bores we had once laughed at, were now running the business – with my name a fading memory. It would all be about margins and bottom lines now, and no longer about the thrill of the chase as it had been for me. I'd treated it as a game, as I did life.

It was she who had suggested the lunch she was now waiting to order. A chance to clear any tension between her and her dining companion – especially as they would be seeing so much more of each other.

Sarah listened to her approaching heels clacking on the wooden floor behind her, before she heard her voice.

'Hello Sarah,' said Emily, looking immaculate as always in dark denim skinny jeans, a crisp white blouse and navy blazer. 'This is a lovely spot by the window.' She leant forward and pecked Sarah lightly on both cheeks before removing her blazer, hanging it over the back of her chair and, finally, taking a seat on the opposite side of the table.

'Thank you for coming,' Sarah said nervously. 'I thought it would be nice to get to know each other a little better.'

'Of course,' Emily replied, seemingly never dropping her professional guard. Sarah tried to imagine the relationship between this emotionally controlled woman in front of her and Ben who wore his heart on his sleeve. She hadn't worked the dynamic out yet, but Ben's happiness was all too obvious.

The women busied themselves for a few minutes discussing the menu but, once their order was taken, there was no hiding from the realisation that they would now have to carry a conversation together for over an hour. Sarah wondered if Emily was as aware as she was of the tension between them; a case of two queen bees in the same hive, jostling over power – of Ben.

'How are you feeling?' Emily asked.

'Oh, fine. A little tired and a bit achy but I still feel pretty good. Only eight weeks to go now so I guess I'm just bracing myself really.'

Another embarrassed silence followed with Emily fearing she had just used up her only point of conversation. With nothing else coming to mind, she decided to shoot from the hip.

'Ben's told me about the problems you've been having with your ex-colleague. Are you certain he's the father?'

Sarah visibly recoiled in shock at the sheer temerity of the question, considering they hadn't even received their starters. She had two options though; either tell Emily to mind her own business or answer the question. Remembering that she was on fragile ground with Ben, she chose the latter.

'It would seem the odds are stacked that way seeing as Harry and I were experiencing problems conceiving.' She looked around uncomfortably before continuing.

'Look, I know it isn't pretty, but there were reasons that I had a one-night stand. Being faced with not being able to have a child was challenging to say the least and, at my lowest ebb, I did something stupid.'

'I'm not judging you, Sarah,' Emily said earnestly. 'I can imagine your torment. I had to accept a few years ago that I would never become a natural mother.'

'But you still could, surely? It's not too late.'

'I've had the tests, Sarah. I can't conceive.' Emily put her head down for a few moments leaving Sarah to wonder whether she was upset or indicating she didn't want to say any more about it.

'I'm sorry,' Sarah replied, still unsure whether to move on or ask her more. In the end, she thought maybe Emily might want to open up to another woman. 'Had you been trying before you had these tests?'

'Yes,' Emily replied distantly. 'With my former partner. But it wasn't to be.'

An awkward silence fell between them again before the waitress appeared with their bread and drinks which they watched her set down in front of them. Alone once more, Sarah decided to risk posing another personal question which she thought was only fair seeing as Emily had thrown down the gauntlet so early in the conversation.

'Things seem to be pretty serious between you and Ben?'

She could see Emily squirm a little at the prospect of having to discuss her relationship so it didn't surprise Sarah when she opted for a typically vague response.

'We enjoy each other's company, yes.'

'So, do you think you'll move in together then?' Sarah was enjoying the shift of power.

'We've discussed it.'

Sarah suddenly wished she hadn't asked the question. She felt more than a little crushed at the idea of Ben living with Emily. Still, she realised she would have to look happy, so she smiled unconvincingly and said: 'That's nice.'

Sensing the tension rising again, Emily decided to broker the peace between them.

'I know Ben is very keen to support you with the baby and in whatever lies ahead. For what it's worth, that goes for me too. If there's ever anything I can do to help, just let me know.'

'Thank you,' Sarah replied, genuinely touched. 'You surprise me, Emily. You're not the hard-nosed businesswoman I once thought you were.'

'Ditto,' Emily shot back playfully and the two women laughed together; something Sarah couldn't have imagined an hour earlier.

～

Ben quickly glanced over the CV that had been left out for him ahead of his meeting with Jayne Byers, one of the young mothers from Sonja's group. He saw from her date of birth that she was 17, but had left school at 16 when she got pregnant – still managing to take with her an impressive array of Standard Grade exams, or National 5s as they were now calling them, including good results in English, Maths, Biology, History and Modern Studies. His eyes then quickly progressed to the 'Career Goals' section, where she had said, simply: 'To be a lawyer'.

Ambitious, Ben thought; his admiration for the girl growing by the minute as he spotted under 'Personal Details' that she was bringing up her six-month-old baby girl, Layla, alone, sharing a home with her mother who had also been a single parent.

He was trying to work out whether the girl was just a dreamer or really had the drive to do this when he heard a loud knock on the door.

'Come on in,' he said, hoping he didn't sound like a school headmaster.

A very presentable teenager popped her head around the door before stepping into the room.

'I'm Jayne,' she said confidently, before holding her hand out for Ben to shake.

'Take a seat, Jayne,' he smiled, gesturing for her to sit down in the chair in front of his desk. 'I see from your details that you have a baby girl. Congratulations.'

'Thank you. She's pretty good so I think I'm quite lucky.'

'She's not keeping you up all night then?' Ben joked.

'No, she goes down before 8pm and sleeps through.'

'Wow,' Ben raised his eyebrows. 'I'm no expert, but that sounds impressive to me.'

'Yes,' Jayne giggled politely.

'I also see from your notes that you want to be a lawyer. What sparked that ambition?'

'I want to help people, but I also want to make something of myself,' she replied firmly. 'I know that having a baby at sixteen maybe isn't the best idea if you want a career, but I'm still going tae try.'

Ben noticed her Leith accent poking through as she started to get into her stride and he realised that she'd been trying to smarten up her speech for his benefit. And somehow this impressed him more than anything because it showed just how much she wanted this. She wasn't satisfied with the life she and her baby currently had. She knew they could have more and she also knew what she had to do to get it.

'You have some good Nat 5s, but you'll need to sit five Highers and pass at A or B level to stand a chance of qualifying for a Scottish law degree course.'

'I know that,' she said. 'But we don't have a computer at home and I've no idea where or how to apply for colleges. I'm also going to need help in sorting out funding and childcare.'

'You've come to the right place then. We can help you with funding and applying to further education colleges – and we'll put some thought into childcare. You may be able to get help through your college, or we could look at how we might be able to contribute too.'

'Thank you,' Jayne said, looking both relieved and grateful. 'My mum can help a bit, but she works, so she can't take Layla every day.'

'We'll work something out,' he reassured her. 'I'm still curious though as to why you're so determined to study law?'

'Where I'm from no one studies law,' she said, her tone once again resolute. 'So I'm gonnae do it, because I'm not letting my child grow up in the same estate that I did, where no one believes they'll ever make anything of themselves.' She looked away for a moment as though she had finished speaking, before adding: 'And because I'm just as entitled as anyone else to have a law degree.'

~

Emily tidied the small number of papers littering her desk, filed them into her drawer then reached for her coat. But just as she headed out the door of her office her direct line started to ring. While her first thought was to ignore it, habit forced her to reach out and pick up.

'Emily DiRollo,' she answered briskly.

'Yes, hi Emily,' said an American voice. 'This is Mark Weiss.'

'Oh hi,' she said, switching her tone.

'I wanted to say thank you for letting me know about Jason Weir. His pictures arrived here yesterday and I'm blown away.'

'I'm so glad you like them.' Emily gushed. She knew for Jason to get international recognition at this early stage in his career would be remarkable – and it would do her reputation no harm either. Emily had often thought about making a foray into the US market, brokering Scottish art to American dealers, and this connection with Mark Weiss was just the start she needed. She held her breath waiting for him to continue.

'I'd like to take a couple more drawings from you – I'm especially keen on the sketches he's done of friends and family. And, if you can get a few pieces together in time, I'm organising a little private viewing here at my gallery for a couple of my newer artists in November. I'd like to include Jason's work.'

'That's amazing,' said Emily. 'He'll be thrilled.'

'I'm inviting a few friends in the business and also a couple of critics I know too. I'm pretty sure they'll want to see this.'

It took Emily every ounce of willpower not to whoop down the telephone. Instead she clung desperately to her reserve.

'That won't be a problem,' she said calmly. 'I have another couple of drawings here that I can send you and Jason is working on more. Do you have a date in mind for the private viewing?'

'Yeah, I'm looking at November 20th. Will I see you here?'

Emily paused for a moment. That idea hadn't struck her yet, but she liked it. She could meet Mark face-to-face and go and check out some other galleries.

'That's a nice thought. I'll talk to Jason and Ben Melville, who's from the centre that discovered him, and I'll let you know if we can make it. I'm sure Jason would love to see New York and your gallery – I know I would.'

'Well, you'd be welcome here. Talk to you soon, Emily. Have a good evening.'

Emily made it round to Sarah's just in time to sit down for dinner. Ben had been there for over an hour and she could tell they were both ravenous but were too polite to start without her. She wanted to blurt out the news about the Mark Weiss private view as soon as she got in the door but decided to hold back so she could spin the story out over dinner. She found her moment once they had all started to eat and the edge had been taken off their hunger.

'I got a call from Mark Weiss today,' she began, her voice nonchalant but her eyes betraying her excitement.

'Oh yes?' Ben said, urging her on.

'He wants me to send a few more of Jason's drawings… because he's going to host a private viewing on the 20th of November for some friends in the business, including a few critics.'

'Wow,' Ben laughed in surprise, his eyes wide with excitement.

'He also asked if we wanted to go along, with Jason too,' she added casually.

'Well, that would be great but we'd have to think about the expense,' Ben warned, his face turning serious again.

'Why?' said Sarah, jumping in. 'I'd be happy to help. It's not like I'm going to be living it up over the next few months so I might as well put my money to good use.'

'I can't let you do that, Sarah. That's way too generous – and it's too close to when the baby's due. I need to be here,' Ben protested, clearly agitated by the speed with which the idea was progressing. He never felt comfortable with quick decisions.

'You're scared to get on the flight, aren't you Ben?' Sarah challenged him.

'No. I'd happily fly but I don't want you spending your money when you're about to have a baby.'

'I'm a multi-millionaire, Ben. Paying for a short trip isn't even going to make a dent. In fact, I'd also like to pay for Jason's mum and dad to go too.'

'Sarah, that's amazing,' Emily said, while Ben sat scowling in the middle of the table, flanked by the two women at either end.

'What's the problem?' Sarah probed Ben again.

'There's not a problem. I just need to have a think about it.'

'Are you afraid of flying?' Emily asked.

'No… well, a little,' he finally conceded. 'I haven't flown in a very long time.'

'Jason would want you there.' Emily put her hand out and placed it gently on top of Ben's before giving it a firm squeeze.

'I know.' He stared at his plate for a few moments before looking up at Emily. 'I guess it's time for me to rejoin the jet-set then.'

Sarah had just closed the front door behind Emily and Ben when she heard the home phone ringing. She raced back into the living room to try and catch it only to wish, moments later, that she hadn't bothered.

'Evening, Sarah,' Paul said in a faux-cheerful voice. 'I hope I haven't woken you. It's a little late, I know.'

'Well, I was just about to go to bed actually,' she replied frostily.

'It makes me so sad to think of you there all alone – a mother-to-be rattling around in that big, empty house with no one to look after you.'

Sarah bristled at his jibe but was determined to keep her cool. 'I'm managing just fine, thanks Paul. Unlike you, I have many friends I can call on.'

'Friends and relations, huh? That's nice. But it's not quite the same as having the father of your child share in the joy of your pregnancy and pending birth, is it?'

'What is it that you want?' she demanded.

'I'm wrestling with my conscience.'

'In what way?'

'I can't help but feel that your efforts to deny my paternity of our child and try to pass him or her off as the child of the late, great Harry Melville, isn't in some way against the public interest.'

Sarah's blood ran cold as she tried to work through the options of where he was going with this. 'What do you mean, 'public interest'?'

'I mean, every time I sit down to have a drink with my old journalist friend I just feel like I'm colluding with your silly scheme by not telling him. If you continue to deny my rights, I don't think I'm going to be able to hold back.'

Now gripped with terror, Sarah struggled to retain her composure.

'I've already agreed to a paternity test, Paul, but you have no rights to this baby until that test is carried out. You may not be the father of this child, so you won't be getting any access until we get the results back – threats or no threats.'

'You're denying me my right to see my child born,' he shouted angrily.

'You don't have a legal right to be there, Paul. You have to wait for the results of the test.'

'You know, and I know that I'm the father. You're playing for time and behaving like a selfish bitch.'

Sarah was shaking now, unsure of how she was going to get this man off the phone whilst persuading him against going to the press, so she took a gamble.

'I know this is hard on you, Paul, and I'm sorry. But this is how it has to be. Now, I'm in a good position financially, so if I can make things easier for you in the meantime then I'm willing to do that.'

The line was silent for a moment as he considered his position. Sarah had always suspected he was motivated by money, now she was betting on his greed to salvage the situation.

'I could have a human rights case here you know, Sarah. I wouldn't hesitate to pursue a case against you if it saved another man from going through this – and I don't want your money. I want our baby.'

Sarah took a deep breath. 'Look, Paul. I don't want to fight like this. Maybe we could go for a coffee and try and get through all this as friends?'

'Well that sounds like the first sensible thing you've said to me in a long while, Sarah.'

'Good,' she said before forcing herself to add: 'I'll text you a date and time later then.' Still shaking, she put the receiver back in its cradle, sat down on her sofa and sobbed.

She had no intention of meeting with Paul, but he was closing in on her and there was no obvious means of escape.

CHAPTER thirteen

BEN AND SARAH APPEARED on the surface to be two entirely different creatures, and yet their newfound kinship was in some ways evident before my death. During the height of my paranoia, I convinced myself that Ben was harbouring a crush on Sarah, and while that thought is natural to me now, it certainly wasn't then.

Following our bonding session (or as close as we ever came to one) over my fertility problems, I had invited Ben out for a curry near my office in town. At that stage I viewed him as the perfect confidante. He had no friends with whom he could gossip about me and he was a good listener. From time to time, he also came out with some pretty good advice.

Ben arrived that evening looking more dishevelled than usual and, as I leaned in to give him a hug, I could smell whisky. While I knew he liked a drink, he was usually very good at hiding it. He also appeared agitated and distracted and, looking back now, I can't think why I didn't ask him if he was alright. But then I don't think I ever asked Ben how he was doing. The idea never really crossed my mind, so after exchanging small talk I very quickly started to moan about Sarah's apparent lack of appreciation for all I had given her.

'She told me the other night that I didn't take a big enough interest in her. Can you believe that? After all I've done for her.'

'Yes,' said Ben, 'but was she not just saying she'd like to spend more time with you?'

'She didn't say she wanted to spend more time with me, she said I didn't show enough interest - that is, I don't buy her enough expensive gifts.'

'Is that what she actually said?'

'No, Ben, but that's what she meant.' I pulled a face at him straight out of our childhood, as if to say 'catch up', before knocking back what was left of my glass of red. I was regretting sharing this with Ben now, annoyed that he wasn't instantly taking my side.

'Not taking an interest to me suggests she'd like you to ask more about her or how she's feeling, how her day's gone. That kind of thing.' I now see he was suggesting this in what was supposed to be a helpful way, but at the time I took it to be deeply patronising.

I laughed dismissively in response. 'Good, God. You should write for Cosmopolitan seeing as you seem to understand women so well. But then you always have been the sensitive sort.'

'What's that supposed to mean?'

'It means you've always been into feelings and expressing yourself - it's your artistic streak. Nothing wrong with that,' I'd smirked, before gesturing to the waiter for another bottle.

'I'm just trying to point out what's in front of your nose, Harry. Sarah actually seemed pretty down the last time I saw her. I've been worried about her.'

He'd further taken me aback by fixing me with a no-nonsense glare which I countered with vitriol. Ben's bad mood was starting to really piss me off.

'Clearly, you think I'm some kind of Neanderthal who doesn't even know his own wife, is that it? Or are you just wishing she'd given a creative, tortured soul like you the chance so you could have counselled her with hours of emotional therapy each day?'

'Are you finished, Harry?' Ben had asked with miraculous composure.

'I think so.'

'Good,' he'd smiled. 'Then I'll sensitively fuck off.'

I wish I'd asked him to stay, that I'd listened to him for just a moment. So much could have changed in that instant if I'd only swallowed my pride. We could have formed a closer relationship, but instead we just drifted apart. If I could have stopped talking about myself for one minute I might have been able to find out what had been troubling Ben for so long. Why he seemed so down. I had never stopped to think about how desperately lonely his existence must have been and how his lack of self-esteem must have been crippling him. I could only ever think of myself. Ben had of course been right, as he usually is when it comes to people. All he had ever needed was for someone to show a little faith in him and give him a chance instead of just assuming he was an eternal loser. But sadly I'd had to die to wake up to life.

~

November had arrived and was making its presence felt, the bitter wind causing Ben to grimace as he walked up the High Street towards Emily's studio where Jason was completing the collection of work for New York.

It had been several weeks since Ben had last seen him and he was growing concerned for his young friend. Usually Jason would send him a text just to check in now and then if they hadn't spoken in a while, but he'd received nothing.

He had messaged Jason the other day to see how he was and received a short reply, 'Fine, just wrecked!', which told him very little. So here he was to see for himself.

He buzzed at the studio door and only had to wait a couple of seconds for Jason to reply.

'Hullo.'

'It's Ben, thought I'd drop in and see how you're getting on.'

'Come on up. It's chaos mind.'

Ben jogged up the single flight of stairs and opened the door to find Jason standing by a desk that was surrounded by piles of paper that looked like they'd been tossed onto the floor either mindlessly or out of frustration.

'How you doing?' Ben asked, taking in the scene of artistic carnage around him.

'Bad day,' Jason mumbled. 'I've only got a couple more pieces to do but I'm struggling. I'm not used to working to order and with important people expecting something of me. No one's ever expected anything of me before.'

Ben picked up some of the papers on the floor and noticed Jason had started to make sketches on them but had abandoned them after a few strokes of the pencil.

'I've done so many faces, I need to do something different.'

'Have you drawn a pregnant woman yet? I'm sure Sarah wouldn't mind if you think that would work.'

'I couldn't ask her, that doesn't feel right.'

'She'd let you take some pictures of her, I'm sure. I can ask her today if you'd like?'

'That would be brilliant, thank you. She would be amazing to draw.'

Ben noticed how Jason's eyes lit up when he talked about Sarah; he clearly admired her. She was undeniably beautiful after all, and she had the strong, distinctive looks that were an artist's dream. It was a reminder to Ben that she wouldn't stay single forever, and he bristled at the thought.

'No problem.' Ben moved quickly to change the subject. 'I brought over a couple of things I've been working on if you have time to have a look. I thought it might take your mind off work for a few minutes.'

'Did you bring some of your sketches?' Jason said, moving closer to see what Ben was pulling out of the leather folder he had brought with him.

'Just two that I've been working on recently,' he said, handing Jason a couple of sketches he'd done of the harbour at Newhaven that he so loved to look out over.

'I'd recognise those rocks anywhere,' Jason smiled. 'You've done a beautiful job.'

'Well, my talent isn't a patch on yours.'

'I wouldn't say that. What else you got in there?' Jason gestured to the folder, eager to see more.

Ben pulled out a crumpled piece of paper that he'd carefully tried to smooth out the other evening, with little success. He handed it to Jason who looked momentarily stunned.

'It's very like your work,' isn't it?' Ben said.

Jason was eyeballing Luke's drawing with something that appeared like suspicion.

'This was drawn by a boy who Harry once tried to help. I'm afraid he was a bit of a lost cause though,' Ben informed him.

'Shame,' Jason said, handing him back the picture.

'I just wanted to show you it because it struck me the other night that this feels like serendipity in a way. Harry wasn't able to help Luke fulfil his dreams, but we're getting a second chance with you.'

Jason looked down at the floor, emotion getting the better of him. 'I'm really grateful.'

'I couldn't be happier for you,' said Ben, reaching out to pat his young friend reassuringly on the back. 'You look really tired so I'm going to go and let you get finished.'

'Sorry Ben. My conversation's been crap, I know. I'm just worried about New York. I'm not sure I'm good enough.'

'Good enough? You'll blow them away. I don't think you have any idea how talented you actually are, Jason. But you're about to find out.'

~

They made a fantastically mixed bunch at the airport. Ben and Emily were dressed in regulation middle class uniform, each having opted for a slight variation on casual trousers and fitted shirts. Next to them in the check-in queue stood Jason who by now was beginning to do quite well for himself as was illustrated by his outfit; an impressive ensemble of designer T-shirt and jeans, paired with very expensive-looking white trainers. Behind him, Gary and Sandra Weir were squabbling over who was supposed to have been looking after the passports when Sandra suddenly produced them from the bottom of her over-sized gold bag and waved them excitedly in front of her husband's ruddy and angry face. They too had dressed for the trip. Gary was spilling out of a blue polo shirt that was way too tight around the waist, while Sandra was similarly pushed for space in a pair of figure-hugging, white calf-length trousers and a bright pink blouse.

Jason had told Ben that his mum and dad leapt around like lottery winners when he'd announced Sarah would be paying for them to travel business class to New York so they could attend the private view. His mum wept with joy and his dad threw his arms around the pair of them. As for Jason, he could barely contain his pride that finally he and his family were going somewhere in life.

But he felt ashamed by how much he wanted to distance himself from them as they swore and cackled loudly through the airport causing all around to stop and stare at the unruly duo holding up the queue. Despite their lack of social grace, he was pleased they were able to come with him on this trip which officially marked their rise out of the depths of poverty and into the ranks of civilisation where you at least had a fair shot at actually living your life. He had vowed to himself that he wouldn't stop working for a minute until he had bought them a house in a good area, where they could live in peace and without fear of the drug dealers down the landing who'd stab you as soon as look at you if you dared challenge them on the many reasons why they were spreading fear and misery.

As they boarded the plane an hour later, Ben and Emily couldn't help but laugh when Gary – having finally found his seat after much noisy deliberation with his wife – loudly announced: 'Sandra, look at this, hen. Leather seats and there's mare space than oor front room.'

From that moment on, every morsel that was delivered to him by the air stewards would be declared, 'absolutely, bloody fantastic'. But Gary saved his best accolade for the evening meal, which he colourfully described to the American businessman sitting across the aisle from him as, 'the best fuckin' chicken I've ever tasted'.

And the pantomime didn't end when the plane touched down. After waiting an hour in the queue at passport control, Sandra nearly got them all put on the next flight back home with her unusual answers to the immigration officer's questions.

When asked where she would be staying in New York, she answered: 'In the pub.' Sadly, only Gary laughed at this joke, prompting a stern response from the officer: 'Mam, you answer the question truthfully or you will be denied entry to the United States.'

'Awright, keep yer shirt on,' Sandra snapped back before tutting loudly.

Ben, Emily and Jason stood wide eyed as they watched the scene unfold. Fortunately, however, the officer seemed to be in a forgiving mood and eventually smiled and waved them on.

Eventually, a heady mix of travel fatigue and booze silenced Sandra and Gary who sat quietly in the people carrier as they headed from the airport to the hotel. It was 7pm local time when they arrived at the Hilton in Chelsea which was only a few streets from the Mark Weiss Gallery where they would be going the following evening. During the flight over, Gary and Sandra had talked endlessly about hitting the bars when they arrived but, after a long-haul flight in which they'd practically drunk Virgin Atlantic out of mini vodkas, neither seemed ready to follow the plan through. Instead, they both said a weary goodnight and headed up to their room. Jason, too, was tired and did likewise. They had agreed to meet for breakfast the next morning, and Ben and Emily were planning to encourage Gary and Sandra to do their own thing during the day so they could do some sightseeing.

Although they were tired too, they decided to drop their bags, freshen up and head out to one of the local diners to get a drink and a snack. Finally free to enjoy their own company, Ben and Emily headed for their room and were just about to swipe the key to get in when Ben's mobile rang. It was Gary.

'Is this oor room?' he demanded without introduction.

'Yes,' said Ben. 'What's the problem?'

'It's a bloody palace,' he barked down the phone. 'We've even got mood lightin' in here. Sandra, that's a fuckin' Jacuzzi.' Ben laughed as he listened to Gary giving his wife a run-down of every new item he spotted. It was difficult not to find their antics amusing – and endearing.

'You like it then,' said Ben, reminding Gary he was still on the line.

'Like it? I'll never get Sandra hame.' Gary finished the call as abruptly as he'd started it leaving Ben to shake his head in bewilderment before opening the door to his own room. Once inside, like Gary, Ben and Emily marvelled at the lavish suite Sarah had booked and paid for – only telling Ben the day before he left that she'd arranged for him to be upgraded. It would have been almost impossible for him to imagine a year ago how much his relationship with his sister-in-law would have changed. Now Sarah, despite her failings, was the closest thing to family he had.

Enjoying the moment, he put his arms around Emily's waist and drew her to him.

'Isn't this wonderful? I can't believe how different my life is now.'

'Mine too.' She kissed him softly on the lips, deciding it would be a better idea to stay put and skip dinner.

~

Sarah stared at the digital clock next to her bed and watched the time turn from 2.59am to 3.00. She let out a long sigh for what seemed like the hundredth time before finally admitting defeat and switching the bedside lamp on. She looked around the dimly-lit room and admired her own good taste as she took in the printed wallpaper along the front wall of the bedroom and the painting on the white side wall she had so carefully selected from a gallery in Barcelona we had visited two years previously. The memory of the trip forced an emotional dagger through Sarah and she shut her eyes quickly, bracing for the pain. Her life had been so easy then. She didn't have to explain herself to anyone or question anything. She was an attached, wealthy lady with only the inner-workings of her marriage to worry about. Maybe she'd dwelt on our problems too much, she mused. Perhaps, if she'd had more important things to worry about there wouldn't have been so much tension.

She thought of Ben and Emily, just starting out in their relationship with all the excitement that brought. She checked the clock again. 3.05am. They would have arrived in New York by now and would either be out somewhere together, or spending time in their room. Another dagger worked its way in, more slowly this time, twisting in her stomach. She realised she felt horribly jealous of Emily. And the more she thought about it, the worse her jealousy got.

She looked down at her swollen belly and was once again confronted by her fear of being alone with a baby she had no idea how to care for. She wished Ben wasn't so far away. She could have called him first thing – and had the comfort of knowing he would talk her down again. Make everything alright.

She closed her eyes and breathed deeply, trying to relax, but just as she started to drift to sleep she felt her stomach muscles start to tighten before taking a firm grip. She sat up quickly, panic rising in her chest. She'd been experiencing these 'Braxton Hicks' for a couple of weeks now, but in the last few days they'd been increasing in frequency and intensity. 'Don't come now, baby,' she said out loud. 'I'm not ready yet. Let's just wait for your uncle to get back first.'

She closed her eyes again and continued her deep-breathing. Within minutes she felt her mind drifting back towards sleep, her train of thought moving between the real and the unreal as she became increasingly drowsy.

It was then I saw my chance to reach out; to cut in.

In her dream she was walking by the shore, close to the lighthouse. She saw me walking towards her in the distance. I was smiling and waving – I was the old Harry, she thought, the happy-go-lucky one she fell in love with. Sarah waved back, unsure how to react when, even in sleep, she knew I was dead. Yet in this dream it felt natural to see me. I picked up my pace, as did she, running free from the constraints of heavy pregnancy. Then briefly we held each other tight, her arms clasped so firmly behind me I thought she would never let go.

~

With breakfast out of the way, Ben wanted to make the most of every moment of the free time he and Emily had in New York – the city he had already fallen in love with. He was in awe of the sheer number and variety of stores, delis, restaurants, nail bars, coffee shops, pet salons – anything you could think of, in abundance. On top of that, the people were so alive and dynamic. They appeared to have no sense of self consciousness, as if just being an inhabitant of this great place brought with it an endless supply of confidence and ambition. He and Emily spent much of their time walking in silence, hand in hand, taking in the constant action all around them.

Their first stop was a large gallery in Chelsea, which had a special exhibition featuring the work of an American artist who Emily was particularly keen on. Inside they found an incredible sequence of oil paintings depicting what at first seemed like fairly grotesque images of childbirth, naked figures wrestling, a mutually obese couple embracing on a bed, but, on closer inspection, Ben realised they were actually rather beautiful. They were certainly earthy and full of character. While my brother sat down to read a leaflet about the artist, Emily excused herself and went to seek out the gallery owner. Half an hour later and Ben was running out of leaflets to read and art to look at. He moved to sit on a leather sofa near the front window and watched New Yorkers pass him by on the street outside as he waited.

He thought of Sarah and wondered what she'd be doing. He suspected she might even be having a post-lunch nap as she was growing increasingly tired these days, and he made a mental note to check in with her later.

After exchanging cards with the gallery owner, Emily finally rejoined him and they moved on a couple of blocks to a second gallery to see a collection of what were described as 'Graphic Primitives – a hybrid of gestural tension and mathematical analysis'. To Ben, these paintings just looked like a mess of structures and colours but, he reasoned, at least they had captured his attention. Emily made notes as she wandered around, eyeing a couple of paintings for her own clients. Then she asked Ben again if he would mind waiting for her while she spoke to the manager. 'Just try and keep it under forty-five minutes this time,' he said, to which she raised her eyebrows.

By the time they had left the second gallery, half an hour later, Ben was thoroughly sick of looking at modern art and persuaded Emily it was time to go for lunch in a restaurant she had visited before and loved, which was only two blocks away.

Once inside the heaving eatery, Ben and Emily were shown to a small table for two in the back corner from where they could survey the scene in full. They watched intently as a group of men – who looked like they'd walked straight off the set of The Godfather

– greeted each other with kisses on both cheeks before taking their places around a table set for eight. Otherwise, the crowd of diners were a mix of large and small tables of families, couples and business men and women. All ate heartily and chatted loudly, adding to the magical ambiance of the place.

Ben and Emily spent a long time pondering the menu before he opted for marinated fresh sardines followed by goose liver ravioli, and she decided on grilled octopus for antipasti, then a wild boar ragu.

Ben's eyes then swept greedily over the dessert menu and he quickly settled on a pumpkin cheesecake which he was determined to leave room for.

'I'm so glad you recommended this place,' he said. 'I haven't even tried the food and already I'm longing to come back.'

'Eating here is an unforgettable experience. And we will come back,' she winked.

Ben felt a sudden surge of hope and excitement – a powerful mix of emotions that had become strangers to him in his adult life. Was it Emily, was it the Melville Centre – or both? Whatever had finally made him so happy, he didn't want it to end. It was time to take a risk, he told himself – to seize the moment in a way that, only a few months ago, he wouldn't have dared.

'Emily,' he said earnestly.

'Yes?' She looked at him with wide open eyes, totally unsuspecting of what was to come.

'Will you marry me?' he asked.

Emily's face flushed with shock. She sat forward in her seat as if buying time to think for a moment whilst trying, but failing, to maintain an illusion of poise.

In the end, she went with her gut instinct.

'Yes,' she replied nervously, her bottom lip starting to crumble.

Ben leaned forward over the table and kissed his new fiancée.

'I didn't see that coming,' Emily laughed, dabbing at her eyes with her napkin.

'Neither did I,' said Ben. 'I just opened my mouth and ended up proposing to you. I guess the words had been hiding in there waiting to come out.'

He reached over the table to kiss her again, then quickly sprang back as he saw a waiter pass their table.

'Can we change our wine order?' he asked.

'Of course,' said the waiter in his gloriously authentic Italian accent.

'Bottle of champagne please.'

'No problem. Are you celebrating?' the waiter asked.

'Yes,' Ben beamed. 'This wonderful lady has just agreed to be my wife.'

CHAPTER fourteen

SARAH DELIBERATELY TOOK HER TIME as she walked the last few winding streets that would lead her down to the shore at Newhaven. It was a route she very rarely took by foot but, inspired by her dream the night before, she had decided the next morning to trace her nocturnal steps. Of course there was the part of her that wondered whether I might appear to her again but, more than anything, she just wanted to feel that connection once more. Just one more moment of that liberating feeling of no longer being alone.

As she rounded the corner and saw the lighthouse at the end of the pier she was reminded of the time, several years ago, she had driven past on her way to a work meeting only to see Ben standing staring out across the water as he leaned on the harbour wall. She had been struck both by his solitude and his serenity. In that moment it had dawned on her that he had given up searching for fulfillment. His peace came from the self-defeatist in him that said, 'don't even bother'. She thought of him now, that same inner-calm providing the very thing that was so important to the future of the Melville Centre – and to her child. She shuddered at how dependent she was becoming on him. How barely an hour went by without her wondering what he was doing, whether it would be okay to call him. She knew she couldn't expect Ben to fill the gap left by my death, but that still didn't stop her thinking about it. They had become ridiculously at ease with one another. Sarah had no idea how it had happened, but it had happened.

She crossed the street and began the walk she had made in her dream just the night before, treading the pavement leading along the shore, half hoping, half fearing, that she might encounter me again – this time in reality. Perhaps I would bring her a message, she hoped, make her see sense, stop her yearning for a different life. Her eyes searched all around for a sign, but her quest was soon thwarted when she was seized by a twist of pain across her stomach, tightening and tightening its grip until she could hardly breathe. She put her hand out to hold on to the harbour wall, and gasped for air. An elderly man passing by rushed to her aid. 'Are you all right, love?' he asked anxiously. 'Is the baby coming?'

'I don't know,' she said, her voice an unrecognisable high-pitched squeak. She took several more deep breaths before straightening up. 'It's passed,' she said, her body flooding with relief. 'Must have been all the walking. I'll take a taxi home.'

'Let me flag one down for you, dear,' he said, taking Sarah by the arm. 'And you should give your husband a phone so he can come back and keep you company. You shouldn't be out on your own.'

'Yes,' she found herself nodding, not having the energy to explain her morbid predicament. 'He's away on business,' she said. 'He's back soon though.'

'And a good thing too,' the old man said, tutting to himself. 'You shouldn't be by yourself in your condition.'

~

Revived by a short nap following their long lunch, Ben and Emily made it down to the hotel reception to find Gary nervously pacing the floor, while Jason stood outside with his mother as she smoked a cigarette.

'The taxi's here,' Gary called cheerfully when he spotted them.

Ben smiled and realised he was growing fonder of his travel companion by the minute who, despite his bark, had a big heart and clearly loved his boy. Gary looked smart in a blue shirt and grey suit and, once outside Ben found Sandra too had pulled out all the stops in a lilac dress. 'You look beautiful,' he told her, giving her a peck on the cheek. She smiled and winked, 'You've scrubbed up alright yersel.'

But the smartest of all was Jason, who oozed cool in a black fitted shirt and pinstripe black and grey trousers with expensive-looking leather shoes, polished to perfection. Emily in a black and white fitted dress with burgundy shawl, was chic and typically understated, while Ben had adopted the male evening uniform of shirt, dark jeans and blazer.

He and Emily had agreed to keep their news to themselves this evening so as not to overshadow Jason's moment. Once inside the people carrier, they kept the conversation to a superficial discussion on where they'd visited that day.

Ben was glad they had all opted to dress smartly as they were soon to discover that the gallery was extremely upmarket – as was the owner. Mark Weiss greeted them personally at the door as they arrived, dressed in an electric blue suit and crisp white shirt. He peered at each of them in turn through his black-rimmed spectacles before introducing himself. He shook hands with Ben, Gary and Sandra but dramatically kissed Jason and Emily on each cheek as if they were long-lost friends.

'You're a genius,' he said earnestly to Jason who was, by now, looking distinctly out of his depth. To everyone's huge relief a girl arrived carrying champagne on a tray which they all readily accepted. Ushering them round the corner into a sectioned-off, but spacious second room, Mark proudly presented Jason's drawings which had been immaculately framed and mounted on the walls to breathtaking effect. In a large space like this and at full size, Ben found his drawings even more spectacular. The detail was extraordinary, especially considering Jason had received no formal training whatsoever. Standing in the middle of the room, Ben understood perfectly what all the fuss was about and couldn't wait to see how the other guests responded to Jason's work.

Gary took one look at the display and burst into tears only to be fiercely reprimanded by Sandra.

'Whit's wrong wi you, Gary? Sort yersel' oot.'

'I just… cannae… believe… this is ma bairn.' Gary sobbed, gesturing towards the pictures on the wall, before flinging his arms around Jason. 'I'm so proud ae you son.'

'Cheers Dad,' Jason said, looking genuinely touched.

'He's an awesome talent,' Mark chipped in. 'As soon as I saw his drawings, I knew he was going to be a big deal. I've got some important people coming here tonight – buyers, critics, some other gallery owners – and I know they're going to be blown away.'

'What do I need to do?' Jason asked, his nerves written in bold letters across his face.

'Just be yourself,' Mark reassured him. 'Your work can do the talking.'

Mark was right, as the forty or so guests dribbled in, Ben watched each of their faces turn from mild interest to a mixture of awe or intrigue – sometimes both.

'He did THAT just with a pen?' One very loud, colourful New Yorker boomed, adding: 'It's as sharp as a picture.'

All the while, Gary stood to the side clutching his glass of champagne and looking like the cat that got the cream.

'Hi. I'm Jason's dad,' he would say from time to time as guests filtered past. 'He gets it frae me, eh,' he'd wink as he nodded towards the pictures, the guests smiling politely back at him not exactly sure what he'd just said.

Jason, as instructed, stuck close to Mark Weiss all evening, meeting the great and the good. Ben marvelled at how well the youngster was coping with such an overwhelming experience. There was clearly a lot of money in the room along with some very influential people from the art world.

Ben overheard a critic introducing himself to Jason and asking him why he had chosen a ballpoint to produce his drawings.

'It was all I had,' Jason replied.

'Then that's all you needed,' said the critic.

Ben also watched Emily as she mingled with the other guests, completely at home in this fanciful world and handing out her business cards like they were sweets. From time to time she would glance over at Ben and smile conspiratorially as if to show him this was just a game. But Ben knew just how seriously she was taking this. She hadn't stopped networking from the second they got in the front door and wouldn't until the last person left.

When the evening was drawing to an end, Mark asked their group to remain behind just for a moment. Gathered together, Ben could tell just from Mark's face that he was pleased with how the event had gone.

'I want to thank you all for coming – and to thank Jason for your amazing work,' he began.

'Tonight, we sold all five drawings, which is incredible. I wanted to tell you after my other artists had left because I didn't want them to be envious. The drawings were snapped up by collectors who know an emerging talent when they see one. So, I'll be taking Jason's work as fast as he can come up with it and, pretty soon, I think I'm going to have to join the line.' He turned to Jason now and put his hand on his shoulder.

'Buddy, I'm gonna need you to come back over here next year to do a larger exhibition with me, and this time there'll be no other artist involved, just you. You think you can come up with the goods?'

'Aye, no problem,' said Jason, his eyes wide with excitement.

'Terrific.' He clasped his hands together to show his appreciation before bidding each of them goodnight.

Ben tossed and turned in the hotel bed, desperately trying to get rid of the persistent ringing in his ears until he realised it was his mobile. He slowly stumbled out of bed and began the hard task of trying to find his phone in the dimly-lit room. Luckily, he discovered he had left it lying on top of the dresser the night before so it was within easy reach. He glanced at the handset to see it was Sarah, suddenly remembering he'd forgotten to call her the day before. 'Hi,' he answered wearily.

'I'm sorry to call you so early,' she said, sounding nervous.

'What's wrong?' He glanced at the clock to see it was only 3.20 in the morning in New York.

'I think I'm in labour,' she said.

'But the baby's not due for another two weeks?'

'I know, but I've been getting pains on and off all night and my waters just broke.'

'Have you phoned the hospital?'

'Yes, I've to go in now to be checked but they may send me home depending on how far on I am.'

'Shit, I'm so sorry, Sarah. I should be there.'

'Don't worry, Ben. My mum is on her way. I'll try and hold out until she gets here.' She laughed unconvincingly.

'But are you going to hospital now on your own?' He felt a pang of sadness that Sarah had no one with her when she needed help most. It would take Angela at least three hours to travel from Cumbria.

'I'll be fine, Ben. I'll let you know what happens. I just don't know what to do about Paul.'

'What do you mean?' Ben asked.

'Hang on,' she said, her voice suddenly strained, 'I'm having another contraction.' Ben felt cold with anxiety as he listened to Sarah puffing at the other end of the phone, clearly in agony.

'Are you okay?' he asked helplessly.

'It's passing again,' she said, her breathing still irregular. 'Paul's been hassling me, demanding that he brings a doctor to the hospital as soon as the baby's born to do a paternity test. He says if I don't do it, he'll pursue me for breach of his human rights. I was supposed to be meeting him for lunch today so I either stand him up or phone him and have to explain I've gone into labour.'

'Stand him up, Sarah. What were you thinking of agreeing to go for lunch with him anyway?'

'I had to do something to keep him off my back, Ben. He's been hassling me to meet him for weeks. He's also threatening to go the press if I don't allow him immediate parental rights.'

'We'll try and get an earlier flight. I'm going to call the airport now. Call me when you can.'

'Ben.'

'Yes?'

'Will you let your dad know? I said I'd call him if anything happened.'

'Of course. And Sarah...'

'Yes?'

'I'll be thinking about you. Hope everything goes okay.'

'Thanks.' She hung up, leaving Ben standing in shock clutching his mobile phone. He turned to find Emily sitting up in bed, looking alarmed. 'What's the matter?' she asked.

'Sarah's in labour. I'm going to see if they can put us on an earlier flight.'

'Why do we need to go back now, there's nothing you can do, Ben, and we'll be home in a couple of days.'

'We're going now,' Ben snapped, his voice full of irritation, 'because she's on her own and is being harassed by that idiot Paul Davis. You can stay if you want but I need to get back.'

'Okay then,' Emily sighed. 'I'll stay.'

Ben swung around to look at her. 'I thought we were supposed to be a couple now Emily. We're getting married, remember?'

'Sarah doesn't need me, Ben. But I've got some more people I want to meet here and I'm not cutting my trip short.'

'Can I remind you that Sarah's paying for this room?'

'She's not the bloody queen, Ben,' Emily snapped, in the first display of anger Ben had seen from her. 'You don't have to jump every time she asks you to.'

He started stuffing clothes into his travel bag, not even stopping to look at her as he mumbled, 'Suit yourself then. I know where your priorities lie.'

After much haranguing of the airline, Ben managed to get himself on to the 7am flight that same day which meant he'd get to Edinburgh in the evening. He'd only had a minute to bid an uncomfortable goodbye to Emily before he rushed off to get a cab to the airport. He didn't know where their row had left them but he was too angry to care right now, and too intent on getting home.

Leaving the hotel so early also meant he didn't have a chance to explain to Jason, Gary and Sandra or even to say goodbye. Instead, Ben scrawled a short note which he pushed under Jason's door on the way out.

'Had to get on earlier flight. Sarah having baby. Emily staying here. See you back home. Ben.'

He didn't imagine Jason or his parents would see daylight for a while. They had all gone on to a wine bar the night before, across the road from the gallery. While Ben and Emily had left at midnight, the Weirs looked as though they still had a couple more rounds in them as they celebrated their son's success.

Ben had thought he'd heard their voices in the corridor at around 1.30am. Still half asleep, he'd registered Sandra shushing her husband who was drunkenly serenading her, before their room door slammed closed.

Now in the cab, on the way to the airport, Ben watched the night scenes of New York from the window and hoped he would be back to see the city properly again before too long. He reminded himself he'd made the right decision leaving; that it was what I would have wanted him to do, especially with Paul Davis on the prowl and ready to pounce. Just the thought of him was enough to turn his stomach. He represented everything Ben disliked in life – self-interest and a total lack of regard for anyone else's feelings.

And in many ways, Paul reminded me of my old self. So I didn't care for him much either.

CHAPTER fifteen

WE HAD SOME BITTER ROWS, Sarah and I. The victor would usually be me – often by overstepping the mark and saying the unsayable, shocking her into storming out. Our first year of marriage was spent bickering almost solidly over the tiniest things. There were the domestic disputes in which I would usually be accused of not doing enough around the house, while Sarah saw herself as the hard-pressed working woman pushed to the edge of exhaustion by a selfish husband. She had a point, but once she started pulling me up on the fact that I was leaving things lying around and not doing the dishes, I dug my heels in until eventually we upped our cleaners' hours, putting an end to that argument. In subsequent years she would complain that I no longer showed her enough attention and seemed to be more interested in the other (female) guests at a dinner party instead of her. Again, she had a point, but I saw myself as a harmless flirt. And I thought flirting helped fan the flames of passion that were so much part of who I was. Sarah, though, had a much more traditional outlook on things. Looking back, I guess I could describe that as loyalty. But the more she moaned about my flirting, the more I did it. It became a bit of a sport – and a dangerous one at that. Then two years ago, just as things were really beginning to crack on the fertility front, I remember waving goodnight to our hosts after one particularly raucous dinner party – which I'd thought had been thoroughly good fun – only to be berated by Sarah the whole way home in the taxi.

'What's your problem, Harry?' She'd pressed herself into the side of the taxi seat, arms tightly crossed in front of her.

'What you talking about?' I slurred.

'You flirted with that stupid woman Gloria all evening?'

'Glorious you mean,' I chuckled heartily at my own joke. Sarah hadn't found it funny.

'Don't you even see me at all now, Harry? Have I become so insignificant to you that flirting outrageously with other women in front of my face becomes fair game? Because if it is, I don't want to play. I'd rather be on my own again.'

Being drunk and unable to understand the gravity of the conversation I ended up nudging Sarah like a cheeky schoolboy before clumsily trying to put my arm around her.

'Don't,' she hissed. 'Don't touch me, you drunken, stupid bastard.'

Stupid bastard. The words bounced around my head, dislodging my senses and before I knew it I had grabbed Sarah by the arm and yanked her towards me.

'Don't you ever call me stupid again, you ungrateful, little bitch. Understand?'

I saw Sarah's feelings for me change in that one moment. And I think I knew even then that it was irreversible. My temper had got the better of me again. I'd used pride to justify attacking my wife. Of course, I hated myself for lashing out, for showing true colours I didn't even realise existed within me; and so I entered the vicious circle of anxiety, paranoia and self-loathing. I was walking a path of psychological decline.

~

Sarah took a cab to the hospital – a 30-minute journey that seemed to last a lifetime. Shortly after she put the phone down to Ben her contractions had started in earnest, around 20 minutes apart to begin with but now very close together and growing in intensity. She writhed around in the back seat trying not to draw attention to herself while the taxi driver talked endlessly of his wife's three labours and how he'd essentially spent most of them watching football. 'Well, good for you,' she wanted to yell sarcastically at him, but instead she stayed silent, trying instead to focus on her breathing. When the pain hit it was totally overwhelming, drowning out everything around her apart from her overriding sense of fear and loneliness. Before long she started to sob, quietly at first and then loud, drowning out the sound of the taxi driver trying to reassure her, saying it would be okay. She was longing for someone to be by her side, holding her hand, sharing this moment. But while she knew that someone should have been me, the person she really wanted with her right now was my brother.

And then the guilt over my death set in again. She didn't know how it could be linked, but it seemed that since that night with Paul her life had spiralled out of control until it brought her here; to the back of this cab, alone and about to give birth to a baby who, at this moment, didn't even have a father. Then another contraction hit and her emotional pain was replaced by a more violent, angry, physical one that was out to punish and brutalise. She wished she was at the hospital puffing gas and air. That moment drew closer as the taxi pulled up outside the maternity unit and the driver leapt out, like a cop on a TV show, racing to her door then helping her out of the vehicle. He supported her as she walked to reception and stood with her when the midwife came to ask her name.

'Sarah Melville,' she said through gritted teeth as she braced herself for another wave of pain.

'Come through,' the midwife instructed, waving her towards an examination room to the side.

'I hope you get on alright, love,' the taxi driver said, his eyes full of concern for this frightened stranger.

'Thank you. I'll be okay.' She pressed thirty pounds into his hand, holding on to him anxiously for a moment before following the midwife into the room.

Sarah's mother, Angela, arrived just as the baby's head was crowning. She found Sarah lying on her back, screaming like a wild animal as she desperately struggled to push her child into the world. Angela rushed to her daughter's side and immediately took up her role as chief encourager.

'Good girl, Sarah,' she said. 'Keep pushing, you can do it.'

'I can't,' Sarah yelled. 'I've been doing this for half an hour and I can't take it any more.'

'You're nearly there, Sarah,' the midwife said. Angela marvelled at how times had changed as she looked at the small, sparrow-like woman who was gently and calmly helping her daughter deliver her grandchild. In Angela's day, midwives always seemed to be austere characters who would bark orders at you. This woman was quite the opposite of that stereotype. Instead she was kind and reassuring. Lucky Sarah, Angela thought.

Suddenly her daughter let out a guttural scream that Angela feared must have echoed around the entire hospital. A few seconds later, however, the midwife held a little dark-haired and red-faced baby up in the air, before declaring: 'It's a boy.'

She then weighed the baby – 7lb 3oz – and wrapped him up before laying him on Sarah's chest.

The new mother gazed lovingly into her newborn boy's eyes. She couldn't believe how perfect and how beautiful this little man was. He had a proud, angelic face and Sarah thought he was everything she had ever dreamed of. She unbuttoned her shirt to allow the baby to feed for the first time and, as she looked up at her mother, she realised they both had tears streaming down their faces.

'Doesn't he look like his daddy,' Angela said, causing Sarah to cry harder with the agony of this statement. Her mother was another person she hadn't told the truth, along with most of her own family and friends. She just couldn't face shattering their belief that she had been a doting and faithful wife. The cruel thing was, that for all but a couple of hours of our marriage, she had been exactly that.

Sarah looked back down at her baby, who was happily feeding from her left breast.

'What will you call him?' Angela asked.

Sarah appeared to think for a moment, although she knew that despite the possible consequences, there was only one name she could ever choose for her baby boy.

'Harry,' she replied. 'Harry John Melville'.

Dad was sitting in his armchair listening to his favourite gardening programme when the phone rang. He was delighted to hear Sarah's voice at the other end as he'd been anxious ever since Ben had called him from JFK airport that morning to tell him she was in labour.

'Hello John,' she said cheerfully. 'It's a little boy and he's gorgeous.'

'Well done, my dear. Are you alright?'

'Yes, I'm fine. A little tired, but everything went okay.'

'Excellent news. And does the little fellow have a name?'

'Yes, he's Harry John Melville.'

John's voice cracked as he tried to get his reply out: 'That's... a very fine tribute... to me and my son. Thank you.'

'I need to stay in overnight, but you're very welcome to come in and see him if you can hop in a taxi?' Sarah asked.

'What a lovely thought,' Dad said. 'I think I'll do that.'

'We'll see you later then.'

'Goodbye dear, thanks for calling.'

Dad sat back in his armchair and smiled. So he was finally a grandfather. A proud moment, he thought. He reached into the cabinet at his side and pulled from it an old tattered photo album which he opened and began leafing through the pages, taking in row after row of pictures of Ben and I from baby-stage up. He would take a couple of photos with him to the hospital, he thought, so they could compare this young newborn with his father as a baby. Dad let the tears fall as the memories rose to the surface. He lingered over a family portrait in which we were all pictured together on our old leather sofa, Mum with her arms around her five-year-old twins and dad smiling proudly to my left.

They were happy times for all of us. These were the days when Ben and I would just muddle along together, sometimes fighting, sometimes rolling around the floor laughing, but always brothers. Just a decade later, and the divisions of rivalry and jealousy would have already set in, severing our bond.

Dad sighed as he remembered his family together and longed for us all to be reunited again, somewhere, some time. His thoughts were then abruptly interrupted by the phone ringing again. He answered quickly thinking it would probably be Ben to tell him he had landed.

'Hello,' he answered.

'Hello. Is that John Melville?'

'Yes, who's speaking please?'

'My name is Paul Davis. I'm an old colleague of Sarah's and I was due to meet her for lunch earlier but she didn't show up. I hope you don't mind me calling. I found you in the phone directory. It's just I'm aware that she's expecting a baby and I wanted to check whether everything's okay?'

'Oh, yes,' Dad replied. 'Everything is very good, thank you for checking. She's had a little boy called Harry earlier today.'

'Harry,' he paused. 'I see. Well, I'd like to organise some flowers for her. Do you know when she'll be home?'

'I think she'll be home tomorrow.'

'Thank you so much. Sorry for troubling you. I was just anxious for news – and I'll be sure to pass it on to all her former colleagues here.'

'No problem at all, my boy. It's very good of you to call.'

'Thanks again then,' said Paul. 'Glad to hear mother and baby are well and I'm certainly looking forward to seeing them.'

Dad put the receiver down again and smiled to himself as he considered what wonderful and supportive friends Sarah must have to be so caring. He found a piece of paper and scribbled down the words 'Paul Davis'. I must remember to tell her that he called, he thought to himself.

Ten minutes later and Dad was pulling on his winter coat, his cab due to arrive at any moment. He wrapped a scarf around his neck and donned his cap before setting foot outside. It was a cold but otherwise clear winter evening and, as he waited for the cab to pull up, he propped himself up against his front wall, partially seated, to take in the night sky. There was a spectacular array of stars above him, all brightly shining and twinkling just like a picture on a Christmas card. As he looked round to his right to examine a particularly dense and dramatic cluster of stars he noticed one fall from the heavens directly above him, leaving a momentary trail. He drew breath at the sight. Shooting stars had always had special significance for Dad because, as a teenager, he had once prayed for God to show him a shooting star to prove his existence. A few weeks later, when he had forgotten about his plea, he was returning home on his bicycle after delivering a tablecloth from his mother to his aunt nearby, when he stopped at the top of a hill to allow a car to pass. Waiting at the side of the road, he briefly glanced up at the night sky and it was then that he saw a shooting star which came and went in the blink of an eye. 'So he does exist', Dad remembered saying to himself. He smiled at the thought. The story of the shooting star was one he would often tell Ben and I before bedtime, and we must have each spent many hours as boys searching the night sky in the hope of seeing one too.

Dad raised his hand to give a wave to the cabbie before climbing into the back seat of the black taxi.

'I'm off to the Royal Infirmary please,' he informed the driver. 'Lovely evening, don't you think?'

'It is indeed. You off to visit someone?'

'Yes. My daughter-in-law. She's just given birth to my grandson.'

'Congratulations. Is this your first?'

'It certainly is, yes, and I'm delighted. Quite a wonderful day this is turning out to be.'

'Very glad to hear it, sir.'

Dad sat back in his seat and relaxed into the journey. Since the hospital had moved to the outskirts of the city, at Little France, it could take anything from 20 to 30 minutes or more to get there, depending on traffic. With rush hour behind them though, Dad hoped the journey would be quick as he was desperate to see his new grandson. He wondered if it would be like the night he first held Ben and I. Despite not being identical, we both had a very similar, almost princely look as babies, with dark hair, refined features and olive skin. Dad had experienced his proudest moment in the maternity ward that day – holding a son in each arm and wearing a smile that filled the room. Sitting in the cab on this winter's evening, he wished he had tried harder to let his sons know how much he cared for them and how wonderful he really thought they were. Instead, he had believed he was doing the right thing by pushing us as hard as he could, thinking this was the only way we would make something of ourselves. Watching Ben descend into depression and hopelessness, it hadn't taken him long to figure out he had got it wrong. And as for me, whatever I achieved, Dad would only ever reply: 'Great. What's next?' It had taken my death for Dad to realise that both boys had needed much more support from him than he'd ever given. He wished now that he'd spent more time listening to us and understanding what it was we really wanted to achieve. Instead he drove us on – and drove us apart. This grandchild would be a chance to put that right. And this time he would only love and never lecture.

Dad plodded further along the maze of corridors, carefully following the arrows directing him to the maternity unit. Finally, he stopped outside the ward and found Sarah sitting up with her new baby in a bed just in front of the entrance.

'Hello there my dear.' Dad greeted her with a kiss and an affectionate pat on the back before turning his attention to the baby fast asleep in her arms.

'Hello,' said Sarah, wearing a warm but weary smile. 'You just missed my mum. I told her to go home because she'd been here since this morning and she looked exhausted.'

'Gosh, that is a long day, isn't it? I bet she's very proud though,' John added peering down at his new grandson. 'And this must be Harry.'

'Would you like to hold him?'

'I'd be delighted.' John set down the photographs he'd brought with him on the side cabinet, and placed his coat over the back of a chair before scooping his little grandson up into his arms.

'Hello, Harry,' he said, gazing down at the infant's tiny, but perfect face. Soon, tears started to tumble down Dad's cheeks, born both out of joy at the new offspring and heartache at the memories of holding his own sons, just like this.

'He's a fine young fellow,' he said eventually to Sarah, who was by now resting back on the bed, taking in the moment.

'I thought you'd like him,' she said, smiling.

'Oh, I do. I can see he has the Melville brow already. I've brought baby pictures of his daddy to show him.'

Sarah smiled, politely humouring him as she had her mother who had also commented on the baby's familial looks just an hour earlier.

'If I can just rest this little chap against my arm here, I can show you,' Dad said, reaching over to hand the pictures to Sarah. 'Do you see the family resemblance now?'

Sarah glanced down and looked into the faces of the two tiny babies lying side by side in their hospital crib, both fast asleep and wrapped in matching white blankets. She looked then at her own son and was immediately struck by the similarity of their fine features and dark hair colour. A lucky coincidence, she thought to herself.

'Do you see it?' asked Dad.

'Uncanny,' said Sarah. 'Thank you for bringing these, John.'

'I thought you'd like to see them, my dear. It's a wonderful comfort to see the resemblance.'

Sarah glanced away, fighting back tears.

'How are you feeling now?' John asked.

'Still a bit tired, but I'm just so relieved that he's arrived safely.'

Dad stayed for another twenty minutes and for most of that time he sat quietly holding Harry, deep in thought and humming to himself. Since repairing his relationship with Ben, Dad felt like a new man with an enormous burden lifted from his shoulders. He realised the mistakes he'd made in the past, but he was ready to make up for them in the future.

With Dad carefully minding the baby, Sarah made the most of her free arms and took the opportunity to go to the bathroom where she washed her face and brushed her teeth ready to settle down for the night and try to get some sleep.

When it was time to say goodbye, Dad kissed his little grandson tenderly on the forehead and whispered to him: 'We're going to be great friends, you and I.'

With the baby settled back in her arms, Sarah leaned over to kiss Dad goodbye.

'Thank you for coming,' she said. 'It was lovely to see you.'

'Thank you for allowing me to come, dear. It was very special to see my wonderful new grandson.'

He folded his coat back over his arm and headed back out into the corridor, busily searching for an exit sign. He had barely taken ten paces out of the ward when two men in a great hurry came bustling past him.

'Is this Ward 24?' one of them asked Dad.

Immediately suspicious – something he had retained from his earlier years serving in the armed forces – Dad asked: 'Who is it you're looking for?'

'Sarah Melville,' the second man asked.

'That's my daughter-in-law.'

'Well then, John,' the second man replied. 'We spoke earlier. I'm Paul Davis.'

'But there was no need for you to come into the hospital,' Dad said sternly, annoyed that the man had chosen to visit at this late hour and without warning.

'I'm here to see my son,' Paul said.

'I'm afraid I don't understand.' Dad replied, straightening up before the strangers.

'Well, it's a little unfortunate that you have to hear it from me. But Sarah and I were intimately involved before your son died and I am the father of her child.'

Without stopping to think, Dad swung his right fist and landed it sharply on the corner of Paul's chin. It was a direct hit that sent Paul reeling backwards and caused Dad to lose his balance before stumbling and falling to the ground.

Ben had just rounded the corner from the lift when he saw a commotion in the corridor ahead. Spotting Dad among the three men, Ben began to run. He was just a few feet away when he saw Dad punch a man – who Ben then realised was Paul Davis – then collapse to the floor.

'What the hell's going on?' Ben shouted as he ran towards them.

'I came with my client here to collect DNA samples from Sarah Melville and her child,' the second man said, pointing to Paul Davis who was clutching his jaw, his face white with shock. 'Mr Davis told this man that he was the father of the child and the gentleman punched him.'

'You fool,' Ben shouted at Paul before dropping to his knees next to where our father was lying face down. He turned Dad's head towards him, but his eyes were set in a fixed glare. Ben checked his breathing and his pulse before frantically shaking his shoulders in an attempt to bring him round.

'Dad,' Ben shouted. 'Please, Dad. Come on.' But it was too late.

CHAPTER sixteen

'HARRY.' I heard my mother's voice calling from behind.

'Harry,' she said again, louder this time. 'Your father is with us now.'

And when I looked back towards Dad and Ben, I saw the scene had changed and Dad was now sitting next to his body in the hospital corridor, calm but confused. Ben was kneeling on the floor in front of Dad's corpse weeping with his head in his hands while a nurse crouched at his side and tried valiantly to console him. Suddenly Sarah burst into the corridor from the ward clutching the baby in her arms, her face a mixture of shock and pain from the effort of rushing to the scene so soon after labour.

Dad smiled when he saw us walking towards him and quickly got to his feet, free now from the shackles of old age.

'Son,' he said, holding out his arms to me. We embraced before he turned to my mother. 'My darling. Thank you for waiting for me.'

~

Ben and Sarah sat together in silence as they tried to process the events of the night before.

She had been forced to return to the maternity ward with the baby while the hospital staff removed Dad's body and led Ben away to a separate room to recover from the shock. Realising the seriousness of the situation, Paul and his lawyer friend had left, but not before vowing to Sarah that they'd be in touch to arrange the DNA test.

She had endured a restless night, listening to newborns crying as she tried to shut out the awful scenes from her mind.

When Harry eventually woke at 6am, she fed him again, changed his nappy and was able to settle him back down again before 7am. By that time, she was beginning to feel like sleeping but it was too late as the ward was now in full swing with a constant flow of staff offering her a breakfast menu, or carrying out checks on her and the baby. When Angela arrived at 9am, Sarah asked to be discharged as soon as possible in the hope that getting out of hospital would help her recover more quickly both from the labour and from the events of the night before.

When they got back home later that morning, Ben was waiting for them. Armed with cups of tea, they had sat down together at the kitchen table while Angela flitted around them, cleaning, washing and generally making herself useful.

Finally, Ben broke the silence.

'I'm seeing the undertaker at three o'clock to make the funeral arrangements. Bob Cuddy will lead the service again. I phoned him this morning and he sounded quite upset to hear about Dad.'

'Will he be buried near Harry and Anna?' Sarah asked somberly.

'Yes. They'll be together.'

Another long pause followed as they each returned to their thoughts. The night before had seemed totally surreal yet the scenes were still so vivid in their minds. Ben flinched between pain and anger as he first relived the moment he realised Dad was dead, and then remembered turning to catch Paul Davis's startled glare. It had taken him every ounce of willpower not to tear that man apart, just as he had torn his family apart.

Ben wondered when Paul would next have the audacity to turn up, and hoped he would have just an ounce of decency enough to give them time to grieve.

In one single blow, Dad had delivered a magnificent parting shot that had put Davis in his place, a thought that offered Ben just a little comfort as he processed the terrible events.

Ben's mind then drifted to Emily who he'd called in New York the night before to tell her what had happened. She had immediately felt guilty about not coming back with him and he hadn't made that any easier on her saying: 'You did what you felt you had to.' The comment was intended to wound as Ben wanted Emily to feel bad about putting her work before their relationship. She was now making her way back from the States, leaving Sarah and Ben sitting alone together with only each other for support.

'I think that John died of a broken heart and it's all my fault,' Sarah blurted out, catching Ben completely by surprise.

'Don't be silly, Sarah,' Ben said, patting her comfortingly on the shoulder.

'The baby was his ray of hope after Harry's death and I took that away from him,' she sobbed.

'That idiot Davis took it away from him, Sarah. Telling him he was the father when he hasn't even proved it yet.' Ben gripped his tea mug, quickly taking another slug of the now lukewarm liquid as he tried to tame his anger.

'I'm going to ask my solicitor to arrange for the DNA test to be carried out this week,' Sarah said glumly. 'I think we all need to know the truth one way or another so we can start to sort this mess out.'

She looked at Ben, expecting to find him nodding in agreement but, instead, she found him lost deep in thought. She saw his eyes close briefly as he seemed to register something painful. When he opened them again he looked directly at her.

'You two are the only family I have left now,' he said, nodding towards the living room next door where Harry was sleeping in his crib. 'It doesn't matter whose DNA is involved. We're family. That's how it's going to stay.'

Sarah leaned forward and put her arms around Ben's neck before holding him in a close embrace.

'I'm so sorry,' she whispered into his neck. 'So, so, sorry.'

~

Three days later, and Ben had the most overwhelming, and not unsurprising, sense of déjà vu as he walked through the doors of Morningside Church again to attend another funeral of a close family member just eight months after they'd buried me.

Today, as then, he took a seat in the front row next to Sarah, this time with Emily sitting to his right. Angela had taken baby Harry for a walk outside the church but they could still hear his cries through the stained glass windows every time she passed with the pram. It was almost as if he was protesting to come inside although it was more likely he was demanding milk.

Harry had proved to be a very hungry young man and was fed every two hours in the day, then screamed for most of the evening before conking out for five or six hours at night, usually waking at four am for another feed.

Ben and Emily had been making the effort to go and sit with Sarah most evenings to help out, taking it in turns to hold Harry while Sarah relaxed in the bath for half an hour or made some phone calls. Despite the crying, Ben really enjoyed his time with his nephew with whom he'd already struck up a bond. And he was comforted to know that Dad had had the chance to hold his grandson before he died. It was something for him to cling on to as he tried to come to terms with what had happened.

Reverend Bob was standing at the alter now, welcoming the congregation to the church. They began by singing one of Dad's favourite hymns: Abide With Me.

Ben picked through the words, searching for comfort or a clue as to where his family were now, leaving him alone in the world. He was drawn to the last verse, allowing its sentiment to stay with him long after they had finished singing.

'Hold thou thy cross before my closing eyes; Shine through the gloom and point me to the skies. Heaven's morning breaks, and earth's vain shadows flee; In life, in death, O Lord, abide with me.'

Ben liked the ease of the transition in the hymn from life to death. He desperately wanted to believe that as the sun had set on his father's life in this world, dawn had broken in the afterlife.

By now, Bob had embarked on a personal tribute to his friend, John.

'He was every inch the family man,' the minister told the congregation. 'Whenever we spoke he would tell me of his sons' latest achievements and his pride in everything they had attained. Harry was, of course, one of life's obvious achievers, building up a successful business and creating a charitable trust in his own name of which John was immensely proud.

'But...' he turned to look at Ben now, who froze under his stare, 'one of the conversations about his sons that I most vividly remember was about Ben, who was then only around twenty two and was living a more...' the reverend paused for dramatic effect, 'rock and roll lifestyle'. The congregation chuckled as Ben's discomfort deepened.

'One day I enquired as to whether Ben had taken up any particular career. John simply smiled and said: 'Right now, Ben's main ambition in life is to avoid having a career. But I know something he doesn't know'.

'What's that?' I asked, hugely intrigued by this comment.

'I know that my son has unique vision and a great understanding of people. He'll find his path eventually and, when he does, he'll do whatever he puts his mind to – just as soon as he's minded to do it.' This raised another few chuckles from the assembled crowd but, by now, Ben was listening too intently to feel any further embarrassment.

'I spoke to John again just a couple of weeks ago after a Sunday service,' Bob enthusiastically continued.

'He raced over to me and waggled a copy of the Evening News under my nose. 'I told you so,' he said proudly. I took the newspaper from him and saw a large article headed: Green Light for Youth Centre Expansion.

'The article told how, under Ben's leadership, the centre had been given permission by planners to expand their premises to enable them to launch a new scheme to help young mothers back into work. It paid a glowing tribute to the man who had turned an already thriving youth centre into one of Scotland's most admired charitable projects. And, to John's particular delight, the article ended by saying that Ben had been asked by the Scottish Government to be an advisor on the voluntary sector so that they could try and emulate the success of these centres elsewhere.

'I'll never forget the pride on John's face that day as he stood waving the article in front of me. He had indeed been right about his son, as he was on most things he took an interest in.'

Ben tightly clenched the order of service in his hand, focusing his gaze squarely on the text as he fought back a river of tears. But his attempts to retain his composure were futile, and as watched the first drop of water plop onto the card he held on his lap, he let go. For several minutes the tears silently poured down his cheeks as he thought about how much Dad must have loved him. To think he had believed in him all those years that Ben had spent doubting himself was as heartening as it was soul-destroying, for with this knowledge also came the realisation that he had wasted many years resenting his father when, in fact, they should have been so much closer. We had all left – Dad, Mum and I - and Ben longed to turn the clock back to feel the comfort once more of his full family around him.

'I'm sorry,' he mouthed. Hoping we would somehow hear him and understand his regret at not being a better son and brother. He would never stop loving us, he vowed. And we would never stop loving him.

It was a bitterly cold day and the crowd assembled by the graveside to lay Dad's body to rest, huddled together for warmth. Ben led the coffin bearers as they lowered Dad's body into the grave, leaving him side by side with Mum and I.

Standing between Sarah and Emily while Bob said a blessing, Ben stared at the two headstones next to Dad's grave, 'In Loving Memory of Anna Margaret… Harry David Melville ..'. Soon a third stone would mark the place where Dad lay, the three of us united with one left behind. Ben felt painfully excluded from the family as he had so often over the years.

He could feel us tantalisingly close, as though he could open a door and find the three of us standing behind it, laughing at our little trick. His soul searched for us but didn't know where to look.

'Send me a sign,' he begged. 'Let me know if you're there.'

∼

Ben was rushing again, as he usually did at this time in the evening, trying to make it to Sarah's house by 6.30pm. His evening visits had, by now, become part of the baby's routine. There was a regular pattern to Harry Junior's day – and his colic – that meant he cried almost solidly between six and ten in the evening then crashed out until around 5am, giving Sarah an even longer rest in between. Ben was inwardly pleased his nephew was crying in the evenings as it gave him the perfect excuse to keep going over there to help out. Emily would join them too sometimes, but was increasingly opting to stay at work or go home to start dinner. Sarah enjoyed the company – and the couple of hours of down time Ben's visits bought her. In between the baby's crying spells, Ben would fill Sarah in on his day while she, in turn, regaled him with parenting woes. She had joined a mother's group who met for coffee each Wednesday morning and would sit and pour their hearts out about their babies' feeding difficulties, broken nights, colic, strange-looking nappy contents, facial expressions, body temperatures, skin rashes, bathing preferences; the list of topics for discussion was endless. Ben gathered that partners came in for a real battering during these coffee mornings and was glad that, with his unique status, he would escape that fate.

He had a set of keys to Sarah's so he could let himself in when expected. That evening, as he pushed open the front door, he could hear Emily was already there – something Ben found annoyed him slightly as she was taking the prime slot of being first to hold Harry that day. He threw his coat over the banister and immediately rushed over to see his little nephew. Peering down into his face over Emily's shoulder, Harry flashed a beaming smile at the sight of his uncle. His happiness was short-lived though as the colic pains soon struck again, starting him off on another ten-minute stretch of wailing. Emily kept jiggling her soon-to-be nephew, while Ben hung around by her side, itching to take over.

'Where's Sarah?'

'She's in the kitchen,' Emily replied. 'She says she has a surprise for us.'

Ben quickly glanced along the hallway to see if he could see what was going on, but the kitchen door remained firmly shut.

'Do you want to hold your nephew?' Emily finally volunteered.

'Absolutely.' Ben held his arms out to take delivery of the baby who had settled down again and was looking sleepy. He rested little Harry over his shoulder and patted his back, while Emily settled back on the sofa to read a newspaper.

A few moments later, Sarah appeared in the doorway holding a tray that carried a bottle of champagne, three glasses and a folded piece of paper.

'What's all this?' Ben asked.

'The results of the DNA test,' Sarah said brightly. Ben noticed a relaxed radiance in her face that he hadn't seen since before Harry's death. She gently laid the tray down on the coffee table before handing Ben the piece of paper. He took a seat so he could settle little Harry on his lap while he read.

The DNA test had been hanging over them for the last fortnight since Sarah had relented to Paul's demands and allowed for a saliva swab to be taken from the baby. From the smile on her face he knew it must be good news, but wondered whether she was just relieved the whole process was over one way or another.

He looked down at what seemed like a complicated set of figures headed with the words, 'Results of DNA Analysis (Legally Binding)'. Ben swallowed hard before looking for the definitive answer.

He could see three columns of numbers representing the genetic information gathered for Sarah, baby Harry and Paul Davis along with the dates the samples had been collected. He couldn't make sense of any of the data so he glanced further down the page where he saw the words 'Statement of Results'. His heart was racing now and he pulled Harry just a little closer to him before reading on:

'Based on the DNA analysis, Paul Davis can be excluded as the biological father.'

Ben breathed an audible sigh of relief as he finished reading the report.

'Harry is the father,' Sarah said, smiling. 'It's a bloody miracle, but it's true,' she laughed, finally looking like a woman without a care in the world after months of torment.

Ben held baby Harry up in front of him and kissed him lovingly on his cheek before holding him close again.

'I was trying not to get my hopes up,' he said. 'But the likeness was hard to miss – he's his father's double.'

'I know, I thought so too,' Sarah giggled.

Emily rushed to embrace Sarah. 'That's such great news,' she beamed before kissing Ben on the cheek.

'My family,' Ben declared proudly looking between the baby and the two women standing in front of him.

Becoming serious again for a moment, Sarah said: 'I'm so sorry for all the pain I've caused.'

Ben too got to his feet now to give Sarah a comforting hug.

'I already told you to forget it. It's in the past now. Have you told Davis yet?'

'Both he and his lawyer will have received copies today too.'

'And you've heard nothing back from him?'

'What is there for him to say now?' Sarah smiled.

'Sorry would have been a good start,' Ben said, before brightening up again. 'Let's get that champagne poured then.'

They clinked glasses and toasted the prospect of a future as a united family, Ben scarcely able to take his eyes off his nephew, now his closest family member and his greatest joy.

~

Ben hadn't initially been enthusiastic when Sonja first suggested a Christmas party at the centre. He had just buried his father and wasn't exactly in the festive mood, but he went along with her suggestion to avoid disappointing the team. Sonja had handled most of the arrangements herself so all that was left for Ben to do was turn up.

But following the previous night's good news on Harry's paternity test, Ben found he was actually looking forward to the do and made a point of finishing work in the office early so he could help set up. When he reached the recreation room he found Sonja and Danny between them just about had everything covered. On Sonja's instruction, Ben headed back through to the office – which was to be used as the eating area – to push the meeting table back against the wall and create a bit of space. Danny bounded up and down the stairs like an excited puppy, carrying various assortments of plates, sausage rolls and bags of crisps – lots of bags of crisps – which Sonja then laid out on the table. The recreation room would have had an environmentalist in a cold sweat there were so many plastic cups and plates but, Ben had to admit, they'd done a good job.

The guests started to arrive just after 5pm, most of them the young people who had used the centre over the course of the year. At their Monday meeting earlier in the week, Sonja had broken the news that in the last year they had seen their success rate in getting visitors to the centre into work or further education increase even further. As a team they had been ecstatic about their progress which had mainly been down to a follow-up programme which meant they not only helped their young people identify careers and apply for jobs or courses, but now supported them through the interview process and the early weeks in their new roles or college places.

Ben made sure he got around all of the guests and was surprised by how much pride he felt at hearing how each of their careers was developing. The sense of purpose and self-worth he noticed in the youngsters made him even more determined to keep going so that, one day, no one they saw would fall through the gap and back into unemployment.

He had just started to hand round the sausage rolls when he saw Jason appearing through the door of the recreation room carrying what looked like one of his larger drawings in a frame. Jason searched animatedly around the crowded room, dodging in and out of guests until he noticed Ben waving at him from the corner. He waved back, smiling warmly as he bounded over to his mentor.

'Hello stranger,' Ben said, greeting Jason with a one-armed hug as he balanced the plate of sausage rolls in the other.

'Sorry, I've not been in to see you in a while, Ben. I've barely seen daylight the last few weeks I've been that busy trying to get more drawings over to the States for Emily. She's selling them like hot cakes.'

Ben smiled at the idea of Jason beavering away in his new flat trying to please an impatient Emily, but it was an equally strange thought to realise how much money she must be starting to make out of him. To Emily, Jason was business. To Ben, he was a friend. Still, as Ben cast his eyes over Jason's designer jacket he could see the young artist was being well rewarded for his efforts.

'Good for you,' said Ben. 'Is this another one waiting to be sent to the States?' he asked, nodding at the large framed drawing Jason was clutching under his arm.

'No man,' Jason held the drawing up in front of Ben now. 'This is for you.'

Ben searched around for the nearest chair to rest the tray on before taking the framed picture from Jason.

'This is amazing, Jason. Thank you so much.' He studied the drawing closely and once again marvelled at the incredible level of detail that had gone into producing it. This one showed a young mother lovingly spooning a teaspoonful of pureed food into her baby's mouth.

'My cousin,' Jason said, pointing to the baby girl in the drawing. 'I thought it could go in your new crèche room when it's finished.'

'What a lovely thought. I've no idea how you found the time to do this when you're so busy, but I'm really touched.'

'You're welcome. I wouldn't be doing any of this if it wasn't for you, so it's the least I can do.' He flashed Ben another beaming smile.

'I'm so proud of you, Jason. You really deserve your success.'

Jason's face crumpled at Ben's kindness. 'I don't know about that,' he mumbled, eyes now cast to the floor.

'Why wouldn't you deserve to be successful, Jason?' Ben asked, confused by Jason's sudden shift in mood.

'I've not always been a good person. I'm not proud of it.'

'Well, there's none of us angels, Jason, and you've not had the easiest start in life.'

'It's no excuse,' Jason mumbled again.

'Look, do you want to talk about this? We could go and sit upstairs if you like?'

Jason thought for a moment before nodding his head. Ben started to lead him towards the stairs but was interrupted by Sonja who had begun pulling on his arm. 'Jayne's just about to leave Ben and she wants to thank you before she heads off.'

Ben looked across the room to see Jayne smiling at him in the doorway. They had managed to help her find childcare while she attended college where she was now studying for five Highers.

Sonja had told Ben the other week that Jayne was already doing really well in her course work so her dream of becoming a lawyer was very much alive.

Ben turned to Jason who was looking flushed and agitated. 'I'll be back in five minutes and we'll talk, okay?' Jason nodded again and Ben made his way over to talk to Jayne. She was full of enthusiasm about her new course and really excited about her future. Ben, anxious to get back to Jason who he could see was troubled, congratulated Jayne on all her hard work and asked after the baby which prompted several minutes of stories about how well her little girl was doing. She was crawling early and had already attempted a few words. Ben would have loved to have given Jayne more time, so he felt guilty when he rushed her a bit by wishing her well and asking her to keep in touch. Still, she didn't seem to notice his keenness to get away and gave him a big hug before she left.

He looked around for Jason again but knew as soon as he saw the empty space where he had been standing in the corner that he'd gone.

~

Christmas was focused on baby Harry who provided a welcome distraction. Sarah and her parents had brought him over to Emily's place mid-morning where they had lavished him with gifts before opening their own. Emily had organised and cooked lunch and they had enjoyed a quiet time together, Ben and Sarah often lost in their own thoughts as they struggled through a difficult day and yet another landmark in their grief.

Sarah tried hard to push the memory of Christmas with Dad and I last year at The Balmoral Hotel from her mind. Ben had joined us for a while there too and it had been one of the few times before my death that she'd spent any significant period of time with him. She recalled how, while I had sat huffily at the bottom of the table, she had laughed for most of the afternoon with my father and brother as they exchanged amusing anecdotes, knocking back champagne and fine wines which I'd later moaned about paying for.

There had been little laughter at the end of the evening - my temper finally exploding with terrifying results. I'd spent the day feeling paranoid and isolated, convinced that Ben and Sarah were laughing about me. As soon as we got home I'd turned on my wife, demanding to know what they'd found so funny. Naturally she was confused, which only wound me up further. In my mind, it was all one big conspiracy.

'I'll make you sorry. I'll make you so fucking sorry you sat there laughing in my face,' I'd shouted as I launched myself at her across the kitchen, slapping her face and knocking her to the floor.

~

It was New Year's Eve and Sarah was sitting alone in her living room rocking her crying baby and reflecting on what had been the worst year of her life. She threw her head back and let out every ounce of pain that had been building all festive season as she tried to keep it together for her mum and dad. She wept for the husband she lost long before he died, for a child without a father and a mother without the love and support of a partner. She wept long past the point Harry had fallen asleep in her arms; she just kept rocking and sobbing until she felt numb. The dark spell was only broken by the sound of the telephone.

'Hello,' she said faintly while struggling to prop the receiver under her chin.

'You alright?' Rosa asked at the other end.

'Yeah, just a bit of a moment that's all.'

'And here's me thinking I had it bad, mopping up toddler puke on New Year's Eve.'

'Are the kids ill?'

'Esther is, yes, so that means Richard's gone to the neighbour's New Year party alone while I sit in like the sad cow I have become.'

Sarah smiled at her friend's efforts to make her feel better.

'You missing, Harry?' Rosa asked, in her usual blunt style.

'I think so,' Sarah sighed, unsure whether that really was why she felt so low. 'I'm sad little Harry will never get the chance to meet his dad, but I also just feel so horribly guilty that he's growing up without a family unit. He only has me and that doesn't seem right.' She started sobbing again but Rosa sensed it was better to let her speak than interrupt.

'Ben and Emily have been great. They do a lot for me and he's round here nearly every night helping me. But in a way, it just makes me feel even emptier. It's like I'm filling in some void in their relationship and I don't like being part of that triangle. It feels temporary and... weird.'

'Hmm. I see what you mean. Why don't you just gently put it to him that he doesn't need to come over so regularly?'

'I suppose I should really,' Sarah sniffed, wiping at her face with a tissue with one hand as she began to regain her composure, and still cradling Harry in her other arm. 'If I'm honest though, I need all the help I can get and... I like his company. But I know he's got someone waiting for him at home – and that he shouldn't really be spending so much time with us.'

'Look. You're hormonally charged and emotionally vulnerable right now. Ben is with Emily, and you need to take control of your feelings or else you're going to get hurt. You will find someone to spend your life with and build a family together, but now is not the time for that. '

'I know, I've told myself that over and over. But I can't stand being alone and I don't want to let Ben go.'

'You're not letting him go,' Rosa insisted. 'Just distancing yourself a little, for both your sakes. Do you think you can do that?'

'Yes,' Sarah said, resolve now finding its way through. 'You're right. I need to learn to cope on my own. I just never thought I'd have to I suppose.'

'It won't be forever,' Rosa assured her.

CHAPTER seventeen

MY MOTHER, ANNA, was the shining light in our lives; always attentive, always interested, always kind.

Like Ben, in whom she saw a kindred spirit, she loved to paint and when we were boys, she would sit us down in front of a puzzle for half an hour and sketch us. She wore such a pure expression of love on her face as she drew her boys that, as an adult, I feared no one would ever look at me with such affection again.

Ben and I shared an unbearable grief when she died, but, typically, we chose to deal with it separately.

For months she had complained of stomach pains and bloating and, despite numerous tests, was told countless times it was only IBS. By the time they figured out it was cancer, it was too late. In the end, she was so riddled with disease they couldn't even tell us where it started out. She died two months after the diagnosis. She had gone into hospital for some palliative chemo treatment and never came out. We didn't get to say goodbye, and my father was devastated that she had died alone. When Ben and I arrived at the hospital we found him sitting beside her body in a room off the ward muttering over and over again: 'I was just a few minutes too late, my love. Just a few minutes.'

He had heard her voice calling out to him in the night and rushed to the hospital, only to find she had gone. He never really forgave himself for that.

In life, I wrestled with my own memories of Mum and my insecurities about her close relationship with Ben which came to a head one painful day when I heard her say something that I spent the rest of my life trying to erase from my mind.

She was staying in hospital after investigative surgery. Ben was sitting by her bedside, holding her hand and reading to her. I had stepped out from behind the curtains surrounding her bed to get some water. I had only taken a couple of steps down the ward when a kindly nurse passed by and offered to refill the jug for me and return it to us. I thanked her and quickly headed back towards my mum's cubicle.

The curtains were slightly ajar and I could see her gently stroking Ben's cheek as he smiled lovingly back at her. 'You've always been special to me, Ben,' she said. 'You're such a talented boy. I don't want you ever to forget that. You'll outshine all of us.'

My body went cold, and the only sound I could hear were my ears ringing with hurt and hate. Why did she have to say that to him? What did she mean 'special'? Weren't we the same to her? Why did they always have to have these private little chats? My head was spinning. I thought about confronting her there and then and asking the questions I'd been desperate to for years: Is Ben your favourite? What did I do so wrong and what did he do so right? Deep down I knew I was being irrational, but I just couldn't crush the overwhelming sense of rejection. I rushed out of the hospital, brushing past my father at the main entrance.

'Harry?' he called after me.

'I have to go,' was the best reply I could manage.

~

Emily let out a long sigh through puffed cheeks as she and Ben took stock of the piles of boxes they were going to have to work their way through that afternoon. Along with Sarah, they had taken the decision to sell John's home and now had the arduous task of clearing it out and redecorating before letting the estate agent loose.

Standing in the doorway of the attic on a chilly Sunday afternoon in January, Ben began to appreciate the size of the job that lay ahead. Not only were they selling Dad's property, but they were selling Ben's flat too. The plan was to buy a new house together, just a few streets along from where Sarah lived in Stockbridge. They would then rent Emily's New Town flat out to bring in some extra income each month. Effectively that meant they had three properties to prepare in the next couple of months. And this was where it all started.

'We'll have to work our way through the suitcases and boxes in the attic first and divide the stuff into three piles; things we're keeping, things we're throwing and things we're giving away.' Emily said, with the tone of authority she usually reserved for the gallery.

Ben had been dreading the clear-out on a number of counts, but primarily because he knew each decision he had to take would be a difficult one. He wanted to hold on to everything that belonged to Mum and Dad; every memory, every trace of them. But he couldn't. He'd used the excuse of looking after baby Harry to put the task off, but after Sarah had sat him down several days before and told him she needed to learn to cope on her own – he no longer had a reason to delay the unavoidable.

He wondered if she'd noticed the hurt on his face when she'd said: 'You've been such an amazing help to me, Ben, and I'm so grateful but, if you don't mind, I think it would be a good idea if you came over just a little bit less. It's not that I don't love having you here. I do. And it's great for little Harry to see you so much... and you are and always will be a huge part of his life... but... you need to be with Emily, and I need to figure out some kind of life for myself. A way forward where I'm not leaning on you too much.'

Had he been imagining their bond? He'd looked forward to every visit – to holding his nephew, to sharing time with Sarah, and now she was turning him away after everything he had done for her. He just couldn't make any sense of it.

'Wakey, wakey,' Emily was calling as she headed for a set of boxes at the back of the attic space, forcing Ben to abandon his thoughts. They began working their way through our parents' belongings, having agreed they could only hold on to about 10 per cent of what was actually there.

Ben was surprised at how easy it was to throw the old trinkets, books, clothes and ornaments away, but he quickly realised that objects held no value for him when there was no memory attached. It was the photos and little reminders of their family life together – the wooden carving he'd made in art class, the 'Player of the Year' rugby trophy I'd been awarded at 15 – that he really treasured and he longed to take those boxes home so he could spend time looking through them and remembering.

As they worked through the afternoon, a huge weight was lifted from Ben's shoulders once he realised they were getting to the end of their task. As Emily sifted through the final two boxes, Ben went downstairs to assess how much there was to clear out from the main living rooms. Dad had lived fairly minimally and, like Ben, hated clutter. It became apparent – to Ben's relief – that they had tackled the lion's share of the work and there was very little to sort through in the downstairs cupboards. The last remaining area to check was a little writing cabinet next to Dad's favourite chair. There was nothing on the surface and only a few pens, the phone, a notebook, writing paper and a reading glass in the upper drawers. As he opened the door to a little cupboard underneath,

Ben found a collection of photo albums. He pulled the front one out and ran his hands over its smooth black leather cover. Inside he found pages of old newspaper cuttings, many of them on my sporting successes with the school rugby team, but also a couple of pieces Ben had long forgotten about that showed him collecting top prize at a nationwide junior art competition, two years in a row. Ben chuckled at how gangly and awkward he had looked, collecting his little silver plate in his oversized school uniform.

What he found carefully arranged in the pages towards the back of the album, surprised Ben even more. Dad had compiled a series of clippings detailing both of his sons' achievements over the years. Admittedly, there were many more pages dedicated to my accomplishments; pictures of me receiving my OBE at Buckingham Palace; countless newspaper articles about the successful entrepreneur with a giving heart. But among them also were some ten or so drawings and sketches Ben had done as a schoolboy – which Dad had even made notes on.

'Wild Poppies at Selkirk, August, 1987. Fluffy the neighbour's cat, October 1988, Chateau de Pressac, Saint-Emilion, July 1990,' and so they went on, until Ben reached a page where Dad had simply written, 'Anna, 1990'. It was a portrait Ben had drawn of our mother on her birthday. She smiled naturally and elegantly, looking straight into the eye of the beholder, her long hair neatly swept back from her face, her faint laughter lines only serving to frame her perfectly-appointed features. That Dad had kept any of his paintings took Ben by surprise, but that he had so carefully recorded them and kept them all these years, took his breath away. He felt he hadn't really known Dad at all. Now, holding this album in his hands, he finally had the sense of who John Melville was. Yes, he had been a tough parent, but above everything he had cared deeply and equally for both his sons. And, yet again,

Ben was struck by the thought it had taken the death of a loved one for him to truly understand them, as though life blinds us to what is there right in front of our eyes if we only took the time to look.

~

Sarah willed the cashier to speed up rather than muck around trying to find a suitable bag for her flowers while baby Harry yelled and wriggled in his buggy.

'Don't worry about the bag. I can carry the flowers like that,' she snapped.

'Not at all,' the cashier said, as if doing her a favour. 'It won't take a minute to fetch a carrier for you.'

As Sarah jiggled the buggy hoping Harry would fall asleep, she looked back apologetically at the row of customers waiting behind her. Just when she thought she couldn't wait another second, a cheerful assistant arrived triumphantly waving a flower bag.

'Hoo, bloody, rah,' Sarah thought as she tucked her purse back in her handbag and headed towards the exit. But, as the glass doors opened in front of her and she prepared to head out into the frosty morning, she saw a familiar face staring back at her.

'Paul,' she gasped.

'Don't look so happy to see me,' he quipped, holding his hands up in a surrender gesture.

'Well, you're not exactly top of my Christmas card list.' She attempted to move past him with the buggy but he deliberately stepped in front of her to block her path.

'How have you been?' he asked.

'Fine. I have to get home, Paul. Harry needs a feed.'

'I'll walk with you.'

'Please don't,' she was pushing the buggy down the street as fast as she could without posing a safety risk.

'I'm sorry about what happened with your father-in-law, but I was only trying to see what I thought was my son. I didn't mean for anyone to get hurt.'

'John didn't get hurt, Paul. He died.' Sarah kept her eyes focused on the pavement in front as she walked.

'Look, I realise it's been terrible for you but I just want you to know that it's been really difficult for me too. First fearing that I wouldn't get to see my son and then finding out that he's not even mine in the first place. But what happened in the hospital was just.. I'm truly sorry. I haven't been able to stop thinking about it.'

Sarah looked up at him briefly and noticed that he appeared slightly thinner in the face – and his already receding hair line had withered even further. She wondered if he had indeed suffered through all this. She'd never even given that a second thought.

'I'm not the monster you think I am, Sarah.' He put his hand out to gently touch her arm, his eyes pleading with her. She thought he might even be fighting back tears.

Behind the sharp suit and polished shoes, she realised the real Paul Davis was far less together on the inside.

She wondered if he felt as alone as she did.

'Can I please just take you for a coffee to explain myself?'

'It's not a good idea, Paul. I'm sorry.'

'Sarah. You never have to see me again after today, but I've barely slept these past couple of months after all that's gone on. There are things I need you to hear. Five minutes is all I ask.' He was staring with such intent that she realised he wasn't going to go away without a scene.

'Five minutes, Paul. That's all I can give you.'

The five-minute coffee had turned into two hours as Sarah listened to Paul Davis pour his heart out to her, little Harry fast asleep in her arms. He had been in love with her for years, he told her, and when they finally got together at that conference he even hoped she would leave me to be with him. He was crushed then, when she'd simply sent him an email telling him to forget it had ever happened. He told her he'd been hugely concerned for her when I died, and then there was a ray of hope when he found out from a colleague she was pregnant. Putting two and two together, he knew the timing was right. He had never intended to upset her, but he couldn't just forget about what might be his only child. In shutting him out she had made him fight for his own rights – he'd had no choice.

He'd hoped right until Dad's death at the hospital that it could all be sorted out amicably, but he realised in that horrendous moment that things had gone horribly wrong. The final blow had been in finding out that the baby wasn't his. He'd been terribly depressed, had taken time off work and had barely seen friends or family. He was so alone. It was so good to see her. She was still so beautiful. He hoped she didn't feel as alone as he did. Was there anything he could do to help?

He talked and talked, and she listened and listened, lulled by his pain, his loneliness mirroring her own.

How I would have loved to step in, to take her aside and say to Sarah: 'Don't you see what he's doing? He's manipulating you.' But sitting in the café that day, she could only hear the sound of her own sorrow.

∼

Emily had just suggested to Ben that they call it a night and head to bed when the phone rang.

'Who would it be at this time?' she said, curtly answering: 'Hello?'

'Hi Emily, it's Sarah. Sorry to call so late.'

'That's alright,' Emily replied, softening slightly. 'Is everything okay? We've not heard from you in a few days.'

'I'm fine, Emily, thanks. We've been out visiting friends. I just wanted to have a quick word with Ben, if that's alright?'

'Of course, he's right here.'

Emily mouthed 'Sarah' to a curious Ben before handing him the phone. She couldn't help but notice how quickly he moved to take the call when usually he would make his displeasure obvious if anyone dared phone after 10pm. Clearly Sarah was an exception she thought, sighing to herself before heading upstairs to bed.

'Hi Sarah. How you doing?' Ben said cheerily.

'Fine, thanks. Sorry for calling so late. I just wanted to let you know that Harry is going to be christened on April 5th at Morningside Parish. Bob's doing the honours.'

'We're keeping him busy,' Ben joked, before pausing momentarily. 'Isn't April 5th…'

'The anniversary of Harry's death. Yes, I know, it was the only date Bob could do in April and, when I thought about it, I realised it could be a positive symbol.'

'I guess so,' said Ben, scratching his head. In truth, he didn't really know how he felt about it. Ordinarily, he supposed, they should be spending the first anniversary of my death quietly but then he figured this is perhaps what I would have wanted.

'We'd be happy to come,' he tried to sound enthusiastic.

'That's great, but I also have something else to ask you,' she paused for what seemed like dramatic effect. 'Would you like to be Harry's godfather as well as his uncle?'

'Yes…I'd love to,' Ben readily accepted. He had wondered if she would ask him and Emily to be godparents. It had seemed like an obvious thing to do considering their involvement in little Harry's life.

'I've asked my friend Rosa to be godmother,' Sarah quickly added.

'Oh,' Ben replied cautiously. It was, whether Sarah realised it or not, a bit of a slap in the face to Emily who had sat with baby Harry many nights, allowing Sarah the 'me time' she had considered so vital. Now it was he who would have to break it to Emily that she'd been overlooked in favour of a friend Sarah hardly saw anymore.

'Rosa's been very good to me over the years and I'm godmother to her little girl, Esther,' she added, sensing his disapproval.

'I see. Well, whatever you think is best.' Ben said unconvincingly, trying to bring the conversation to a close.

'Ben,' she faltered again. 'I also wanted to ask if you'd come over on Sunday – you and Emily.' She sounded nervous now, almost breathless as she added: 'There's someone I think you should get to know.'

'That sounds ominous,' Ben half joked, assuming that she was talking about a boyfriend. It just hadn't entered his head that Sarah would start dating again so quickly. Or maybe it was just a friend?

'Is it someone I've met?' he asked, looking for clues.

'Look, I'd better go,' she said. 'Harry's crying. See you on Sunday. Come over at five.'

Ben felt distinctly unnerved as he ended the call. He could have just been imagining it, but it had sounded as though Sarah deliberately cut the call short to avoid answering his question. This started Ben thinking about who it could be. As he racked his brains, trying to come up with a shortlist of possibilities, Emily wandered back into the room. Now changed into her pyjamas and dressing gown she was busy searching for her book to take to bed when she noticed Ben standing in a daze in the middle of the living room.

'What did Sarah want?' she asked.

Ben stood silently for several more seconds before he appeared to register that he'd been asked a question.

'Erm… She called to invite us to baby Harry's christening which she's having on the anniversary of my brother's death,' Ben announced in a matter-of-fact tone that was densely coated in sarcasm. 'She then asked if I would be the godfather, before telling me her friend Rose or Rosa – I think it's Rosa but I can't be sure because I've barely met her, nevertheless, this friend is to be godmother.'

'Oh…' Emily tried to interject but was cut off by Ben who was saving the best for last.

'And finally,' he laughed half-hysterically as he prepared to tell Emily the final part of the story. 'She asked us if we would like to come for Sunday dinner as there's someone she wants us to get to know. I think it must be a boyfriend.'

Emily gasped. 'Did she actually say she was seeing someone?'

'Well, no. But, what else could she mean?'

'Don't go jumping to conclusions. She may just have a good friend staying or something – or maybe she wants you to meet Rosa properly before the christening,' said Emily, attempting to be the voice of reason.

'Yes, that might be it. I asked her if it was someone we knew and she couldn't get off the phone fast enough. I'm now wondering if she's seeing Danny.'

'Danny?' Emily exclaimed. 'Danny from the Melville Centre? She's almost old enough to be his mother.'

'I know,' Ben said, stroking his chin. 'But I noticed they were chatting for ages when she dropped in a couple of weeks ago. I bet it is him you know.'

'Just wait and see – and don't get yourself all upset. Harry will still need his uncle.' Emily kissed him lovingly on the cheek. 'I'm off to bed,' she said, leaving Ben standing in the middle of the room, staring into space.

~

Ben was half filled with curiosity and half dread as he rang her front door bell, Emily huddled by his side trying to shelter from the cold. While, based on a hunch, he had placed Danny at the top of the list of suspects, he also wondered if she might be seeing one of her neighbours from two doors along called Miles. He was a single guy in his forties who I'd been quite friendly with at one point and had joked to Ben that I thought Miles was using me to get to Sarah as I'd caught him giving her more than one or two admiring glances.

Now, it seemed, was the moment of truth. Ben took a deep breath as they waited for Sarah to answer. She opened the door while balancing baby Harry in her left arm. As usual, he was full of smiles for his uncle as soon as he set eyes on him. Stepping inside the house, Ben immediately held his arms out to take hold of Harry, raising him up in the air above his head before holding him close to his chest.

'How's my favourite nephew?' he asked playfully.

'He's been looking forward to seeing his uncle and auntie Emily,' Sarah smiled.

After greeting Sarah with a kiss, Emily opted to hang behind Ben, sensing the presence of the mysterious 'someone' in the living room next door. She only prayed it wasn't who she feared it could be and hadn't had the heart to even mention to Ben.

She noticed Sarah was looking extremely tense, her hands even shaking slightly as she'd reached to take her coat. This only served to confirm Emily's suspicions and she braced herself for what could be an explosive encounter. The fact the idea had never even entered Ben's head filled Emily with even more dread, for she knew it hadn't occurred to him because the prospect was just too awful. He would have thought, as Emily once did, that Sarah would have run a mile rather than spend another second with the man. It seemed, however, that they were wrong.

'Come through,' Sarah eventually ventured, gesturing towards the sitting room before leading the guests through.

'Paul Davis.' Ben exclaimed, his voice turning to ice as he clapped eyes on the man standing by the fireplace, who had now become his nemesis. 'You're seeing him again after all the shit he's put us through?' He fixed Sarah with an angry glare that sent a shiver through Emily as she watched helplessly from the sidelines.

'Ben, I…' Sarah faltered.

'He killed my father. What the hell can you be thinking?'

'He didn't kill your father, Ben. They had a misunderstanding. John had a heart attack.'

'A misunderstanding? He deliberately provoked a very elderly man who had come to see his grandson for the first time and died wrongly believing the child belonged to that prat.' He pointed accusingly at Paul Davis who hovered uncomfortably by the armchair – ironically, my favourite chair – hands in pockets.

'Look, I'm really sorry about all that.' Paul said in what was supposed to be a conciliatory tone but ended up sounding pretty flippant.

Ben suddenly turned to stare his adversary in the face for the first time since their eyes had locked that night at the hospital. 'You're sorry for *all that*. All that being the death of my father and last remaining member of my immediate family.'

Emily moved closer to Ben's side now and reached for his sleeve as if attempting to pull him back from the conversation.

'I knew you'd be angry,' Sarah interjected. 'But you need to let me explain.'

'Go on then, Sarah.' Ben turned to look at her again. 'Explain to me why you think it's appropriate to start sleeping with a man who almost tore what's left of this family apart and who caused the early death of my father. A man you cheated with on my dead brother. Explain that to me?'

He bounced baby Harry agitatedly on his shoulder, clutching him closely as if shielding him from Sarah's unpopular new partner as she attempted, in vain, to rescue the situation.

'We bumped into each other a couple of weeks ago and ended up having a chat and Paul apologised profusely for the trouble he caused. He said he had been convinced the baby was his and that he just wanted to be a good father – and to be there from day one. When I listened to what he had to say I realised he hadn't really done anything wrong. I just want you to consider his side of things.' Sarah looked at Ben pleadingly.

'You're pathetic,' he hissed. 'Not even a year has passed since Harry died and you're moving on. I want to turn around, walk out of here and never see your face again but I will not say goodbye to my nephew because he's all I have left of my family. Do you understand that?' He turned his back on Sarah, still clutching Harry to him. Emily could see tears of rage in his eyes as he pressed his cheek against the baby's, before kissing him tenderly.

'I would never stop you seeing him.' Sarah said softly.

Ben turned once again to look at her. His voice now breaking with emotion.

'After everything we've been through this last year, Sarah, you've betrayed me. My father and brother would be rolling in their graves if they could see what you were up to.'

'Ben..' Emily put her arm out to try and stop him from continuing but he pressed on regardless.

'Now I have to stand back and watch this snake hang around my nephew.' He jabbed his finger accusingly again towards Paul who by now looked as though he was trying to sink into the wallpaper. Ben pressed his face close to Harry's again.

'He deserves better than this, Sarah.' he said, reluctantly handing him back to his mother.

Ben turned to Emily and ushered her out of the room but before they reached the front door, Sarah ran out after them her face contorted with emotion.

'I can't bring Harry back, Ben,' she sobbed. 'You're not alone, why should I be?'

Emily opened the front door and stepped outside, hoping Ben would quietly follow but instead he turned to have the final say.

'I know what happened between Harry and you, Sarah. I know that my brother was not a perfect husband. But this? All I can say is you deserve each other. I only wish to God my nephew didn't have to suffer that fool too.'

He slammed the front door loudly behind him before marching out into the darkening evening, his heart heavy with the realisation that the regular access to baby Harry he had enjoyed so much, was now a thing of the past. Before him lay a future full of uneasy conversations and false civility with a woman he had only hours ago considered close family.

Emily and Ben walked the short way home in almost total silence as they each mulled over the implications of their bitter fall out with Sarah. Emily had noticed a change in Sarah since Christmas. At first she had seemed slightly distant and less keen for them to help out so regularly. But more recently, Sarah had seemed quite different all together. Her style had changed from demure to glamorous as she increasingly opted for heavier make-up and bolder, more closely fitted clothes. Ben seemed to have accepted these changes without really questioning them, but Emily could sense there was someone else on the scene and had had a nasty feeling it would be Paul. Despite this, she had still found it galling to find him standing in my living room, acting as if he owned the place. While she sensed he probably did feel ashamed of his actions leading up to Dad's death, he certainly hadn't gone out of his way to apologise.

Now a few yards from their front doorstep she turned to look at Ben who was still far away in thought.

'I think I'll keep walking if you don't mind,' he said as they neared Emily's.

'No problem,' she replied, kissing him gently on the cheek before going her separate way. 'I'll sort something out for dinner.'

Ben walked on deciding he would continue to Newhaven Harbour where he could escape the sound of treacherous voices and listen only to the comforting rush of the sea.

Once at the harbour wall, he took up his favourite resting point, which, on a sunny day, would give him a clear view over to the Forth bridges and Fife on the other side of the water.

He looked up at the skies to see they had cleared and, as he listened to the gentle lull of the waves breaking against the shore, he admired the impressive display of stars that seemed to be breaking out in the darkness just for him. The harbour was a place he used to visit so often, yet it had been months since he'd had the chance to spend time alone here.

In the last year his once pathetic but safe existence had been shaken to its core by the death of his brother, closely followed by his appointment as director of the youth centre. His life had gone from strength to strength as he built up professional and personal relationships he could have only dreamt of months before. And just when everything looked as though things were finally coming together, his world had come crashing down again with the sudden death of his father. Now, Sarah had delivered the final blow by taking up with the last person on earth he would have wanted near his nephew. He felt betrayed and, once again, he felt alone, the family he had fought so hard to keep together now blown apart.

He looked again to the sky, taking several deep breaths in an effort to stifle the great surge of emotion that threatened to engulf him and send him crumbling to the ground.

'I'm sorry,' he whispered, both to himself and to his family who seemed so agonisingly far. He was sorry for losing control of his emotions and for losing Sarah, and he was sorry that he may have just thrown away whatever chance he had of helping raise my son – a baby he had come to consider his own.

For several minutes he stood listening to the soothing rhythm of the waves, until his thoughts ceased to race and he became calm once again. As he took in the night sky for a final time before heading back to Emily's, he was struck by a bright cluster of stars directly above him. And then, in just the blink of an eye, he saw one of the stars tumble and trail away. A falling star.

Ben nodded in appreciation. He didn't know whether it was a message or a coincidence, but in that moment he realised he was no longer helpless. If he could teach others to take charge of their lives, then he could take charge of his own.

CHAPTER eighteen

MY LOVE FOR MY BROTHER was pure again. Our connection as strong as it was in the womb. My greatest desire now was to see my son growing up with a stable father-figure in his life – and Ben was the best man for the job. Better than Paul, and better than me.

I had been far from a good husband to Sarah. In fact, I was not the blameless victim in her dalliance with a work colleague that everyone was taking me for. Emily, too, would have been all too aware of this seeing as it was with her that I had betrayed my wife two years before my death. We had met again at a fundraising event for the centre – she had been blown away to see her teenage love again after so many years and was, of course, keen to hear whether I was still painting. Too embarrassed to confess that I had not been the original artist of her most treasured pieces, I simply told her I had very little time for my hobby these days. Sarah and I had been arguing almost constantly in the few weeks leading up to that night as the reality that it was highly unlikely we were going to be able to conceive a child naturally began to hit home. I told her we should look at adoption but she was adamant that we were going to consult the country's top fertility experts until each one of them had bled us dry.

I was sick of being reminded day-in day-out about my inadequacies as a man and I was tired of having to pay thousands-upon-thousands of pounds to give yet another doctor the chance to rub it in.

So, when I asked Emily that evening if she wanted to go on for a drink, I have to confess that my intentions were already utterly dishonourable, because I was just so damned pissed off with my situation and with my wife.

Emily and I had one drink, and then another, and then another, until she became like a giggly schoolgirl, swaying drunkenly out of the bar with me. We went back to her flat and had what I thought was a pretty awkward encounter. But Emily saw it quite differently. When I went to leave at 3am, she took me by the arm and said: 'I always knew we'd end up back together.' I smiled meekly and told her I would call her the next day.

Sarah was furious when I got home and I had to make up all kinds of bullshit about a very wealthy sponsor of the centre convincing me to go to a casino with him and not letting me leave until the early hours. She seemed to believe me, and I had no intention of contacting Emily again and hoped she'd just forget about our night – or few hours – between the sheets. She was attractive and interesting, but I felt no great connection with her and I wasn't about to risk my marriage to sleep with her again.

When I didn't call her she sent me an email telling me she was disappointed that I hadn't got in touch after 'the evening we shared together' but that she understood I was in a difficult situation and that 'we must accept we have to do the honourable thing and stay apart'. Frankly, I found her message a little odd, but I was ultimately grateful that she was willing to let the whole thing drop. What I found odder still though, was that she had then become a major supporter of the centre, donating thousands of pounds in funding each year. I guessed it was her way of reminding me she was still around. It felt like a little power game, but money was money and I didn't really care where it came from.

Seeing the way she was now with Ben, I realised her fascination with me had almost been entirely about the fact she believed I had an amazing talent. Almost as soon as she found out it was my brother, she transferred her admiration to him.

The truth about Emily, I had come to see, is that her greatest love will always be art – and furthering her career in it. No human would ever get in the way of that.

∽

Two long weeks passed during which neither Ben nor Sarah picked up the phone to one another. He realised she had the upper hand. She would no doubt know he was now desperate to see the baby so was likely waiting for him to make the first move. He held off as long as he could, until one Saturday morning in early March he finally broke.

She had taken a long time to answer the house phone.

'Hello,' she said, sounding a little breathless as though she had run to pick it up.

'Hi Sarah, it's Ben.'

'Hi. How are you?' she responded with the professional distance with which one might greet a client.

'I'm fine. I'd like to see Harry.' He had decided to say as little as possible and stick to the point.

'I see. When were you thinking of?'

'Can I come over this afternoon and take him out for a walk?'

'Yes, we're going out to buy some new clothes for him this morning but we'll be back by two if you want to come then?'

'That would be fine.' Ben knew he should say goodbye and quit while he was ahead, but he just couldn't remove 'we're going out' from his mind.

'Will Davis be there?' he blurted.

'No,' Sarah answered curtly. 'My mother is staying.'

A pattern then developed over the next few weeks, whereby Ben would call in at Sarah's every Saturday afternoon, sometimes accompanied by Emily, and would take Harry out for a couple of hours. Ben quickly realised what it was like to be a Saturday dad, grasping for every moment you could bargain out of your former partner, but never feeling it was enough. He was comforted by the fact that little Harry still beamed as widely as ever as soon as he caught sight of his uncle. Ben wondered if Harry smiled as warmly for Paul. He hoped not. He derived more than a small amount of satisfaction that Paul was never there when he called to collect his nephew. He was either too sheepish to make an appearance, Ben guessed, or Sarah had told him to stay away. Either way, it suited Ben fine. The idea of Paul and Sarah together was eating away at him – the thought of him pawing all over her made him feel sick.

Emily would tell him to forget about it, pointing out his anger was starting to affect their relationship. But he couldn't let it go.

As the 5th of April drew close, Ben realised he would have to make a decision on whether or not to attend Harry's christening. As he dutifully returned his nephew home one afternoon late in March, he decided to broach the subject with Sarah.

This time, instead of handing Harry over on the doorstep and turning on his heels – as had become customary – Ben instead asked if he could come in.

'Of course,' Sarah swiftly replied.

Once seated in the living room, with Sarah happily bouncing her son on her knee again, Ben began.

'You asked me some time ago if I would be a godfather to Harry.'

'Yes,' Sarah smiled politely.

'Well, if the offer still stands I would like to be.'

Sarah remained silent but sat with her head tilted to one side, obviously expecting him to continue.

'I'm still very unhappy about the Paul Davis situation,' Ben added. 'But I won't do anything to jeopardise my relationship with Harry so, I want you to know, that I'll be there in whatever way I can.'

Sarah dropped her gaze to the floor, her eyes welling with tears.

'I'm sorry I've upset you, Ben. And I'm ever sorrier that I've lost you as a friend,' her voiced wavered as she fought to stay composed. 'I still want you in my life… and I want you to be close to Harry. I should have made that clear long before now.'

Ben exhaled sharply. It had been so tough not knowing when he could see little Harry, and having to take whatever scraps of time Sarah would throw at him.

'I'm still struggling with what you've done, Sarah. I can't understand it. I had started to feel…' He paused, grasping for the right words. 'Like you were such an established part of my life. Now, suddenly, you're a stranger to me again.'

The tears were rolling freely down Sarah's cheeks as she listened.

'Don't give up on me, Ben.' To his surprise, she reached out and touched his hand causing him to freeze. He stared at his feet and wondered how they'd ever got to this place.

'I'd better go,' he said finally, pulling his hand from under hers. 'I'll see you at the christening.'

~

Ben and Emily arrived at the church twenty minutes early as requested by Bob who wanted to brief Sarah and the godparents on their duties. From what Ben could gather from the short briefing, he was merely expected to sit at the front, stand to

FROM the OUTSIDE

attention when asked to, then take charge of Harry when Sarah handed him over.

Thankfully seated once again, Ben carefully took stock of the guests as they arrived, keeping a look out for Paul Davis. As the church continued to fill out with a mix of friends, family and regular Sunday worshipers, Sarah took her place next to Ben, with Rosa seated on her other side speaking animatedly with a woman sitting behind her. Ben turned to look at Sarah but found her lost in thought, her eyes directed straight ahead. He saw once again her fragility; a mix of anxiety and sorrow etched on her face, and he leaned in close to whisper: 'Are you okay?'

'Yes,' she said, suddenly aware of her surroundings and of little Harry struggling on her lap. She corrected his position and smiled at Ben, but he could see she was still somewhere else.

He cast his eyes fleetingly over her wrap dress, which hung closely to her slim frame, his gaze then returning to her face when he became aware that Emily, who was seated directly behind, was watching. He smiled but her lips gave only a fleeting flicker in return.

'Where's Davis?' Ben whispered to Sarah, unable to contain himself any longer.

'He's not coming,' she replied curtly. 'I need to talk to you later about that.'

Ben wasn't sure whether to feel relieved or fearful at that comment, but he thought it was a good sign that he hadn't come today. Surely, their relationship couldn't be very deep if he hadn't even bothered to attend her son's christening.

The service was mercifully short, due in part to Harry making his feelings very loudly known when Bob wet his head – and then keeping going pretty much for the rest of the service. That's my boy thought Ben, chuckling to himself at the sight of the minister struggling to make himself heard over his nephew's relentless wails.

Once the service was over, Ben looked around for Emily who she spotted greeting Jason and what looked like a very glamorous young woman. Taking Harry from Sarah, Ben headed over to where they were standing.

He hadn't spoken to Jason since that evening at the centre where he'd disappeared before talking through what was troubling him. Ben had left a couple of unreturned messages on his mobile, but Emily assured him Jason had been really busy.

'Well, well, well, if it isn't the world-renowned artist Jason Weir,' Ben joked as he approached the group.

'Hello there big man,' Jason said warmly. 'And this must be the star of the show.'

'Yes, this is little Harry,' said Ben, looking down proudly at his nephew.

'He didn't appreciate getting his head wet,' Jason laughed.

Ben turned to look at Jason's blonde and leggy companion.

'This is my girlfriend Virginia,' he informed Ben.

'Pleased to meet you,' she said, holding her hand out which Ben shook firmly, smiling as he registered the very clipped and polished accent with which she spoke. He looked at Jason and marveled at how far this talented young man had come. What a tragedy it would have been if his gift had been kept hidden forever.

'And where did you two meet?' Ben asked, intrigued.

'At a preview of Jason's work in Soho,' Virginia answered matter of factly.

'Are you an artist too?'

'An art lover,' she replied.

Ben glanced at Jason who winked cheekily in return.

FROM the OUTSIDE

'Well, there's plenty to love about this guy,' Ben said, playfully slapping him on the back. 'Is all well with you?' he asked Jason quietly, hoping he'd understand the implication in light of their last meeting.

'Aye, I'm good pal. Sorry I didn't get the chance to hang around at the Christmas Party, but my mum called to ask where I was. I'd forgotten I'd promised to go over to see her.'

'No problem. Be nice to catch up with you soon though. Will you give me a call?'

'Course I will.'

'Excellent,' said Ben, thinking how much he had missed his young friend in recent weeks.

Still on a high from the christening, Ben mingled happily with Sarah's guests at the reception she had organised at a local restaurant. Those assembled were a bit of a who's who of Edinburgh establishment, and Ben was surprised at how many of them he actually now knew. There was a day, not so long ago, when he would have rather sunk into the floorboards than mingle with industrialists, lawyers and financiers.

As he turned to see Emily merrily hob-knobbing with a well-known media couple in the corner of the restaurant, Ben couldn't help but wonder what had changed within him and why. His life was unrecognisable from only a year ago when he'd been living almost as a recluse. Now here he was; a respected pillar of the community. In the last twelve months, Ben had spent a lot of time thinking about fate and whether certain things were meant to be. He'd had a feeling of destiny all his life, yet he never knew what he was destined for. But the day he walked into the centre, with all his awkwardness and embarrassment, deep down he had known. He belonged there.

He'd had that same feeling the night he first met Sarah. He didn't know what it meant, he only knew that something about his world had changed.

He checked the room again for Paul Davis but still couldn't find him in the crowd. Ben prayed Sarah was right and that he wouldn't show up and ruin this happy day. It then dawned on him that he hadn't seen Sarah – or little Harry – in some time. When, after he'd taken a good look around the restaurant, he still couldn't see them, he stopped the manager and asked if he knew where they were.

'She's with the baby in the side room at the back,' the manager said, in his thick French accent, nodding towards a door at the other end of the dining room.

'Thanks.' Ben quickly took off in the direction he'd been pointed towards.

As soon as he opened the door, he could see Sarah perched on a chair in the corner, leaning over the baby's pram. The room was dim and Ben couldn't see whether Harry was asleep or not.

'It's okay,' Sarah whispered. 'He's out for the count. I was just about to come back through.'

'Mind if I sit with you for a moment?'

'Please do.' She pulled another chair over next to hers while Ben closed the door behind him and sat down.

'It was a lovely ceremony,' he leaned close to Sarah as he spoke, endeavouring to be as quiet as possible.

'It was. And thank you for coming. For a while I was afraid I'd lost you.'

Ben thought for a moment. He was about to say he came for his nephew, but they both knew there was more to it than that.

'I can't lose any more family,' he finally replied.

The two sat quietly for a moment, listening to Harry's deep, contented breaths as he slept, before Ben broke the silence.

'I'm glad we're spending today celebrating, otherwise I'd have sat at home feeling miserable and trying to figure out the most appropriate way of marking the first anniversary of Harry's death.'

'It felt right.' Sarah smiled. 'He knows how much we miss him.'

'He'd have loved little Harry,' Ben said, expelling the emotion with a long and forceful breath. He felt Sarah's hand tuck in under his arm as he stared intently at the floor, trying to keep himself from completely surrendering again to his grief.

'I keep thinking about how much time Harry and I wasted. Too caught up in our pathetic jealousies to just be brothers and help each other out.'

'Well,' she shrugged. 'Maybe you'll get a chance to make it up to each other one day.'

'Do you actually think that? Do you think we'll see him again?' Ben turned to look at her, desperation flickering in his eyes.

'Yes. I still feel him around us,' she smiled. 'Two nights after Harry was born, I was sitting on the side of my bed watching him sleeping as we are now and I could swear I felt his father's presence in the room. For the briefest of moments, I felt the three of us together as a family… and it was really wonderful.' She looked away, her lip crumbling, paving the way for Ben to let go of what little reserve he had left.

He put his arm around Sarah, resting his head against hers, oblivious to a world outside the room where they sat.

Several minutes passed before their spell of silent grief was broken by baby Harry loudly passing wind in his sleep.

Within seconds they went from tears to laughter. It was the perfect tonic in a deeply gloomy moment. Feeling relaxed and at ease with his former sister-in-law again for the first time in weeks, Ben asked the question he'd been desperate to put to Sarah all day.

'What happened with Davis?'

She shook her head and sighed. 'I realised it was madness, Ben. The act of a desperate and lonely woman. It was over almost as soon as it began, but I've not known how to tell you. I didn't want you to become angry again when you realised I'd put you through all that agony for a quick, pathetic fling. Or should I say another quick, pathetic fling.'

She looked up at him, searching for a reaction. But rather than feeling anger, Ben felt overwhelmed with relief. He instinctively moved closer to Sarah until he could almost feel her breath on his skin. He was aware of his heartbeat quickening with every passing moment and wondered if it was so loud that she could hear it. She didn't move away. He reached to touch her face and began wiping her tears with his thumb, but when their eyes met and he saw her confusion he snapped back into reality.

'Sorry, Sarah,' he said, feeling his face flushing. 'Got a bit lost in thought there.'

'Don't apologise,' she whispered, silence falling between them again. She reached out slowly and took his hand in hers, holding it for a moment with the familiarity of a child clutching a comforter. 'We'd better go back into the restaurant,' she said finally.

'Yes,' said Ben, forcing himself to stand and walk out behind Sarah into the crowd when all he'd wanted to do was stay with her in the private world they had shared for just a few minutes.

And as he made his way slowly through the guests he caught Emily's gaze across the room. She quickly averted her eyes and continued her conversation. A silent statement, Ben thought, that spoke louder than words.

Although only a ten-minute journey, the taxi ride home from the restaurant felt so much longer to Ben and Emily. With Ben's flat now sold, he had moved lock, stock and barrel into her home with the plan being to start looking for a new property to buy as a couple. Just weeks ago Ben had been excited about their new life together and their wedding which they had discussed holding around Christmas time at a castle in Perthshire. But the excitement had faded as he became more and more consumed with the whole spectacle of Sarah and Paul Davis. In truth, he hadn't really taken the time to analyse his feelings and had simply thought he'd been outraged about her choice of partner rather than the fact she was seeing someone. He also knew the fear of losing his nephew had been a major factor in his anguish. But sitting next to Emily now in the back of the cab, it was becoming all too obvious to both of them what the real problem was. It had been silently eating away at their relationship since New York.

'The day seemed to go well,' Ben said as chirpily as possible, trying to ease the tension between them that couldn't have been broken with a hammer.

'Yes,' Emily answered curtly.

'You certainly knew a lot of people there, didn't you?'

'Yes,' she snapped again. 'And it was just as well considering you shut yourself away in a room with Sarah.'

Ben could feel himself reddening with embarrassment. 'We only chatted for a few minutes while she tried to get Harry to sleep.'

'You barely spoke to me all day, Ben. You were too busy either fawning over your sister-in-law or over the movers and shakers you were trying to squeeze cash out of for the centre.'

'Did you ever consider that you might just not be that fun to talk to?' Ben was looking at her directly now, but she quickly turned her head away and stared purposefully out of the window.

'Sorry. I didn't mean that.'

'She has something I can't compete with, Ben.'

'What are you talking about?'

'I'm talking about you and Sarah and the baby.'

'He's my nephew, and he comes first. That's it.' Ben looked at her defiantly.

They spent the rest of the journey in silence – both wondering what tomorrow would bring now the unsayable had been said.

Once home, Emily decided to go for a bath and have an early night, leaving Ben to stew on his own in the sitting room. He spread out across the sofa and switched the TV on hoping to find something good to distract him. Flicking through the channels he found only reality TV shows, lame comedies and dramas, none of which interested him. He settled for watching the news, but despite trying to follow the ins and outs of the latest political crisis he soon found his mind straying to Sarah and their bewildering encounter that afternoon. He couldn't help but wonder what would have happened if he'd actually kissed her. It would have broken every rule in the book and meant that he'd not only betrayed his future wife but his own brother too.

He closed his eyes and exhaled loudly as he realised the magnitude of his situation.

He would have to try and control his feelings for Sarah in the hope that they'd eventually go away. And he'd have to face up to the reality that there would no doubt be another man on the scene again soon. How long had these feelings been there? Since the day he met her, was his answer. He remembered how I had proudly presented her at the restaurant all these years ago with a look that told Dad and Ben that I'd landed the big prize – a beautiful, intelligent woman. The fact she'd cheated on me had come as a major blow to Ben, but not a major shock. The few times he had seen her in the last few years before my death she always appeared troubled. Where once she had shone in her own bright light, she had eventually been forced to step back into my shadow.

Ben had feared in the early months after the car crash that Sarah was leaning on him too hard; that replacing me with my brother was the urgent emotional substitute she needed while carrying a baby. Now, he realised what he had really feared was how easily he could have fallen into that role. How natural it all felt, yet how unnatural it would seem to an outsider. And so he had resisted.

As Ben's mind continued to churn over his feelings, his tiredness got the better of him and he began to drift off to sleep until he found himself in an armchair in his old flat where I was sitting opposite him on a wooden stool by the window, smiling.

There were no words spoken as we sat together, yet in those few subconscious seconds Ben understood completely.

He woke with a start at the sound of Emily opening the bathroom door. As he took in his surroundings, he couldn't shake the aura the 'dream' had left him with; the images so vivid, so unlike anything he had experienced before. He tried to recall what had happened between us, yet all that remained was the sentiment I had expressed. That I was on his side.

He heard Emily's footsteps in the hallway and steeled himself at the thought of what she was about to say. He knew how hard this must all be on her. It felt like the two of them were cornered and surrounded with no obvious way out. Until she spoke.

'I can't carry on like this, Ben. I feel like Lady Di with Charles and Camilla.' She smiled at her own joke, clearly trying to make things easier for both of them. God, she was a trouper, Ben thought.

'What do you want me to do?' he asked.

'I think you should go in the morning. I don't think you belong here any more. You can sleep on the sofa tonight.' They looked at each other, the finality of their situation dawning on both, before Ben nodded.

'Okay,' he said. 'I'm sorry it's ended like this. You deserve a lot better.'

'It's not your fault,' she replied matter-of-factly. 'I guess you could call it karma.'

~

Jason took a few steps back to assess his latest piece of work destined for New York. This one was a special request from a long-term client of Mark's who had sent him a picture of his two young sons laughing and tumbling around the floor together, which he'd asked him to recreate as a large pencil drawing. While Jason had been unsure about how the drawing would work out, looking at the final article he was pleased with what he'd done. He thought the client would be too.

He glanced at his watch and realised he was running late for meeting a friend, so he ran out to the hallway of his flat and grabbed his jacket from the coat hook. But when he opened the front door to leave, he found his dad struggling to the top of the stairs, red-faced and out of puff.

'Alright Dad, I'm just on my out. Can I walk you home?'

'No son, I'm on my way tae Tesco's but I need tae speak tae ye.'

'What's the problem?'

Gary looked around him to check if there was anyone else in the stairway before stepping closer to Jason.

'We cannae lie any mare son,' he said quietly.

'How, what's happened?'

'I bumped in tae Billy Mackay fae the old estate yesterday and they've aw been talkin' aboot seeing ye on the news. Someone's gonnae say something tae yer man Ben soon enough and then he's gonnae put it aw together.'

Jason swept his hand roughly through his hair as he thought for a moment. He knew his dad was right, but he had no idea how he was going to tell Ben. He'd already tried once before but couldn't go through with it. He knew their friendship would be over the instant the truth came out – and Jason could also be looking at a stretch in prison. But his past was closing in on him and he couldn't put his parents through any more worry. He was going to have to face the music, whatever the cost.

CHAPTER nineteen

IT HAD BEEN A COLD but bright spring morning when I had driven out of town to Livingston to view a new office complex. We were looking at relocating our YourLot.com HQ, the rapid expansion of the business meaning we were outgrowing our central Edinburgh offices. I wanted to more or less take over the entire building, anticipating that growth would continue as we diversified. I'd been pretty pleased with what I'd seen so I made a call from the street outside to Doug Henderson, our head of operations, to let him know I thought the move was a goer. I'd just hung up and was returning my mobile to my pocket when I became aware I was blocking the path of a passer-by. I stepped to my left and smiled at the man apologetically, only to find something very familiar about this stranger.

It was the eyes that gave him away – eyes I had seen in my nightmares many times – but otherwise Luke appeared like a different person. The skeletal frame and deathly white skin had been replaced with a healthy physique and almost olive complexion. His once shaven head now covered with a trendy crop of brown hair, and even his broken nose fixed. Despite the shock of seeing him, I couldn't help but be impressed with the transition. I could tell by his startled glare that he was trying to decide whether to run or stay-put so in the end I made the decision for him.

'Keep walking,' I said. So he turned and headed off in the other direction, rounding the corner quickly. But although out of my sight, I knew I would never be able to shake that boy from my mind.

Luke had become my nemesis – and I his. We had brought out the very worst in one another, though he had been nothing but a child and I the adult who should have known better. And on that chilly morning in Livingston, I finally had to confront the real Harry Melville. The one who had taunted a desperate teenage drug addict into pulling a knife and stabbing me in self defence. Because when he'd turned up after dark outside the Melville Centre, Luke had been hoping to make amends, to start again. But my ego had been way too big to let that happen. I'd taken a chance on him before and he'd thrown it in my face. The sight of his pathetic, wasted figure hovering in the darkness that fateful night just made me see red. I had lunged for him, grabbed him around the neck and shoved him against the wall. He was struggling for air but I didn't care. I was angry and violence felt good. I wanted to squeeze and squeeze and squeeze until I'd wrung out every bit of rage in my body and silenced his lack of respect for me. Fortunately for both of us, Luke reached for his knife and stabbed me, allowing him to get away alive and me to keep my spotless reputation intact. The stabbing in fact did so much to boost my heroic image that I was awarded an OBE shortly after it.

But I was no hero and I knew it.

Having watched Luke disappear from my vision, I quickly headed back to my car and sped off from Livingston towards the M8 motorway into Edinburgh.

I wanted to get home as quickly as possible – to the woman I had deceived and who was beginning to drift further and further away from me with each passing day. I was losing her, I knew. But I couldn't bear the thought of life without her.

I was paying the price for a life of complete selfishness. For putting myself above everyone I ever loved in favour of furthering my own ambitions.

As I put my foot down and accelerated towards home, I couldn't erase the memory of the first person I'd stepped on to reach pole position – Ben.

My jealousy of Ben had been compounded in our teens when I found my father one night, hunched over a scrapbook, painstakingly pasting another of my brother's drawings onto its pages. For me, it was time to act. Ben, as I had known for many years, had the kind of talent that could take him all the way – with the right encouragement. But I couldn't allow him to emerge from our family as the highest achiever. That title was mine.

'What's that you've got there, Dad?' I had asked.

'Just keeping a few memories on file.' My father smiled as he smoothed the edges of the drawing he'd just pressed onto the page.

'He's good at drawing isn't he? I remarked, casually hanging over my father's shoulder.

'He certainly is.'

'I suppose we'll just have to accept he'll be a different Ben once he goes to art school.'

'What do you mean?' my father looked at me quizzically. 'I haven't talked about art school with him.'

'Oh,' I laughed. 'Ben's already decided he's going.'

'Really,' my father raised a skeptical eyebrow.

'Yes. He's going to join the punks and other social misfits down at the Edinburgh School of Art. Then he'll be able to paint pretty pictures to his heart's content and become a professional waster,' I added, fully realising I had delivered a killer blow to my brother's plans.

The next day Dad confronted Ben about his intention to apply to art school and they'd had a raging argument which ended in my father telling him he'd never be allowed back through the doors of our home if he even attempted it. That was Dad – you could wind him up like a clockwork clown then set him off.

As I neared the junction that would take me back into the city I applied more pressure to the accelerator. The speed was a partial release from the guilt I was battling, a tirade of memories tumbling through my mind, and all pointing to the fact I had stuffed my brother well and truly then left him to rot in a pool of misery while I dined out on his failure. I wasn't the talented one, but I was the dominant one. And, if that wasn't enough, I was now crushing my wife's only dream of motherhood. All this money, this so-called success, but why did I feel like I'd messed everything up?

Luke's face as I held him against that wall. His terror. He was just a boy, but I'd enjoyed it. I floored the accelerator. I needed to silence my thoughts.

The roadside barrier loomed ever closer and I wondered how it was all going to end.

First with an impact, then darkness. Then there was light.

~

Sarah could never work out how many layers of clothes a baby needed in spring weather. Harry always seemed either too hot or too cold in whatever she dressed him in. Being a sunny day, she decided to stick with a light jacket but covered him with a blanket as she sat him up in his buggy. Just getting out of the door was a major upheaval these days, with bottles and nappies to remember, not to mention her own purse, mobile phone and house keys. Relieved to be finally heading off, she pulled the door closed and was locking up when she heard fast footsteps approaching behind her. Gripping her bag as tightly as she could, she swung around to challenge the man whose heavy breaths she could hear getting ever closer.

To her relief, it turned out to be a familiar face.

'You scared the hell out of me.'

'Sorry,' Ben puffed. 'I knew you were going out at ten so I had to run most of the way so I wouldn't miss you.'

'You going somewhere?' Sarah asked, pointing to the large holdall bag slung over his right shoulder.

'I was hoping I could stay with you for a while, actually.'

'What about Emily?' she asked, her voice quiet and unsteady.

'Things haven't worked out between us,' Ben looked at the ground for a moment, searching for an appropriate explanation. 'We had a row and she asked me to leave.'

'But what about the wedding?'

'It's off.' He dropped his bag on the ground, realising the conversation could last longer than he expected. 'I didn't have anywhere else to go, Sarah. I hope you don't mind.'

She stood staring at him for several moments, unsure of the implications. Then he met her gaze and broke into that open, all-consuming smile she had grown to love about him. It was the smile that let her know she was no longer alone.

'I suppose you'd better come in then,' she laughed. 'I've a ton of DIY jobs for you.'

Three weeks later and Ben had made it home from the centre just in time for Harry's bath – a nightly ritual that always started at 6.15pm sharp. He flung his jacket over the banister then raced up the stairs, reaching the bathroom to find Sarah lowering the baby into the water. She looked up and smiled: 'You're just in time. Do you want to do the honours?'

'Yes please,' Ben grinned, rolling his sleeves up then kneeling down next to Sarah to take Harry from her.

'How was your day?' Sarah asked, throwing her arm around Ben's neck and kissing him.

'It was good. Looks like we're going to get some extra government funding for the centre next year. We might even be able to take on another full-time staff member.'

'That's great news. You're taking that place from strength to strength. You were born to do it.'

Ben laughed. 'At least I'm good for something,' he said, beaming down at little Harry who was enjoying relaxing in the warm bath water.

'You're good at a lot of things,' Sarah said, playfully pulling on his shirt to draw him towards her. He smiled and kissed her firmly leaving her with a lingering look, before turning his attention back to baby Harry in the bath.

'How's he been today?'

'A little angel. He's barely cried once.'

'You're such a good boy,' Ben cooed.

The doorbell sounded downstairs. 'I'll go,' said Sarah, quickly getting to her feet. Ben heard her footsteps on the stairs and then the creak of the front door opening.

He strained his hearing to see if he could work out who she was speaking to, fearing at this time of night it might be the police to tell them the centre had been broken into, as had happened a few months back. He was relieved then when Sarah shouted up to let him know it was Jason.

He gently plucked Harry from the bath and wrapped him in his towel before heading down the hall where Sarah was waiting at the top of the stairs to take the baby from him.

Ben found Jason standing near the front door, hands stuffed

awkwardly into the pockets of his jeans, and looking unusually downbeat.

'Jason, how you doing?' Ben asked brightly.

'I'm alright,' he mumbled like an awkward teenager. 'I went round to Emily's and she said you'd moved out.'

'Yes, a couple of weeks ago. Did she tell you I was here?'

'She did, aye. She said you'd broken up. Sorry by the way,' he shuffled from one foot to the other. 'Hope you don't mind me bothering you but I need to speak to you about something. Can we sit down?'

'Of course,' Ben said, confused and slightly worried by Jason's obvious nervousness.

He showed him through to the living room where they sat on the sofa next to one another. 'Has this got to do with what you were trying to tell me at the centre before?'

'Aye,' said Jason. 'This is not going be easy for me Ben so I'm just going come right out with it. I've not always been called Jason. I used to be Luke – and I knew Harry.'

He didn't have to say another word. Ben immediately knew who he meant. He thought about the pictures he had found in my filing cabinet – their likeness to Jason's work. And then he remembered me telling him about the night I was stabbed. How I'd named the attacker I was protecting - Luke.

'What the hell's going on here?' Ben asked coldly.

'I was a drug addict, Ben. I was getting in to all sorts of trouble but that wasn't how I wanted it to be. I showed Harry my drawings and he said he'd help me, but he had to kick me out the centre when I kept taking heroin. I was trying to get clean, substituting drugs with drink. I was passing the centre one night when I saw Harry locking up outside. I was just trying to be friendly, to see whether he might give me another chance, but he went for me and started choking me. I thought he was going kill me, Ben, honestly, he just had a look in his eyes like he wasn't going to stop.'

'So you stabbed him?'

'So I stabbed him, aye. Like the rest of my so-called pals back then, I carried a knife for protection, but I never thought I'd use it.' Jason said mournfully. 'As soon as I did it I felt terrible. I called an ambulance and I stood in a doorway at the bottom of the road and watched them take Harry away.'

'Why are you telling me this now?'

'I need you to know the truth. My mum and dad have been through hell with this and we're all sick of lying to you. They've had to move estates so that I could come back home from Livingston and try and start again. I cleaned up my act, the way I look, the way I speak, everything, because I wanted to do something with my life – and stay away from the lads that got me into trouble in the first place.' He turned to look deliberately at Ben. 'I'm not who I was, but if you decide to tell the police I'm willing to take what's coming to me. I mean that.'

Ben exhaled, long and hard. 'I'm not going to tell the police… Luke. I guess that's what I should call you.'

Bowing his head, he replied. 'I'm not Luke. I left him behind a long time ago. I'm Jason now.'

'Okay, Jason, I'm not going to tell the police.'

'Why you not angry with me, Ben?'

'Though I never allowed myself to fully piece it together, I think deep down I knew. . I couldn't get over how like Luke's drawings yours were. And there was something about you when we first met, but I couldn't put my finger on it. There was something about the way you spoke so differently from your mum and dad, like you'd made a deliberate decision to be different.

'Harry told me about you and what happened, but he didn't tell me he provoked you. I guess he felt too guilty to go to the police, probably didn't want your version of events coming out. The trial, the negative publicity, he wouldn't have wanted any of that.'

Jason tilted his head back and looked up at the ceiling as he let the relief sink in. 'Thank you for believing me,' he said. 'I feel like the whole world has just been lifted off my shoulders.'

'You've been through a lot in your life and you're still so young. I know what it's like to be lost, to feel like you're good-for-nothing and the whole world is against you. I'm just glad you found your way.'

Jason smiled, grateful for Ben's understanding.

'Why did you put yourself through all this?' Ben asked. 'Why not just go to someone else for help?'

'I changed my name because I wanted to rid myself of my past. My mum and dad barely recognised me when I turned up on their doorstep after six months clean, teeth and broken nose fixed, so I thought nobody else would.

'Don't ask me why, but I just knew you would help me. I didn't expect my career to take off so quickly, but it all got out of hand when suddenly I was in the papers and on TV. When that happened, I knew it was only a matter of time before I had to tell you the truth – before someone else did it for me. I tried to tell you before when I came to the centre that day, but it's taken me until now to pluck up the courage.'

Jason studied Ben for a moment, wondering if his apparent forgiveness was simply just shock, but my brother was calm and seemingly completely unfazed.

'Can we really still be mates, Ben?' he asked. 'It's more than I ever expected after what I did?'

Ben paused for a moment to question his own reaction. After

all, Jason had stabbed his brother and then lied to him for the sake of his career. But Ben could see the full picture, because there wasn't a part of Jason's story that he didn't fully understand. 'I have nothing but admiration for you, Jason. You came from a place where you seemed destined for failure. But you fought it and you dug your way out of a very deep hole. I see so much of me in you. We were both outsiders, we were life's losers, but we've come in from the cold.'

Jason smiled, 'We have, aye.'

'And you know what,' Ben added, 'we deserve our second chance. And this time no one's going to blow it for us. We earned our happiness.' Ben got to his feet. 'This is where I should get you a beer or a glass of wine to celebrate new beginnings, but I can only offer a cup of tea. Want one?'

'Perfect,' said Jason, following him into the kitchen.

And that was where I left them, two men utterly transformed by the self-belief they had given the other.

I had seen enough to know Ben didn't need me anymore. He could take care of himself and his family now. Our family.

I had watched and I had learned. I had faced up to the man I was, as difficult as it had sometimes been. I had mended what I'd broken, including me.

Acknowledgements

This novel, although entirely fictional, was inspired by experiences I've had in feeling connections with loved ones who have passed away. No one can be sure what's on the other side, or even if there is another side, but those of us who have had even just a fleeting moment of connection have little doubt.

In writing this novel I didn't set out to answer questions, but to pose them. It's a piece of fiction that doesn't fall neatly into a literary genre and for that reason I owe huge thanks to Kerry-Jane and Matthew at Urbane for their belief.

Thanks also to the fiercely-talented author Shari Low who was one of the first to read the final manuscript and who gave it such whole-hearted support.

Clare Johnston is a journalist and content specialist, and a frequent contributor on radio, having appeared on Radio 4's Woman's Hour, The Kaye Adams Programme and comedy satire show Breaking the News on BBC Radio Scotland.

She is a former editorial director of Press Association Scotland and weekly columnist with the Daily Record newspaper, and is now Commercial Editor with the DC Thomson publishing group.

Praise for Clare Johnston's first novel, **Polls Apart**:

'A political thriller fraught with twists and turns. AWESOME book!' *TV presenters Colin and Justin*

'A smart, razor-sharp novel that makes a massive impact.' *Shari Low, Daily Record*

'A gripping piece of contemporary fiction. I couldn't turn the pages fast enough.' *onemorepage.co.uk*

URBANE

Urbane Publications is dedicated to
developing new author voices, and publishing
books that challenge, thrill and fascinate.
From page-turning thrillers to literary debuts,
our goal is to publish what
YOU want to read.

Find out more at

urbanepublications.com